DAVID OF KI

E F BENSON

New Introduction by
Peter Burton

Millivres Books
Brighton.

Published 1991 by Millivres Books
33 Bristol Gardens, Brighton BN2 5JR, East Sussex, England

David of King's first published by Hodder & Stoughton Ltd, 1924
Copyright this edition, (C) Millivres Books, 1991
Copyright Introduction, (C) Peter Burton, 1991

ISBN 1 873741 01 4

Typeset by Hailsham Typesetting Services, 4–5 Wentworth House,
George Street, Hailsham, East Sussex BN27 1AD
Printed by Billing & Sons, Worcester

Distributed in the British Isles and in Western Europe by Turnaround
Distribution, 27 Horsell Road, London N5 1XL

Introduction

Originally published in 1924, E F Benson's *David of King's* has been unavailable for half-a-century. The sequel to that popular classic of homoerotic public school literature *David Blaize* (reprinted 1989), this novel was almost as successful as its forerunner, going into four editions in as many months.

Following chronologically on from *David Blaize*, *David of King's* commences with the six foot blond hero celebrating his nineteenth birthday. He is at the beginning of his three years as an undergraduate at King's College, Cambridge (at which his creator also completed his formal education and which was later to become so strongly identified with E M Forster who entered the college in 1897). David Blaize's years at King's more-or-less accurately correspond with those of E F Benson and in some respects – though totally devoid of any overt homosexuality – *David of King's* is the most obviously direct ancestor of Forster's *Maurice*.

To anyone who has dipped into the many auto-biographical books by E F Benson (*Our Family Heritage, Mother, As We Were, As We Are, Final Edition,*) or the biographical studies (Betty Askwith's *Two Victorian Families*, David Williams' *Genesis and Exodus*, Geoffrey Palmer and Noel Lloyd's *E F Benson: As He Was*) it is immediately evident that, like *David Blaize*, David of King's is highly autobiographical – a work, in this instance, stirred by the success of the earlier novel and a continuing sense of nostalgia for a simpler past.

However, although the events in *David of King's* directly follow those of *David Blaize*, anachronistic references to events which were contemporaneous with the composition of the novel have been allowed to creep in – the discovery in 1922 of the tomb of Tutankhamen, for example.

It is clear that the portrait of the snobbish and tricycle-riding Cambridge don `Alfred Gepp', known to his familiars as `AG', must have been based upon the immensely snobbish and tricycle-riding Cambridge don Oscar Browning, known to his familiars as `OB', who had been dismissed as an Eton schoolmaster in 1875 because of his over-familiarity with the future Viceroy of India, Lord Curzon, and had washed up and found safe haven at

King's College, Cambridge. Browning died in 1923 and it is possible that his death may have stirred memories of undergraduate days which quickly formed themselves into *David of King's*.

Though at Cambridge David continues his intense homoerotic relationship with the three years older Frank Maddox, he is still untouched by `beastliness' – which in the first book implied homosexuality and in the second seems to refer to both homosexual and heterosexual conduct.

I suggested in my Introduction to *David Blaize* that in that book E F Benson split himself, as it were, in two to create the characters of David and Frank Maddox. Geoffrey Palmer and Noel Lloyd have propounded a similar – yet crucially different – theory in which they suggest that whilst Benson used himself as the model for David in *David Blaize*, he used himself as the model for Frank in *David of King's*. `It is in Frank's character, and in his achievements, that Fred can be more clearly identified,' Palmer and Lloyd write, `his fondness for younger boys, his knowledge that he would lose his friend to the heterosexual world in which he felt an alien...' It is my contention that *David of King's* is yet another example of Benson expressing the duality of his nature – athlete and aesthete, masculine and feminine – which is evident in so many of his books, including the enduring Mapp and Lucia sequence. Although there is more than enough evidence to suggest that `Fred' Benson was emotionally homosexual, there is little to indicate that he physically fulfilled his desires. It may be worth considering that the duality so constant in his fiction was a safety valve for his life.

David of King's provides a fascinating picture of the homoerotic world of the Cambridge undergraduate at the height of the Victorian era – one which (for me, at least) is a deal more readable than Forster's anguished out-pourings and wish-fulfilment in *Maurice*.

Peter Burton, Brighton 1991

First Year

IT would probably prove to be useless in the long run to attempt to conceal the fact that the street down which David Blaize was walking on this damp and dispiriting morning in November was the King's Parade at the University of Cambridge, or to try to delude the intelligent reader into believing that it was Queen's Parade at Oxbridge or Prince's Parade at Camford. It was nothing of the sort, nor was it Queen's College Chapel that reared its fretted pinnacles so loftily into the sombre and ugly sky, but King's College Chapel, justly appreciated by Mr. William Wordsworth and celebrated by him in one of his more successful sonnets. It never entered David's head, with regard to it, to disobey Mr. Wordsworth's bidding and to tax the Royal saint, who was responsible for it, with vain expense, for he had no idea how much the chapel had cost, and so could not possibly find fault with King Henry the Sixth's extravagance. Besides it was very pretty.

David had no cigarettes with him and wanted to smoke so much that he would certainly have cried aloud with unappeasable desire had he not, at the moment when his need was the sorest, seen Frank Maddox walking in the roadway some twenty yards ahead and in the same direction as himself. Between them, and just in front of David, was a large, con-

venient furniture-van also moving that way, and so
he put himself directly behind it, found a very old
golf-ball in his pocket, and lobbed it over the furniture-van with such fortunate accuracy that it fell
precisely on the toe of Frank's right foot as he put
it forward to take a step. From his ambush David
could see him jump like a large startled fawn in a
great coat, and, standing on his left leg with the
other drawn up like a Fakir in meditation, look
wildly round to see where this inexplicable missile
came from.

So the driver of the van said " Hi, Mister ! " in
an offended voice, for Frank blocked his fairway.
Upon which Frank moved on, and David, still in
ambush, searched in his pockets for something else
to throw. A half-penny and some shillings and half-
crowns were the only suitable missiles he could find,
and he threw the least expensive of these coins.
This was not such a success (though quite pleasant),
for its sharp edge alighted on the hind-quarters of
the van-horse. This animal was clearly neuras-
thenic and easily startled, for it broke into a fantastic,
lolloping trot. Consequently Frank had to step on
to the pavement and the van passed him.

He turned in at the gate of King's, and as he
crossed the pavement he looked round and saw the
disclosed David. David, of course, was now saun-
tering absently along, and appeared not to perceive
him till he came opposite to him. He then executed
a small, well-feigned start, and dropped the volume of
Thucydides's interesting History of the Peloponnesian War which he was carrying into the gutter.
It fell face downwards and open.

" What a pity ! " said David. " Hullo, Frank ! "

" Hullo ! You can't lend me an old golf-ball, can you ? "

David felt in his pockets.

'Fraid not. Have you got a cigarette ? "

" Yes, thanks. Plenty."

" Oh, don't be humorous. Besides, it's my birthday, and if you'll give me one, I'll—I'll come and dine with you this evening. Thanks awfully. What time ? "

" Oh, summer-time," said Frank.

" Right-oh ! Nine o'clock then, as we're in winter-time."

" No, seven," said Frank.

" Not if you mean eight."

Frank pulled out his watch, and put one finger firmly on eight.

" You're perfectly idiotic," he said. " Look, there's eight. Well, we put our clocks on an hour at the end of summer-time, so eight's really seven."

" But we didn't put them on ; we put them back."

" Then we put them on when summer-time began, so it's the same thing . . . or is it nine ? "

David picked up his Thucydides by the corner of the cover, and looked about for something to wipe it on.

" You take a piece of paper when you get in, and work it out," he said. " What am I to do with this book ? Oh, there's a brown horse with no one looking after it. Just the colour of mud. Isn't that lucky ? "

David made a soothing groom-noise to the mud-coloured horse and wiped his book tenderly on its back.

" Been having a lecture on the plague in Athens," he said, " and I believe it's given it me. I'm full of the symptoms of it. If anybody wrote such a foul description now it would be suppressed, or published privately at a high price, and called 'very curious.' The plague began with ineffectual retching——"

" Are you coming into college, or are you going to drivel ? " asked Frank, thrusting his hands into his pockets.

" Both. I say, fancy my being nineteen. It's a great age. You know I always used to think that by the time anyone was twenty-two or so, life was practically over. You couldn't possibly be fit for much then, and might as well die. So now there are only three more years to roll in which to do all the things I don't mean to do. I say, there's the Provost coming, and I shall have to put my cigarette in my pocket. Though why one shouldn't smoke in Court I don't know."

The Provost had something to say to Frank, and stood talking for a few minutes. Out of David's coat-pocket where he held his concealed cigarette there oozed thin blue whorls of smoke. The Provost perceived this, and with a pleasant contralto hoot of laughter made an apt Homeric quotation, which David didn't catch, and passed on.

" Think he saw ? " said David.

" Considering he quoted to that effect, you may take it that he did," said Frank.

" Oh, that was what it was about, was it ? I wish I could laugh like that."

" You will in time, if you go on trying," observed Frank.

" Then you've recognised it. Ha ! About dinner this evening. Now I come to think of it——"

" Don't come to think of it. I haven't," said Frank.

" Well, then, you needn't. Because now I remember that Bags said he would give me a birthday party, if he didn't tell me to the contrary by this morning. And it is this morning," said David lucidly, " and he hasn't."

" Bags is becoming rather a blood," observed Frank.

" Rather," said David, " and now he'll become much bloodier. Lord, it was funny ! Bags came into my room this morning while I was still in bed, and said quite suddenly, ' My uncle's dead.' Well, if you're told anything, bang, like that, of course you laugh. So I laughed. That made Bags laugh, too, and there we were with awful giggles because his uncle was dead ! "

" What did he die of ? " asked Frank.

" That's just what I asked, and that made it worse still because he died of measles. Fancy dying of measles when you're nearly seventy ! There was an obituary of him in the *Times* ; but the *Times* only said ' a short illness.' Naturally it wouldn't say measles."

" But why does all this make Bags bloodier ? " asked Frank.

" Why, because his uncle was a lord, and hadn't any kids—only measles. So now his father's a lord, and Bags is an honourable. He looks just the same,

though. Honourable Crabtree : Lord—Lord Lob-
sterbush and the Honourable Percival Crabtree.
His father's a clergyman, too. Does a clergyman
get hoofed out of the Church when he's hoofed into
the House of Lords ? That stumped Bags ; he
didn't know."

" Bishops don't," said Frank.

" Oh, but they're different. If they weren't
Bishops they wouldn't be there at all. They get in
because of it. Bags's governor didn't get in because he was a clergyman, but because his brother
measled."

They had passed down the side of the back lawn
at King's and gone into the buildings by the river
where David kept. Frank had not had the smallest
intention of coming so far, but it was always so
much easier to remain with David than to go away.
Indeed, it was a sheer waste of time not to be with
David when you could be, for the old love, born in
the days of school, had never waned, and at nineteen
(just) and twenty-two they were still knitted into
each other with that taut bond of boyish affection
which early manhood had done nothing to slacken.
It had grown, indeed, in closeness and comprehension,
when, last October, David came up to Cambridge
where Frank, having already completed his third
year and taken his degree, was staying up for another
year to go in for a second tripos in Archæology with
the view eventually of getting a fellowship. For
this year, then, they would be together at King's,
and that was sufficient for the present. . . .

A cold and discouraging lunch was laid out on
David's table. There was a " loaf of bread, a jug

of wine " (or more precisely a small opaque remnant
of port in an otherwise empty decanter), a piece of
cheese, and some marmalade. The Thucydides was
the " book of verses."

" Sit down and have some lunch, Maddox," said
David fatuously. " Don't spare the bread, especially the crumb, or we shall quarrel. You shall have
precisely half the port—it's only a week or two old,
and was a fine vintage in its time. I will eat marmalade on cheese."

" There's a pie of sorts in my room," said Frank.

" Then don't sit down," squealed David. " Go
and get it."

" If you'd said that as we passed my room——"
began Frank.

" But how could I when I didn't know it was
there ? "

" Toss up who goes," said Frank.

He lost and went, and as David rummaged in his
gyp-cupboard for cutlery and plates, he planned a
pleasant afternoon. When lunch was over they
would play a game of billiards, not go out at all, have
muffins for tea, and drop into the ante-chapel to hear
the anthem at evening service. Then—— A voice
like a foghorn sounded in the court below, hooting
at intervals.

" David . . . Mr. Blaize . . . Blazes . . . Dean
David " (the last was an allusion to David's father).

David opened the window.

" What's the row ? " he asked. " Come and have
—oh, no, don't ; there's not enough. What is it,
Tommers ? "

Tommers (alias Tomlin) seemed to like the sound

of his own voice, for he chanted " Mr. Blaize " once
more. Then he spoke in ordinary conversational
tones.

" I say, David, do come and play Rugger this
afternoon," he said. " It's only against Cat's and
I've been trying all morning to get——"

" No," said David and shut the window.

Instantly the foghorn began again.

" Master David Blaize . . . Da—a—vid ! Once
in royal David's . . ."

" Oh, blast him ! " said David, opening the window again.

" —Somebody to play three-quarters, and I can't
find anybody," said Tommers, going on precisely
where he left off. " I say, do play. It's absolutely
impossible to get anybody else, or I wouldn't have
asked you. At least, I don't mean it quite like
that, you know. You see what I mean."

" But I hate Rugger," said David. " Have you
tried——"

" Yes," said Tomlin. " Ages ago."

David hesitated ; he didn't really object to Rugby
football, if he wasn't in the scrum.

" Well, if you promise you won't put me in the
scrum under any circumstances," he began.

" Rather not."

" Or full-back," said David.

" I swear I won't. You are a ripper."

" I know that. Where and when ? "

" Two fiff. Our ground. I'll call for you."

Frank came back with the pie of sorts and a tan-
kard of beer.

" My pleasure's completely spoiled," said David.

"I meant to play pills with you in a jolly fuggy
room. Now I've promised to play Rugger."

"Filthy game," said Frank. "Hairy people rub
your face upwards. Couldn't they get anybody
else?"

"Of course they could. Everyone was fearfully
keen to play. But they wanted me. Why shouldn't
they? Besides, I'm not playing in the scrum. No!
Three-quarters. I'm a smartish three-quarters with
a rooted objection to being collared. I played for
the school once, and I should have got a try if I
hadn't been knocked down and trodden on."

David had not quite finished lunch when the foghorn began again, so Tommers came up and waited
for him, while he changed in front of the fire.

"Who've they got?" asked David, taking his
trousers off. A pocket got upside-down, and all his
money rolled about the floor.

"Nobody of any class, except Alston," said
Tommers. "Oh, do be quick; I'll pick them up for
you."

"Alston?" shrieked David. "Lord, I wish I
was dead, but I soon shall be. I bet you he's opposite me. There's another half-crown. I'll give it
you if I needn't play, Tommers."

"What's the matter with Alston?" asked Frank.

"Oh, nothing. He offered to take the place of a
bull in a bull-fight once," said David, "but they
wouldn't have him because he was too savage.
That's all."

Frank strolled up to the field with them, David,
between the two, being led like a large yellow-haired
lamb to the slaughter, and sure enough Alston was

opposite him in the three-quarter line. This young gentleman was quite square, as broad as he was long, and of the build of a luggage-engine. If David's seventy-two slim inches could have been cut in half, without inconvenience to him, and the severed halves fastened together side by side, he would have had much the same sort of figure.

David did not possess the grim but cheerful temperament of the football player, and he had a strong objection to being collared somewhere about the knees and thrown flat on his face, which was exactly what Alston proceeded to do to him three times in the first ten minutes. The fourth time that this brutal rape appeared imminent, David gave a loud hoot of despair, and hurling the ball wildly away with no thought but to get rid of it, found that he had made a marvellously neat pass to his centre-three-quarters. From twenty yards off the ball went into his hands like a bird into its nest, and the luggage-engine thereupon left David and steamed after the other, who with great dexterity passed back again to David.

" Oh, blast," thought David, " I've got it again, and here's this blighter coming for me."

He raced on, and thump, thump came the awful Alston after him. David again passed to his centre (this time it was on purpose), who dodged the full-back, and got a try right between the goal-posts.

Now just before, Tarler and Towling, two great football bloods, captain and secretary of the University team, strolled on to the ground. There was a fearful dearth of talent this year: Rugby football was darkened by the most gloomy eclipse, for the incoming tide of freshmen went and played golf, that mild and elderly pursuit which from the football point of view was a decadent and effeminate sort of croquet. The three-quarter line, indeed, in the University team was at present a mere derision, and Tarler and Towling, known as the Tooties (two T's), who lived so entirely for Rugby football that if there had not been any they would have evaporated like morning dew, occupied their off-afternoons in looking on at College matches in the hope, at present vain, of discovering some faint indication of talent. They were large, strong, taciturn people, much like each other, and their idea of Eternal Bliss was to be tightly wedged together in a steaming scrum shoving hard with their big legs. . . . At David's exploit they simultaneously took their pipes out of their mouths.

" Pretty neat piece of passing," said Tarler.

" Who's that lanky Kingsman on the right ? " said Towling.

" Never saw him before," said Tarler.

" There's Maddox," said Towling.

" Might ask him," said Tarler.

They strolled on to where Frank was standing.

" Hullo ! " they said simultaneously.

" Hullo, Tooties," said Frank. " How's your golf getting on ? "

The Tooties gave a polite grin, but couldn't make jokes about the beastly game.

" Who's that tall youth playing three-quarters for you ? " asked Tarler.

" On the right," added Towling.

" Blaize," said Frank. " Freshman."

" Thanks. So long," said the Tooties and moved
on again.

" Might watch a bit," said Tarler.

David, unconscious that the joint eyes of the
Tooties were firmly fixed on him, was rather pleased
with himself. There never had been a more outrageous fluke than his first pass, for his whole intention had been to rid himself of that ball for the sake
of which Alston had already thrown him down on
his face three times. The result of those assaults
was that he was already completely covered with
mud : his knees were caked with it, so was his face,
and on his arms Alston had imprinted two impressions of his large hands, like the crest of a baronet
in black. But nothing ever made David look dirty ;
he might be wholly encased in mud, but the mud
appeared to have nothing to do with him. · It just
happened to be there, but he remained clean and
ruddy below. It had begun to rain, and rain and
perspiration, which made other people look dirtier
than ever, only seemed to wash him. Anyhow, in
spite of Alston, this was much better than being
in the scrum over which a thick and sweaty steam
arose, out of which every now and then Tommers's
face appeared, black and radiant. He had seen the
Tooties, and was playing up for all he was worth in
order to catch their distinguished eyes, and was
blissfully unconscious of the fact that they were
taking no notice whatever of him.

It was a cheerful sort of game. The gentlemen of
St. Catherine's College were getting a shade savage
and rough, which Tommers always enjoyed, since
no one ever could hurt him, while the King's three-

quarter line, in which David had to be included, because he couldn't get anybody else, was doing itself proud. And here was half-time already—though who'd have thought it ?—and on resuming it was clear that their opponents meant to make the game more open, for they were not scoring much in the scrum. Things therefore became vastly more hectic for David, for the ball kept coming out with odious frequency. It had become thoroughly slippery now, and was as hard to hold as an eel, while running was a skidding progress on this greasy ground. Here it was coming out to him again, and he just touched it as it bounced in front of him, and then somehow managed to gather it. He wriggled free of the embrace of one of their forwards only to hear the thump-thump of Alston coming up on his left and intercepting him. He was all alone, too, and there was no chance of passing anywhere. Like an orphan.

Now David could, on emergency, run like a hare. He did so at cricket when despair winged his heels with the terror of being run out ; but unless he was thoroughly frightened, he was only a moderate sprinter. But now a spasm of this admirable panic seized him ; there was this infernal luggage-engine stamping and snorting and breathing hostile steam, and the only possible chance of avoiding being run over and squashed and squeezed and flattened was to flee like a bird. And like a bird he fled, his yellow hair standing straight up on his head, and his blue eyes wide in an ecstasy of cowardice. Alston had only got to steam along a radius, so to speak, while David must traverse an arc of circumference, and close by the touch-line was standing Frank with a

friend or two, who, knowing David's power of pace
when and when only he was thoroughly alarmed,
broke into loud laughter and encouraging cries.

" Spurt for your life, David," shouted Frank,
" or he'll get you."

" Don't funk, whatever you do," screamed Bags,
who had come down when he heard David was
playing.

Then Tommers's foghorn boomed out from where
the broken-up scrum were racing after him.

" Run like Blazes," he shouted. " He's catching
you up."

David was beginning to laugh himself, but he had
enough speed to curve round Alston like a yacht just
clearing the mark.   Alston's hot breath was on his
shoulder, and he felt himself grabbed by his jersey,
which tore from neck to waist with a zipping noise,
leaving his back quite bare, while the flap of it waved
like a victorious flag. The spectators generally had
caught on to the joke, for there was David, the
picture of headlong terror and amusement, with his
jersey slipping off his arm as well, and the vindictive
Alston plying his short stout legs so swiftly that their
motion could hardly be followed. The Tooties alone
remained perfectly grave, because under no circum-
stance could you laugh at Rugger, and Tarler took his
pipe from his mouth.

" That's a sprinter," he said.

Towling put his pipe back in his mouth.

" Just a bit," he observed.

David had left the luggage-engine definitely out-
paced and distantly snorting, and now he was
aware of the full-back immediately in front of him,

dancing on his toes like a mongoose ready to spring this way or that and collar him. He tried to run round him to the right, but there wasn't room between him and the touch-line, and slipping on the greasy ground recovered himself by shooting out his left leg, and found himself clear of his man, who had pounced towards the right, with the goal open in front of him. The manœuvre looked like the most superb swerve, but was really nothing of the sort. Next moment he was safe behind the goal-posts.

"Ripping good swerve," said Tarler solemnly. "Try him in the picked game on Saturday. Forgotten his name."

"Blaize of King's," said Towling. "No-one else worth spitting on. Let's toddle."

David was happily unconscious of the awful and undeserved honour in store for him, and when the game was over hurried back to enjoy the remainder of his carefully planned and Sybaritic evening. The first item must certainly be a bath so hot that to move in it was torture, and only by lying quite still could the heat be tolerated. Then when it began to get a little cooler he turned on the hot tap again and sat on the edge whistling loudly, till the temperature had risen sufficiently to produce the requisite agony. Then when he was bright red all over and sick with heat he let the water drain away, and turned on the cold tap. He dressed and went over to Frank's room to eat muffins till it was time to go into the ante-chapel and hear the anthem.

"A large tea," he said, "is the right thing to give you an appetite for a large dinner. It prepares the inside for what's going to happen to it. I say, that game was rather a lark. I've never been so frightened. Blowed if I ever play Rugger again; it takes years off one's life, or adds them on."

"Don't be too sure," said Frank. "The Tooties were there, and asked me your name. That was when you threw the ball away, and Cartnell happened to be there."

"Just a fluke," said David.

"Rather. But it looked neat. Did you know that you can always tell Rugger blues by their faces? They look like leather, and their ears are always close to their heads from being squashed in the scrum. And their noses spread sideways over their faces for the same reason."

David gave a loud sigh of content.

"Funny things!" he said. "And it's funny to see you making tea and toasting muffins for me. I used to have to do that for you when I was your fag."

"You did. Good Lord, that's five years ago. You haven't changed an atom, except that you're about a foot taller."

David drew his hand over his chin.

"Rot! I shave now," he said.

"Only for swank."

"Not at all. If I didn't shave, I should have a honey-coloured beard and a moustache. Let's grow beards and whiskers and be known as the Hairy Horrors. More lumps of sugar, please."

David slid from his chair and sat on the hearth-rug.

"It's all very well not to think about it," he said, "but we're growing up. I shall have to have an aim

in life soon, and I'm blowed if I know what it's going
to be. Bar fooling round with you and playing
games, I suppose I like fooling about with words
better than anything else. I make beautiful sentences in my bath, and forget them afterwards.
And then I suppose I shall marry. Fancy having a
wife. Or kids. What a frightful responsibility. I
fell in love at school once, at least I thought I did,
and her name was Violet. And then I fell out
again, and haven't thought about a girl since.
Perhaps I shan't marry. Don't let's marry. What
are you laughing at ? "

" You, of course. You get attacks now and then
of thinking what you're going to do when you grow
up, and it comes out like a sneeze and you don't
think about it again for months."

" But it's important," said David. " My father
talked to me about it the evening before I came up.
He's just like a boy still, you know, but he told me
that I wasn't a boy any longer."

Frank interrupted.

" I read a story in *The Cambridge Observer*," he said,
" called 'The Life that was Never Begun.' Something like this. There was once a little boy just
going to a private school. His father told him he
wasn't a child any more, but was entering on his
boyhood which was the seed-time of life. So he
went to his private school. Three years later he
went to a public school, and his father told him that
he wasn't a little boy any longer, and that these were
the years in which character was formed. All sorts of
temptations would now assail him, and life was beginning to open for him. When he went up to the Univer-

sity his father told him that he was going out into
the world at last.   All the years that had passed
were only a preparation for the life which, as
before, was just opening for him.   When he left
Cambridge, his father told him that he was *in
statu pupillari* no longer, and instead of being
sheltered and looked after as he had always been,
he was going to begin to fight life's battles.   When
he was engaged to be married his father told him
that he was now entering on manhood with all its
sacred responsibilities and duties.   Life at last was
opening in front of him.   And when at the age of
eighty-seven he lay dying, the parson knelt by his
bedside and said, ' Dear friend, this world is only
the dream, the probation, the prelude.   Now you are
called to enter into the true life, and through the
gate of death you will begin really to live.'   The man
gave a hollow groan, and muttered, ' Good Lord,
haven't I begun yet ? '   Then he fell back dead."

David cackled with laughter.

" Poor old devil ! " he said.   " Couldn't get going.
But I see what you mean : the best thing to do is
just to go ahead and not mind whether you've finished
or haven't yet begun.   Sort of tract.   Let's write
some tracts, Frank, ' Septic tales for serious people.'
Hi !   It's half-past five : we shall miss the anthem
if we aren't quick."

They sat in the dimness of the ante-chapel, David
still occasionally bubbling with laughter at the
tragedy of the poor gentleman who was always just
going to begin.   The screen with the organ towering
above it cut off the sight of the choir, but beyond,

the soft shining of the candles with which it was lit mistily illuminated the tracery of the windows now black against the night outside, and glowed in the cells of the fan-vaulted roof. Like some mist of sound, too, were the preluding bars of the anthem, with one low pedal note held on the open wood, scarcely audible, but drowsily pervasive, making the leaded glass to quiver. Then like light piercing a depth of dusky water came the first notes of the soprano solo.

David gave a little wriggle of delight.

" O-o-h ! Cold water down my back," he whispered.

" Anything you like. Only shut up ! " said Frank.

They sat on when the singing was done, while the remaining prayers were intoned, waiting for the crimson curtains in the entrance of the choir to be drawn ; then a flood of mellow candlelight poured out into the antechapel, and as the organ muttered and modulated into the key its master sought, the procession of singing boys and men followed by a few fellows in surplices streamed out in pairs. David, always vivid in perception and emotional in mind, basked in the soft, solemn splendour of it all, and yet even while he absorbed and loved it, he couldn't help thinking of the silly line, " The animals came out two by two—hurrah ! hurrah ! " . . . Then other animals came out one by one, for a verger with a silver poker preceded the Provost to the door. His bald head shone faintly like a moon in the candlelight. . . . Hurrah ! hurrah ! How ripping it all was, and he wedged his shoulder against Frank's, for

he must be in touch with him when he enjoyed himself particularly.

The organ had found its key. Dr. Mann paused a
moment before he gave out the subject of a Bach
fugue. It was really a Fugue for the Well-tempered
Clavier, but the wizard who presided over those
banks of stops and triple keyboard had designed the
painting of it with all the orchestral colour of the
organ. It was well known to David, for his sister in
schoolroom days had been set to learn it, and to
enliven her task she and David had created absurd
words for it which fitted the subject.

" Why, it's Margery's," he said, and made a fluting noise that followed the rhythm of it.

> "John Sebastian Back
> Sat down on a tack,
> Sat do-own on a tack and said ' Wow ! ' "

" Now he's going to sit down again : he keeps
sitting down on a tack ; there's a tack for him every-
where. Isn't it ripping ? "

The second voice announced this interesting feat,
and the two discussed it. Then a baritone joined in
and affirmed it, and the melodious riot grew ever
more rollicking. The treble kept on insisting on it,
though no one contradicted him, and the bass gave
out peals and roulades of laughter. Then a fluty
alto, who had hitherto not had any finger in the pie,
bore witness to it, and the bass, having laughed
sufficiently, tried several times to say the same
thing but was always interrupted after announcing
" John Sebastian Back " by hoots from the treble.
All the time the banks of stops were being pulled out
and the volume of sound symmetrically swelling like

a huge blown soap-bubble. Then at last the bass
called the pedals to help, and boomed out what
John Sebastian had done so thunderously that
nobody else had the slightest chance, and held on
to the last "Wow" in a stupendous roar. Upon
which every stop in the coupled keyboards combined against it, the deafening yell of the tubas
was unloosed, and with one more repetition they all
came to agreement, and blared out the major chord
of C.

"O Lord, what fun!" said David. "Worth
while sitting down on a tack, if it makes you sing
like that. I must learn music. I must be a composer. How do you set about a fugue?"

David of King's   *II*

THERE was no time after chapel to settle down to
work, for David said that snippets of work were no
good. You had to sit down with a solid couple of
hours in front of you if you were to make any sort
of headway. There were, as a matter of fact, just
about a solid couple of hours in front of him before
he need dress for Bags's birthday party, but after
a stroll round the quadrangle and a little discussion
on this point the hours were solid no longer, and it
was wiser to play piquet. He and Frank had a
running score over their games, and were supposed
to play, like the heroes of Ouida, for sovereign points.

Up-to-date David had lost on balance rather over five thousand pounds, but to-night he got a few hundreds back, and felt quite rich when he went to dress.

Bags had blossomed in the most exotic manner since he came up to Cambridge, like a plant taken out of a nipping garden-bed and put in a hothouse. He was one year senior to David, and from having been nobody in particular at school, because he was short-sighted and could not play games with any success, he now found that there were many other lines for development and expansion besides the athletic. During the last long vacation he had been abroad, learning French, and now shamelessly inter-larded his conversation with expressions in that elegant language, even when there was a perfectly appropriate English equivalent. He said " Tiens " and " Mon Dieu " ; he even talked with a slightly foreign accent till David imitated him with such withering felicity that it was really wiser to adopt the more familiar pronunciation. He read quantities of the most amazing books which threw a flood of lurid light on the possibilities of life and sex, and made him certain that the only shocking thing in the world was to be shocked at anything in the world. You had to taste existence in its most curious essences. . . . One day David, waiting for him in his rather exquisite rooms, picked up a small volume with a great deal of margin and very little printed in the middle of the page by a man called Baudelaire, which even with his limited knowledge of French he could perceive was something quite unusual, and with a dictionary to help he proceeded to follow his

meaning more closely. He was not in the least
shocked (thus avoiding the really shocking thing in
the world), but gave loud cackles of laughter, and
murmured " Hot stuff ! " But it soon palled, and
when Bags entered a few minutes later David threw
the book at him, and said, very carefully and slowly,
with a puckered brow :

" Il aime le smut. Son vrai nom est Bawdy
Laire. Bawdy Laire, votre ami, sait une chose ou
deux. I say, Bags, what awful piffle ! "

Bags tried to look slightly superior.

" Of course you've got to know French to appreciate him," he said. " His sense of beauty is quite
unrivalled. There's not an English poet to touch
him."

" Je crois que non," said David, " not a with pair
of tongs. I say, Bawdy Laire, you know. Jolly
funny. I wonder if they'd take me on to the staff
of *Punch*. Cushy job ; you make a joke or two like
that every week, and they pay you a salary, and
you get *Punch* free."

" *Punch* ? " said Bags. (This was before David
cured him of talking French.) " Ah, oui ! Ce journal
comique."

" Oui ; mais non si comique que—— "

" Pas si comique," said Bags.

" Non ! Je préfère non. Non si comique que
Bawdy Laire. Ne me interruptez pas, and let's
talk English again ! "

Then Bags, slightly cooling towards French as a
ladder to culture and a medium for English conversation, had taken to dress too beautifully for words
with a tie carrying out the scheme of his socks and

buttons, and David, coming into his room one morning
as he was dressing, insisted that his drawers were the
same colour as his hair and his sock-suspenders.   And
Bags belonged to a very select dining-club and talked
Port, and cultivated the Society of long-haired poets
with pale green ties, and that of horsy young gentlemen who went to Newmarket.   He liked athletes, too,
though he couldn't play any games himself, and never
called them flannelled fools or muddied oafs.   He
kept a horse with a mouth of cast-iron, and a playful
habit of bucking whenever it met with the slightest
opposition to its whims, and then Bags's faultless
riding-breeches would be seen sitting in the air and
subsequently on the ground, and his riding-crop
flew west and his cap east.   But at bottom his horse
was perfectly good-natured, when it was allowed to go
where it liked at the pace that suited it.   So on the
whole Bags quite enjoyed his riding, and subscribed
to the drag, and even on the days when he was not
taking equestrian exercise he often strolled down to
the Pitt in his breeches and beautiful gaiters without
the risk of being bucked off anything.

Bags, in fact, just now was being highly experi-
mental, and having discovered that it takes all sorts
not only to make the world, but the University of
Cambridge, was sampling everything within sight with
a zealous appetite.   So you never could tell whom
you were going to meet at Bags's parties, and David
as he set out for his dinner was equally prepared to
hear recitations from Swinburne's Poems and Ballads
(or the poems and ballads of the bard's disciples),
or to listen to the latest odds on horses he had never
heard of, or to drink port for a long time after dinner

and talk about vintages. But it was sure to be fun,
for David always enjoyed everything, and besides
Bags was one of the best fellows in the world.

Bags had provided an elegant and sumptuous
repast, and had written the menu-cards out himself
in French. But as his gyp had put them all upside-
down, nobody was any wiser than they would otherwise have been. He himself wore a purple padded
smoking-coat with a sapphire solitaire in his shirt,
and there was a poet there called Stapleton whose hair
was so long that it fell into his eyes, and gave him the
appearance of an anæmic Aberdeen terrier. Then
there was a golfing-blue called Gowles, who hit the
ball so much further than anybody else that it was
quite impossible to believe in equality, and who,
when David entered, was embarked on his usual
story without an end about his game that afternoon.
Then there was one of Bags's sporting friends called
Vyse, who when he was spoken to said " Quite," and
when he wasn't, crooned on about the respective
chance of Armadillo and Belisarius for the Grand
National, and an elderly don of Bacchic and genial
disposition, who was much younger and stouter than
anybody else had ever been. His name was Alfred
Gepp, and he was known as A. G.

" Well, at the second hole," said Gowles, " I made
a decent sort of drive and my opponent was sixty
yards behind. May have been seventy. So he took
his brassy——"

" Capital," said Bags, " Do you know Mr. Blaize,
of King's ? "

" How-de-do ? He took his brassy, and moved his
ball while he was addressing it, but insisted that it

hadn't rolled over. ' Right you are,' said I, and he just reached the green with his second, which was really his third. So I took an iron and laid mine dead."

A. G. tucked David's hand into the crook of his own arm.

" Ha, ha, Blaizides and his birthday," he said. " How awfully jolly to be just nineteen. You can eat and drink whatever you like without thinking that you're going to die to-morrow. Let us eat and drink, for to-morrow we haven't the slightest intention of dying. And at nineteen whatever you do hasn't any consequence at all. Consequences! Let's play Consequences till dinner's ready. That daring game when Mr. Something or Other meets Miss Other or Something in an organ-loft peeling potatoes with— with a theodolite. The consequence was that they became as bald as me and the world said ' That Kruschen feeling!' Now it's Vyse's turn. What does Tommy Vyse say ? "

" Quite," said Vyse. " But my name's Robert."

The amazing A. G. put his other arm round Vyse's waist. The three looked rather like a Laocoon group without their snakes.

" Oh, well, somebody else is Tommy," he said. " You're just a centaur, dear boy. You spend your beautiful life in riding over gates and bullfinches, instead of opening the one and putting the other in a cage. The idea of mounting a horse at all appals me, and the horse would hate it. I rode a horse once if it wasn't a mare, and it gave me the sense of ' fallings from me, vanishings,' as Wordsworth says on the less important subject of Immortality, while the horse, I feel sure, felt the 'mute misgivings of a creature.' "

" Then at the third hole," said the inexorable Gowles, who had got Stapleton fixed in a corner, " we both got pretty decent drives, mine with a slight pull on it, which carried the little pot-bunker. He was on the far side of the green with his third——"

Stapleton swept his hair out of his eyes.

" I don't understand a single word," he said in a loud, lamentable voice. " I don't know what you're talking about. If it's golf, it isn't any use to me."

Gowles wheeled round to David.

" So I made a perfect chip-shot with my niblick," he said, " and lipped the hole."

Bags was a perfect host.

" That was splendid," he said. " Serve the other Johnnie right for going so far with his third. Jolly good match. I think dinner's ready."

The genial A. G. was always delighted to talk about any subject. Golf would do as well as anything else.

" Tees and bunkers ! " he exclaimed. " What a perfect title for a novel that dealt with the start of some fair and flourishing career which ended in complete disaster ! I used to play golf in a red coat, and it would have been awfully jolly if I could have hit the ball. Psychologically, of course, golf is all wrong from beginning to end. Every hole, of which there are far too many—is it eight in a round, or eighty ?—every hole is a process of diminuendo, whereas it ought to be a crescendo. As it is you start with a great glorious drive, and after some brassy shots there is an approach, not so strong and free as the drive, and then there's a putt which isn't so long as the approach, and then there are some more putts each of which, if you're putting well, is shorter than the last. Instead you ought to start with a short putt, and then make a longer putt, and then play some approaches, and finish up with a great glorious drive on to the tee. How much more exhilarating and expansive and exciting and excellent ! "

Gowles knitted his brows over this revolutionary project.

" I don't quite see how you would manage it," he said.

" Ha, ha ! nor do I, my dear Teddy," said A. G., who had suddenly remembered his Christian name. " But I don't see how to manage golf as it is. Golf and the Infallibility of the Pope are affairs which transcend the powers of my mind. You ought to call a Symposium of Golfers, and drink quantities of golden wine—everything is done by Symposiums now —and, and get it all altered. Almost everything I know ought to be altered : we're much too Conservative, and the world will never get on till we've remodelled it entirely. Yes, champagne please : perhaps champagne needn't be altered. We might leave champagne alone, which I haven't the slightest intention of doing."

He emptied his glass so quickly that there was practically no pause between the last sentence and the next.

" We should begin by turning every institution upside-down," he said, " and get out of all our hide-bound notions. Greek, for instance, oughtn't to be compulsory or even voluntary, but absolutely prohibited, and then you would get everyone to study it with the zest that always attaches to the forbidden. That was the cause of man's first disobedience, and it will certainly be the cause of his last. We all want to be wicked, and so few of us know how. That's why poor Bernard Shaw is so popular, for he tells us that we are wicked, and that mothers are nasty, foul-minded old women, and sweet English girls are liars and hypocrites. Anyhow, the present company are the best and most delightful people ever brought together under one roof. Awfully jolly."

Stapleton waved his fork in violent disagreement, and a small dollop of spinach fell on his soft shirt.

" I entirely disagree," he said. " I'm not quite sure what you mean, but I entirely disagree. I think that's a *bourgeois* point of view."

" Quite," said Vyse. " I say, you've some spinach on your shirt."

" Well, at the third hole," said Gowles—" or did I tell you about the third hole ? "

" Yes, dear boy, you holed out in—in dormy two from a bunkered stymie," said A. G. " How rich and delicious words are when you haven't the slightest idea what they signify ! That is the whole secret of Stevenson's popularity. He leads up to a matchless situation, and then being quite unable to handle it, makes his characters talk Scotch, and the reader interprets the unintelligible dialogue which follows by the light of his own emotion. Other authors, when they can't get on, or are getting on too far, put rows of asterisks, and we fill them up for ourselves. How beautiful to publish a book of thousands of pages consisting completely of asterisks ! Most

3

books are far too long, for you have to wade through
dreary events and the ill-digested impressions of the
author, but the book of asterisks could never be long
enough, for the reader would put into each line of
stars some passionate and unprintable experience.
Only a title would be necessary, with perhaps a
sub-title to explain what the asterisks were about.
'Toques and Trousers,' for instance. 'A Revelation
in the Relations of the Sexes!' Who will collaborate
with me in a lurid volume of asterisks ? "

Gowles had despaired of finding any listener, so he
went on quietly talking to himself about what happened at the fourth hole, in order to get it ready for
the next occasion on which he would find a sympathetic audience.

"Or 'Toques and Togas,'" continued A. G.
"The title of a book, so one of our leading contem-
porary novelists told me, is the only thing that
matters. Certainly his books do not. David would
look awfully jolly in a toga. Why doesn't everybody
wear togas and cothurnuses or something of the sort ?
and I would give my lectures on Theocrites on the
banks of the Cam, and we would all swim about when
I got too dry. Nobody would learn anything, but life
would become quite preposterous and Athenian and
exquisite. I wonder who invented that dreadful
maxim 'Live and learn.' The whole point of life is
to refuse to learn anything that can possibly be of
use and thus hamper your natural style. I did not
know that when I was young, and balefully amassed
a quantity of useful information which I thought
would help me in after-life. It has done nothing of
the kind ; it has hampered me at every turn, and in

my most joyous and *allegro* hours I can never quite get rid of the incubus of it."

A. G. was now firmly anchored to the subject of himself and went on with extraordinary gusto.

" I might otherwise have become the apostle of the new civilisation," he said, " which I firmly believe is dawning at last, and in which everybody will be young and useless and ignorant. As it is, the drudging habits of my early years continue to reassert themselves, and I go round and round like a squirrel in a cage industriously grinding out the meal of instructive information to bored and bright-eyed undergraduates. Who, after all, was the wisest man the world has ever seen ? Socrates, of course, who spent his entire life in convincing the youth of Athens that neither he nor they knew anything whatever. They sat under plane-trees, and it was all awfully jolly. What a drab age is ours ! An age of blue-books and Pelmanism which, I am told—and I am afraid it is quite true—enables you to remember anything you have ever learned. Let us start an Anti-Pelman Society, which enables you to forget anything you have ever learnt. It will purge our minds, as by a great golden pill, of all the stored-up waste-products of information, which if allowed to accumulate poison the system and make us stiff with educational acids. Ha, ha ! "

" Quite," said Vyse. " By the by, Bags, I got a tip from the Charlton stables that the Queen of Sheba's got a swelled fetlock, and probably won't run on Tuesday. Hope you haven't backed her."

Stapleton, who had removed the spinach, was feeling less contradictory, and was now listening to A. G.'s sonorous periods with quivers of delight, like a terrier who smells something interesting and ratty. He drew in his breath with a hiss and a shudder at the introduction of this barbarous and horsy topic, but A. G. patted Vyse's shoulder appreciatively.

" How splendid and exotic and oriental," he said. " That is the sort of information I delight in, for though it conveys nothing whatever to my reason, it evokes endless imaginative visions. I seem to see the Queen of Sheba telling King Solomon that she proposes to run all day next Tuesday. Hardly had she spoken the vainglorious words than she was seized with a dull ache in her rosy and royal fetlock. The king's physicians, hastily summoned, pronounced that the place was distinctly swollen, and that any notion of running on Tuesday was out of the question. That, no doubt, was why there was no more spirit left in her——"

" Quite," said Vyse, " but the Queen of Sheba I was telling Bags about is a mare."

No amount of literalness ever daunted A. G.

" The doctrine of the transmigration of souls," he said. " How fascinating, but how very improbable. I entirely believe in it for that reason. An eminent transmigrationalist, the other day, assured me that I had been one of the later Roman Emperors, whose soul had been kept, so I understood him, in some sort of spiritual cold-storage till I was ready for it. I wonder, if I behaved like Heliogabalus, whether the University authorities would admit the plea of identity as an adequate excuse for imperial excesses."

David's health was duly drunk at the close of dinner ; A. G. proposed it, and as David was totally incapable of making a public oration of any sort, since the moment he opened his mouth, all ideas escaped from his mind like a flock of startled birds, A. G. also replied for him. He professed, on David's behalf, a stern determination to keep himself pure from the malady of learning anything, and assiduously to devote the golden days of youth to unfitting himself for any future career, keeping the prismatic colours of his soul as bright as an awfully jolly rainbow. . . . Then he forgot that he was speaking for David, and gave them some incredible reminiscences of the late Kaiser. . . .

Bags was in his element to-night, entertaining a party of this kind. He was, to begin with, richly endowed with the ancient and honourable virtue of hospitality, and liked nothing better than to see people eat and drink at his expense. The more incongruous and dissimilar his guests were the more he enjoyed it, and it really was a rich variety of human nature that was now smoking his cigars. There was Vyse, who thought about nothing but horses, and Gowles, whose little life was bounded by a bunker, and Stapleton, who didn't know a horse from a golf-ball, and A. G., who was a reincarnation of Heliogabalus. Finally, there was David, in whose honour the feast was set, and David somehow was in acuter contrast with each of them than any of them were with each other. He could hugely shout with laughter at A. G.'s amazing conversation or take the deepest interest in the exposition Gowles was at this moment giving him with the aid of a poker and a match-box as to how to explode a ball out of sand. (Just then he hit the match-box so venomously that all the matches

exploded.)   Or if Vyse recounted to him the pedigree
of the Queen of Sheba, or Stapleton recited to him
some outrageous poem, David would consider it to be
wonderfully gifted of them and attend with all his
might.   That was so characteristic of him : he cared
for what interested other people, just because it
interested them, and that was why everyone wanted
to get hold of him.

For the moment all Bags's guests were engaged
with each other—Vyse had gone to telephone to
somebody, Stapleton was gesticulating about the
colour-value of Paul Verlaine's lyrics to A. G., and
there was Gowles gardening with a poker on the
hearthrug.   Yes, that was the difference between
David and them : they all had their own stunts,
while David hadn't any stunts at all, except the
stunt of being an ardent well-wisher to other people's
stunts.   And it wasn't as if he was not keen enough
on his own affairs : he played games as if his eternal
salvation depended on them ; but anything that
concerned his friends mattered so much more to him
than what concerned himself.   You really couldn't
call him unselfish, because it interested him more,
and though he was as good as gold and as wholesome
as bread, there was no one less meek—fancy a meek
David !—or pi' or priggish.   But you couldn't
shock him.   Bags had tried once by giving him some
lurid hints about the Moulin Rouge and other gay
resorts in Paris, and David had only yelled with
laughter and said, " O Lord, I wish I'd seen you Don
Juanning with two coc—what are they ?—cocoons !
You must have looked funny."

" Cocottes," said Bags.

" No, I think cocoons. Tell me some more about the cocoons," and he gave a large yawn.

There wasn't really anything particular to tell, and Bags felt that his hinted devilries had fallen rather flat. . . .

David understood all about niblick-shots by now, and Bags thought it was time for drinks and diversions. There was a piano and some packs of cards, and A. G. was soon overbidding his hand at bridge and talking the whole time except when he warbled the simple and moving air of Chopsticks, as performed by David and Bags on the piano.

" Awfully jolly," he said. " Let me see, have I revoked or have our adversaries ? Oh, here the card is. When I was in Venice last year we used to play bridge in a gondola. Tum-te-te, tum-te-te, tum-te-te. A little faster, my dear Bags. Somebody ought to set words to Chopsticks full of subtle innuendos. Ha, ha ! I trump that, so why isn't it my trick ? Oh, I see, dear old Teddy has overtrumped it. There's many a slip betwixt trump and trick. Has the ace of trumps been played yet ? Dear old partner, your hand seems to be at sixes and sevens, and we're two down already on my sumptuous call. Well, I've got the last heart ; anyhow that will make. No, the ace of trumps has not been played. Why didn't you kick me very gently under the table ? That makes us a hundred and fifty down, but I had three trumps, all of which were honours. How awfully jolly it all is ! Why doesn't our beloved David have a birthday every day, and Bags ask us to dinner every night ? I once played bridge at Aix-les-Bains with two

Queens, which with the four in the pack made six.
They are both dead now. I can't take any tricks,
partner. Ought I to have said four diamonds ? I
had five headed by the nine. Five and sixpence,
is it ? I shall get a barrel-organ and a monkey and
sing in the streets of Cambridge, or else cut down my
subscriptions. Perhaps that would give least pain
to the greatest number."

" Quite," said Vyse.

A. G. was easily induced to sing a little, though not
in the streets of Cambridge and without a barrel-
organ, before going to bed. A copy of the *Immortal
Hour* was found, and he accompanied himself in a
fortuitous but optimistic manner. But sitting at the
piano with occupied hands he could not produce the
glamour and atmosphere of Dalua in the pine-wood,
and so he got Bags to play for him, and standing on a
footstool to add majesty to his presence, he wrapped
himself in Vyse's black gown, and put out all the
lights except the candles on the piano. It would have
been more impressive had not David, when Dalua
pointed at him and declaimed " Laugh not, ye out-
casts of the invisible world," been seized with violent
hysterical laughter which he was quite unable to
check. However, he behaved like a man, and
smothered his face in a sofa-cushion, and the concert
proceeded. But he was still rather shaky, and when,
with a good deal of supplementary falsetto, A. G.
went on with " How beautiful they are, the lordly
ones," his efforts at self-repression completely gave
way, and with the cushion still over his mouth, he was
softly led away on to the landing outside.

After this musical conclusion the party dispersed. Vyse, who was in Trinity, suddenly remembered that he was gated at nine, and as it was close on midnight, he would obviously have to run very fast to get back there in time. A. G., whose flippancy had quite evaporated in the deep impression his own singing had made on him, waddled downstairs with David tucked close into him, and explained how rare it was to find exquisite words set to exquisite music, in which happy circumstances alone was the singer capable of doing justice to either.

"Fiona Macleod!" he said. "I am convinced that if that wonderful poetess and I had ever met, I should have found that she was the one woman in the world. Or was Fiona Macleod William Sharp? How exceedingly disconcerting!"

The rain of the afternoon had ceased, the clouds had blown away, and a large quantity of stars, sadly dimmed by a powerful moon a few days after the full, covered the sky. It flooded the great court with light, brightly illuminating the south side of the chapel, and A. G. as they emerged turned his solemn imperial face skywards. He began humming "How beautiful they are" again, and David, unstrung by hysterical laughter, felt his ribs beginning ominously to shake. The identity of the one woman in the world with William Sharp had already unsettled him, and he knew that any more music or high romance would be devastating. But instead A. G. turned a magisterial and disapproving eye on the moon.

"Of all the countless mistakes made in the six days of creation," he said, "that tawdry object always seems to me the worst. Look at it, my dear David, and tell me if you ever saw anything so lop-sided and shabby. It shines with a light that is not its own, like some inefficient plagiarist, and as it waxes and wanes, it does not swell and decrease symmetrically, but plasters fresh pieces on to one side or takes parings off it. It surely would have been possible to make a symmetrical moon which would increase evenly all round up to the full and then diminish evenly, if you wanted an adjustable light, now bright and now dim. The most ordinary lamp-maker will supply you with a burner which turns up and down without going out on one side and flaring on the other. Take it away."

He walked on a few paces, and as David hadn't taken it away, he went on with his criticisms.

"And the quality of the light, too!" he said. "It is the ruination of all colour, and your delightful ruddy face appears at this moment to be ashen in hue. And why could not that ill-drawn ovoid be made to keep pace with the other stars? It goes scurrying along without paying the faintest attention to the general tempo, much in the same way as I play the piano. And why its light is supposed to be suggestive and amorous and romantic has always baffled me. Yet so it is: I imagine the moon has been the cause of more imprudent marriages than any terrestrial stimulus. Every marriage traced to the influence of the moon ought to be dissolved at the pleasure of either party."

He was staring at it now with a fat and fixed malignity.

"Shakespeare, of course, saw what a fraud the

moon was," he said, " and ridicules her with his
most pungent sarcasms in *Midsummer Night's Dream*,
where, as you probably don't remember, he introduces
the moon in the person of the seediest of Bottom's
company, and Thisbe bitterly and deservedly apos-
trophises her, ' And thou, O moon, O base and wicked
moon,' or something of the sort. Indeed it is a
debased and wretched object ; it looks as if it was
covered with spots and was moulting. ' And thou, O
moon, O measly moulting moon ! ' Ha, ha ! How
wonderfully Shakespearean ! Observe too the effect
of that decrepit luminary on the complexion of the
chapel ; how it turns limestone or granite or whatever it is made of to the semblance of greenish and
putrid cheese. . . . Dear me, what a quantity of
things I have said about the moon, but I dislike it
so intensely that they come flooding to my lips. I
shall not sleep to-night, but lie awake hating the
moon, like the second Mrs. Tanqueray. Why do
not all the poets make a dead set against the moon,
and abuse her till she suffers a permanent eclipse ?
I will write a Platonic dialogue about her in which
Socrates, who is me, forces Blaizides, who is you, to
admit that the moon is a mad, measly, mangy,
moulting, melancholy, misbegotten mummy. Dear
old boy, good night ! How awfully jolly it has all
been. Come to breakfast to-morrow at half past
eight."

DAVID presented himself at the rooms of the moon-hater within a few minutes of the appointed hour next morning, but instead of finding his host and breakfast, found only a table sparsely laid for one, and a bed-maker with a duster tip-toeing about her duties.

David explained that he had come to breakfast, and in answer she pointed dramatically to a piece of paper pinned up on the door of Mr. Gepp's bed-room, on which was inscribed in large, legible letters, " Do not wake me till half past nine." This seemed to indicate that his virulence about the moon had caused him to forget about his invitation. But whether or not he had lain awake all night hating it, he was certainly awake no longer, for through his bedroom door came comfortable noises which proved it. So underneath the order not to call him till half past nine, David wrote, " I didn't ; and thank you so much for my nice breakfast.—D. B.," and went to the college kitchen to see what of a suitable and substantial nature could be provided without delay.

David was quite pleased to have got up so early, though the immediate cause for his having done so had proved futile. But otherwise he would certainly have turned over with a groan when his gyp called him, have gone to sleep for another hour or two, and have scrambled through a hasty breakfast in order to be in time for Mr. Crowfoot's lecture on Cicero's letters. As it was, the act of rising had

been attended by no pang, since it was to be succeeded by breakfast with A. G., and he had now a
couple of hours clear before he need be moving. It
would be an ample sacrifice on the classical altar if
at ten o'clock he began devoting himself to the study
of such letters of Cicero as Mr. Crowfoot would be
expounding at his lecture, and two consecutive hours
occupied with that diffuse and pompous correspondent would be as much as anyone could hope to
survive.

Cicero wrote the worst possible sort of letters:
there was no lightness about them ; they were interminable discussions on heavy topics, politics and
Roman history, and he ought to have foreseen what
a nuisance they would be if anybody kept them.
He ought to have said, " Destroy them at my death."
. . . As it was, they formed, in Mr. Crowfoot's hands,
a vehicle for the consumption of Roman history.
However, as you could seldom hear anything Mr.
Crowfoot said, for his words ran into each other in
a swift, strange gabble, broken every now and then
by shrill clearings of his throat, there was not really
much consumption of anything. His speech, in fact,
was to the ear what writing becomes to the eye,
when after having written something with a broad-
pointed pen and plenty of ink, you fold it down the
middle and press the two sides together. Written
words lurk somewhere in the spine of the strange
insect which is then disclosed, just as words, no
doubt, lurked in the core of the confused noise which
Mr. Crowfoot made, without pause, for the space of
one hour twice a week. The erudite could identify
fragments of what he said ; David himself was

getting rather good at it, and his conjecture that what sounded like " fish-sauce " (an expression which had occurred several times in Mr. Crowfoot's last lecture) signified " official sources " was certainly correct.

But there was an hour yet before he need turn his mind to the infamous letter-writer, and David settled himself comfortably in a large arm-chair in front of the fire, with a foot on each side of the fireplace, and proceeded to perform the first indispensable duty of the day, which was smoking his meerschaum pipe. A cigarette, of course, would have tasted much nicer, but if you had a meerschaum pipe there were duties as well as glory attached to the ownership of it, and it had to be coloured. Its virginity was still almost distressingly white, but up the neck of it, as far as the amber mouthpiece, and up the bowl of it as far as the plug which occupied the bottom of it, David's optimistic eye detected a faint yellowish tinge, like threatenings of jaundice, which he hoped were the first manifestations of its colouring. By and by, if he persevered, that tinge would deepen into a rich chestnut hue, and would eventually become a bright and lustrous black. What would happen after that was uncertain : some said that the stain would spread to the top of the bowl, others that above the plug it would always remain white ; but all were agreed that every now and then, when the pipe got warm, the stem of a wax match should be carefully and lovingly rubbed on it. The odour of the liquefied wax mingling with that of burning tobacco was wonderfully nauseating ; but the match could be applied when the pipe was

finished, and so he was not obliged to go on smoking
in the aroma of that oily stench. Luckily a meerschaum must only be enjoyed two or three times a
day, and must be allowed always to cool before it
was smoked again. David was glad of that.

He applied himself to the ritual, which was girt
with ceremonial observances. You must never,
when it began to get warm, touch the bowl or the
stem of it with the finger, because fingers left an
impression on that sensitive skin ; you must never
smoke fast and get it over, because that fevered the
delicate creature ; but you must never smoke so
slowly that it went out, because then it had to be
relit, which was bad for it, and tasted disgusting,
which was bad for you. Luckily it did not need to
be waxed this morning, for it had been waxed yesterday ; but, unluckily, it had been waxed yesterday, and as it warmed up the smell of the remelted
grease began to diffuse itself. Often and often
David wished that Bags had never given it him, but
Bags had discovered that about forty years ago it
was rather chic to have a well-coloured meerschaum,
and had bought two of these woeful badges of an
antique mode, and had given David one. Once
started on their career, the two pipes had become
rival beauties, and had been, for some inconjectur-
able reason, christened Angelica Crabtree and Perpetua Blaize. Angelica, so David had jealously
observed last night, was quite unmistakably browner
than Perpetua, but she had distinct signs of a nasty
sort of pale rash coming out on her bottom, which
was a consolation.

Perpetua was sweating heavily this morning from

her waxing yesterday, and had a creaking sort of
cough when she was sucked. It must have been
some diphtheritic trouble, for a blob of bitter mem-
brane got loose in her throat and flew up the stem
into his mouth. David got rid of that by the obvious
expedient of spitting between his legs into the fire,
and this emission seemed to have relieved Perpetua,
for she coughed no longer and only sweated. He
blew down her to assure himself that her air-passages
were now clear, and the burning tobacco flew out
like a cork from a soda-water bottle and lodged in
the hearth-rug. David shovelled it back and burned
the top of his finger, and the singed fabric of the rug
made a new sort of smell. Then Perpetua began to
burn lop-sidedly : one side of her glowed with incan-
descent fervour and was probably very heating for
her, while the other wouldn't burn at all, and probably gave her a chill on her liver. David muttered
" Blast the silly wench ! " and stirred things up
with a wooden match. In his vexation with the silly
wench, he used the inflammable end of it by mistake,
and the head of it went off in the middle of Perpetua's stomach and scattered her burning bowels
on the hearth-rug for the second time.

A loud tattoo sounded on his door and Tommers
entered. When Tommers tapped it did not imply
that he was asking if he might come in, but that he
was doing so. He wrinkled up his freckled nose.

" Lord, what a stink ! " he said. " What's wrong
with Perpetua ? "

" She's got the Athenian plague, if I remember
the symptoms rightly," said David.

" Well, the sooner it's fatal the better, I should

say," said Tommers. "You don't get well when you're as bad as that."

"Oh, it's the hearth-rug partly," said David, stamping on glowing fragments of Perpetua's inside. "Wow! There's a piece on my trousers."

David slipped from his chair as a fragment of burning tobacco produced a sharp, stinging pain in his knee-cap, and extinguished it.

"Fire on one knee," he said fatuously, "and I believe I've got water on the other which I put into Alston's face yesterday. And as they were both covered with earth, there are the three elements for you."

"Element's embrocation," said Tommers, after a little thought.

"Jolly smart, Tommers," said David.

"I thought you'd like it."

"Awfully jolly," said David in A. G.'s voice. "He was priceless last night. He sang most of the *Immortal Hour*, and I got the most hopeless giggles. When he wasn't singing he didn't stop talking."

"What about?" asked Tommers.

"How should I know? That's the charm of A. G.'s conversation; by the time you think he's talking about one thing, you find he's talking about something perfectly different. He was saying something about books entirely consisting of asterisks, and I'd hardly got on to that when it was Toques and Togas, and Stimies and the Queen of Sheba and Socrates and the transmigration of souls. Coming back across the court he certainly stuck to one subject, and violently abused the moon, which didn't pay the slightest attention. But Angelica's got a

rash—I guess she'll soon be in a greater mess than
Perpetua."

" Oh, do stop jawing about your putrid pipe,"
said Tommers.

" Putrid she is, but I haven't said anything about
her yet.   And then A. G. asked me to breakfast, but
he was snoring, and as he hadn't asked me to snore
with him I came away.   That's why I'm up.   And
there's a hole burned through my beautiful old
trousers, and if you look closely you can see me
coming through."

" Indecent exposure," said Tommers.

" Yes.   I shall have it patched, and claim the price
of a pair of new ones from the Fire Insurance."

" Do.   As a genuine antique.   I believe they were
found in Tutankhamen's tomb."

" They were.   While they're being patched I shall
wear a toga.   A. G. said I should look awfully jolly
in a toga.   And then there's the hearth-rug.   All
seems to lead us back to the subject of Perpetua.   I
must fill her again, I suppose.   Lord, how the poor
maiden sweats ! "

Tommers had dived underneath one of David's legs,
and now filled up the triangle they made with the
fireplace.

" I wish you'd chuck her into the fire," he said.

" Can't see it," said David.   " Oh, is it behind
you ? . . .   Do shunt, Tommers.   It's beastly
cold."

" I know ; that's why I'm standing close to the
fire," he observed.

David suddenly leaned forward and dexterously
pulled Tommers's trousers, which were now toasted,

close against the back of his thighs.   He gave one loud squeal, and burst out of David's encircling legs.

"Thought that would do it," said David.   "Now, don't rag.   My health is precarious this morning. Besides, in two minutes I want to begin to work, and ragging always takes more than that."

Tommers sat down on the sofa.   It had only three legs, but he made a temporary fourth with a Greek Lexicon and Dr. Smith's larger Latin Dictionary.

"Right.   I didn't come to rag.   I came for a little quiet conversation.   I awfully want you to do something."

David cocked his head on one side like a canary, and a gleam of suspicion came into his eyes.

"If it's anything to do with Rugger, I won't," he said.

"Well, it has partly."

"Then I won't have anything to do with that part. I hate Rugger ; it's a mucky game.   I only played at school because I had to.   What's the other part ? "

"Oh, it's the other part that's about Rugger," said Tommers.   "I wish you'd play regularly. We're quite a decent College team, but we're stodgy somehow.   We're all industrious, but there ain't any snap.   Now, you funk, of course ; I never saw a large tall thing funk so frightfully——"

"Oh, go on, don't mind me," said David.

"I don't—you funk, I was saying, but you do surprising things.   You can go like hell, too, when there's something savage after you.   You won the match for us yesterday, however much you hated it. Do play regularly for the team."

" No," said David.

" It's rather rotten of you, then. It's a jolly
good game ; you'd get to love it. Besides, *esprit
de corps*——"

" Esprit de skittles," said David. " I play games
because I like them, not because of any espreeze.
Besides, I'm no earthly good. But cricket now—if
nobody else in the world played cricket, I should go
on playing it all by myself."

" Jolly clever of you," said Tommers.

" I know. But I should. I should bowl a very
slow ball, and then run like the wind to the other
wicket and hit it. Then I should drop my bat and
go and field it——"

" How about runs ? " asked Tommers, momentarily distracted from his real topic.

" Oh, that ! I—I should get someone to run for
me. You may always have someone to run for you
if both captains consent. I should be both, you
see. . . . Or I could spoon up an easy chance, and
just as I thought I was going to catch myself, I
could call no-ball. . . . Oh, why do I talk such utter
piffle ? It was your fault, Tommers, for asking me
to play Rugger in the College team. Firstly I don't
want to, and secondly I'm an absolute stumour at
it——"

" But you can run," said Tommers. " We want
somebody who can do more than trot."

" Only when I'm frightened," said the wily David.
" You said so yourself ; and if I played a lot, I
should probably cease to be frightened. No ; you
get some bright industrious lad who likes being
clasped round the knees and thrown flat on his

face and kicked in the eye. For them as likes that sort of thing, Rugger's a ripping game—none better."

The College porter came in with a couple of letters for David, and a card. He took this first and read it, and an expression of blank perplexity came over his face. It was printed, with the date and his name written in, and ran :

C.U.R.F.C.

DEAR SIR,

Will you play for Stripes in the picked game on Saturday next at 2.30 on the Corpus Ground ?

E. TOWLING (Hon. Sec.).

Then the obvious explanation struck him.

" Bally ass," he said to Tommers. " But not a bad try-on. Where did you get the card from ? "

" What are you babbling about ? " asked Tommers.

David held the card lightly between thumb and finger and flicked it at him. It was a perfect shot, hitting Tommers precisely on the nose and falling on to his knee.

" That's what I'm babbling about," he said. " Childish jape."

David began to laugh.

" It took me in just for a second," he admitted.

Tommers looked at the card.

" But I swear I've had nothing to do with it," he said. " It's all genuine. Why, of course, the Tooties were looking on yesterday when you made your great funk. I hoped they were looking at me, and played up like billy-oh. And they'd got their limpid eyes on you all the time."

" But it must be a joke," said David. " If it's not you who's done it, it's some other blighter. I shan't take any notice : I simply shan't go ; and I bet you a bob the Stripes aren't a man short."

" Done," said Tommers. " O Lord, how funny! You were actually saying that you weren't good enough to play for the College when the notice to play in the picked game arrived."

David heard Frank's whistle from the court below and went to the window. When he was excited he stammered a bit. " Yes, c-come up," he shouted.

Frank came in. David had refilled Perpetua and was smoking her violently in his agitation.

" Frank, d-did you do it ? " he said. " I believe you did. Show it him, Tommers."

Frank read the card and burst out laughing.

" Of course I didn't," he said. " And as I told you, the Tooties asked me who that lanky devil on the right was. That's what comes of funking, David. If you hadn't got terrified you wouldn't have run so fast or chucked the ball away, and the Tooties would have let you alone."

Now, though David professed to dislike Rugby football, he could not help being pleased at this invitation to play in a picked game. He was quite convinced he was a wretched performer, but he loved having impressed the Tooties, even though terror had been the first cause of this distinction.

" I suppose it is genuine, then," he said. " Lor ! Picked game ! More than ever happened to you, Tommers ! "

" In an access of fright the brilliant young freshman three-quarters then ran round——" began Frank.

" Oh, shut it," said David. " I say, I shall go into training till Saturday. I shan't smoke Perpetua. Give me a cigarette, somebody. What did you come about, Frank ? "

" Nothing particular. Chiefly because I didn't want to begin working. The claim of friendship took precedence of intellectual interests."

" Speech," said David.

" I was going to ask you about yours last night."

" Oh, A. G. made it for me. And he forgot towards the end and produced reminiscences about the Kaiser. A. G. had been told that he had been a Roman Emperor in a previous incarnation. I think he told himself. When anyone says ' I'm told,' it means he's invented it."

" Cynical dog is David," said Tommers.

" Huh ! That's taut—tautology. Comes in grammar."

" And what's tautology ? "

" When you say the same thing twice over. Cynical means doggy."

" So's your room," said Tommers.

" Lord ! What brilliance ! I say, nobody need go away unless they want to, but I'm going to work. Where's Cicero's letters ? Where's my Latin dictionary ? Where the hell's my Latin dictionary ? It was on the table just now."

Tommers sidled in a casual manner to the corner of the sofa, so that he concealed the biblical leg he had made for it.

" Dematerialization of a dictionary," he said.
" That's the sort of thing that the spirits of the
departed occupy themselves with in the next world,
in order to demonstrate their existence."

David caught sight of the corner of it.

" And then materialize it again to show there's no
malice," he said. " Oh, get up, Tommers. I'm
going to work, I tell you. I don't often get up early,
and the golden morning——"

Frank moved towards the door.

" Come on, Tommers," he said. " He likes Cicero
much better than us. You're playing tennis with
me at two, David."

" Oh, ripping. I'd quite forgotten. I'll call for
you."

The two chattered downstairs.

" Funny about the picked game," said Frank.
" David half thinks there must be some mistake even
now. But he looked pretty useful in that match
yesterday."

" Of course he was. He got one of our two tries
himself, and made the opening for the other. But
he never thinks he's any good at anything. Rotten
modesty."

" Yes. Rather jolly, though."

Tommers laughed.

" And, by Jove, can't he sprint when he's got the
wind up," he said. " I hope somebody will frighten
him thoroughly on Saturday."

Mr. Crowfoot, under whom David was to sit and possibly learn that morning, was a bustling, chirpy little body, who always dressed in a tail-coat, a bowler-hat, and buttoned boots which turned up at the toes. He had a round face, the lower portion of which was covered with a round beard, and he wore round spectacles of peculiar construction. They had extra lenses like blinkers hinged to their outer margins, and these could be turned back over the others, so as to give an additional magnifying power. He whisked these backwards and forwards as he lectured, using one pair for the larger type of his text, and adding the second for the smaller type of his notes, and poured forth a swift gabble of confused exposition, as if he was just going to catch a train and had only a minute or two to spare.

He had never been seen otherwise than in a hurry, which caused him constantly to drop whatever he was carrying. To-day as he scurried up the lecture-room a cataract of books and papers spirted from below his arm, and as he gathered them up and put them back they kept pushing each other out and falling down again. A pencil popped out of his waistcoat pocket as he bent down, like a torpedo from its tube, and his watch fell out and dangled by its chain in the air. He continued to clear his throat and smile and murmur, " Dear me ! how awkward I am ! Very tiresome ! Thank you, Blaize," as David helped him to recover and retain these treasures.

Mr. Crowfoot was full of what he called " dodges,"
like the White Knight in *Alice in Wonderland*. On
the writing-table in his rooms where he corrected
Latin proses, and made memoranda and never could
find what he had put there, was a row of ink-bottles
which you could upset without anything coming out,
containing polychromatic fluids, purple ink, green ink,
red ink, everything but black ink, and it was popu-
larly supposed that he was thinking out a dodge of
using black paper (which would probably be cheaper
than white, owing to its not being bleached) and
writing upon it with white ink (which would probably be cheaper than black, because it hadn't got
any colouring matter). These inks he used week
by week in rotation for his correspondence and the
correction of proses, red ink one week and purple
the next, so that merely by looking at the colour
you could ascertain the date of the piece in question.
There was a pen by each ink-pot, dedicated to its
use alone ; but being always in a hurry, he usually
dipped the red-ink pen into the green-ink bottle and
the purple-ink pen into the red-ink bottle, thus producing curious colours of mixed date, and all the
nibs had to be cleaned. He had a drawer full of
small hanks of string which he unravelled from parcels
received and used again. They were seldom, of
course, precisely the length required (that would
have been too much to expect), so he knotted a
couple of them together, or three if necessary, and
there you were! But he ceased to be quite so
much there when the knots came undone, for the
contents of the parcel fell out, and he had to begin
again. In another drawer were sheets of brown

paper, which had already been through the post but could be turned inside-out and used again. If too small, two pieces could be gummed together ; if too large, one piece could be torn in half. More ingenious yet was his cuckoo-clock, which was adjusted to strike the hour two minutes before the right time.

" Because," so he gleefully explained, " if you want to do something at eleven o'clock—or say ten —it's too late to get ready for it when the clock strikes and it's time to begin. But if your clock strikes two minutes before the hour, there you are all cool and comfortable." In practice, Mr. Crowfoot generally began to do something else when this dodgy clock struck, because there were two minutes to spare yet, which it was a pity to waste. After that he forgot the time altogether until the cuckoo performed again, and he found that he ought to have begun the first thing fifty-eight minutes ago.

Below his table was a fur foot-warmer (why not fill it with ice in the summer ?) in which he inserted his feet while he worked. But the buttons or the turned-up toes of his boots often got caught in the torn lining of it, so that when he tried to stand up he sat down again, or lurched forward among the ink-bottles. In extricating himself a button or two sometimes came off the boots, which he put in his waistcoat pocket and forgot about; so that when, in a great hurry, he took out his pencil-sharpener, which was like a small candle-extinguisher and cut your finger instead of the pencil unless you knew the dodge of it (and sometimes even then), the buttons came out too, and rolled about the carpet like the bright black eyes of birds. He picked them

up and put them on the chimney-piece, and naturally
forgot to sharpen the pencil with which he was just
going to make a most important memorandum
concerning a motion of his at the next Council
meeting.   He had always half a dozen motions down
on the most various subjects, such as the cutting
of the lawn, the cleaning of the lightning-conductors
on the chapel, the quality of the beer supplied by
the buttery, or a scheme for feeding the fish in the
Cam and fattening them for the use of Fellows.
Sometimes his own arguments converted him to the
opposite way of thinking, and he voted against the
motion which he had himself proposed.   Especially
was this the case when A. G. agreed with his original
motion, for he would do anything rather than be
agreed with by A. G. . . . Whenever he was in the
company of his fellow-dons he was rich in incoherent
arguments about some abuse that needed rectifica-
tion, and got up round-robins, and had hares to
start and bones to pick, and schemes to moot, none
of which ever came to anything.

Mr. Crowfoot was of a highly social disposition, and
his favourite hospitality was the glee-singing parties
which he gave in his rooms after Hall every week.
They took place on Wednesday in the summer and
Thursday in the winter, and he had some reason,
which no one could ever remember (so abstruse was
it), why Wednesday was more suitable to the long
days and Thursday to the short ones.   He had collected an enormous quantity of old English glees
and madrigals, and his guests, who were entirely
undergraduates (except when A. G. came in unasked),
sat round his dining-room table, and with him as

conductor and chief vocalist produced very pleasant
and extraordinary noises for an hour or two with
intervals for unusual refreshments. To-night, Frank,
David, and Bags all went together as soon as Hall
was over, and found themselves the earliest to arrive.
This was Bags's first appearance.

Mr. Crowfoot was employed in transporting stacks
of glee-books from the bookcase by the piano to
the table. They reached from the stretch of his
arms to his chin, and he welcomed them over the
top.

" Very glad to see you all, Maddox, and Blaize,
and Crabtree, isn't it ? Help yourselves, won't you ?
There's some Tintara-wine on the table, and let me
see, what have I done with the buns ?—oh, yes, in
the fender to keep warm—and a small Borneo cigar,
won't you, and some chocolates ? I don't think
you've been to my glee-parties before, have you,
Crabtree ? What do you sing ? "

" I think a sort of bass," said Bags coyly.

Mr. Crowfoot was handing buttered buns and
pouring out Tintara, which was mulled and steaming
from having been put close to the fire, and distribut-
ing glee-books and pressing small cigars on everybody, and talking all the time with the greatest
animation and incoherence.

" We'll soon find out ; and then there's Maddox
and Blaize, and I think Tomlin's coming, and me,
and two choral scholars, that makes six, or is it
eight ? —another glass of Tintara, Maddox—and
some more are sure to drop in. And a bun, Blaize ?
Quite alliterative, isn't it ? Alliteration is the key to
poetry : if I say ' pretty tunes,' it's prose, but if I

say 'melodious music,' it's poetry. Let me see: have we enough chairs ? Ah, here are Tomlin and Kenneth, and I forget your name for a moment— oh yes, Horncastle. That's a quorum, isn't it ? Will you help yourselves to cigars and buns and everything, and we might begin."

They began with the famous catch " Mr. Speaker, though 'tis late," with a fine lead for the first voice, which Mr. Crowfoot performed solo, in a high quavering tenor, beating time with a paper-knife. As directed by the composer of this remarkable piece, he gradually quickened the time from *andante* to *prestissimo*, and the paper-knife flew out of his hand and, narrowly missing David's head, crashed among the buttered buns in the fender. But he made no pause, and merely snatched up the cake-knife which flashed like Excalibur in his nimble hand. His voice rang out shrill above all the others as he feverishly declaimed " Order ! order ! Hear him ! Hear ! "; a wisp of his hair fell over his eyes, his face grew red and shining with exertion and pleasure, and it was only when he was breathless and exhausted that he brought the cake-knife down among the ink-bottles, which signified that the catch was finished.

David's methods in the matter of part-singing were sound, though slightly elementary. The object in view was to sing firmly and unwaveringly the notes that were set down for him, and he found that if he put his fingers in his ears, so as not to be distracted by the voices of others, he could keep to his notes pretty well ; but if he heard the air, he could not help joining in it. So he sat during the next part-song frowning with concentration on his page, all other noises completely banished from his sealed ears, making a loud bumble-bee noise and occasionally only looking up at the movements of the paper-knife which had been recovered from the fender and cleansed from the fragments of buttered buns. When they had got well embarked on the glee, Frank said in a voice audible to all but him,

"I say, let's stop singing, but keep our mouths going, and then David will have a solo."

This was done ; David looked up occasionally and saw the paper-knife going, and the mouths of his fellow-melodists opening and shutting. So he went on completely by himself in his booming voice :

> "I loved thee beautiful and kind,
> And plighted an eternal vow."

His own voice, ringing through his head behind his stopped ears sounded wonderfully sonorous and true and he was feeling immensely pleased with himself. As the paper-knife was plied more encouragingly he bellowed with the greater vigour, and at last after singing a page or two he thought he had got so firm a hold of his part that he might venture to uncork his ears. This he did, and was amazed to find dead silence all round him.

"What's happened ? " he asked.

"Ripping good solo : encore," said Frank.

Roars of laughter.

"How long have I been going on ? " he asked.

"Since the third bar."

David howled.

"You utter brute ! Sorry, Mr. Crowfoot. O

Lord, I wish I'd heard it ; it must have been funny ! Jolly good singing faces you all made."

" You ought to be in the choir, David," said Tommers.

" Ought I ?   You ought to be in——" He couldn't think of a sufficiently degraded place for Tommers to be in. . . .

David got his own back pretty soon, for being asked to strike the chord of F on the piano, he gave them a chord two tones higher.   Consequently when the top voices were called upon to sing A, they had to make a shrill approximation to C sharp, and that was a very interesting noise.   This could not possibly be kept up, and they got flatter and flatter, sinking like a barometer before a storm, and carrying everyone with them till they ended in precisely the key they should have begun in.   David verified the amazing fact that they had not sunk a quarter of a tone. . . .

About this time A. G. waddled uninvited into the room and wedged himself in between David and Frank.

" David and Jonathan, ha, ha ! " he said, " and here's Saul among the prophets.   Awfully sorry, dear old boy, about breakfast.   Why didn't you pull me out of bed ?   Come to breakfast to-morrow, or lunch, or anything you like : come to everything ! What are you singing ?   Ah, good evening, Crowfoot.   Let's sing the *Immortal Hour*, as we did last night.   Let's sing——"

Mr. Crowfoot rapped the table with his paperknife.   Gepp constantly came in like this and interrupted the singing with his interminable harangues.

But Crowfoot was host and conductor and leading
tenor, and he did not mean to have his glee-club
turned into a pulpit for his colleague.

"We're going to sing 'Three blind mice,'" he
observed tartly. "Now then! One— two——"

"'Three blind mice,'" said A. G. "A curious
and incredible collection of myopic rodents, ha, ha!
If it had been one blind mouse, or even, in excep-
tional circumstances, two blind mice for whose
melancholy fate you demand our melodious threnody,
I might have been willing to believe you, but when
it comes to——"

"Three blind mice," chanted Crowfoot loudly,
opening his mouth very wide and flourishing the
paper-knife.

A. G. took up the glee-book which David and
Frank had been sharing, and held it at a convenient
distance from his own face. He was almost as fond
of singing as of talking and began at once in his
woolly voice on the wrong beat and the wrong note.
Instantly Crowfoot banged his paper-knife on the
table and stopped the singers.

"Gepp, will you either sing second or first or
third," he said, "and not in between? And the
note is *La*! Now let us start again."

Mr. Crowfoot continued to beat time pointedly at
his colleague, who took not the slightest notice but
sang "Three blind mice" or "See how they run"
or "Awfully jolly, David" whenever and however
these sentiments occurred to him. Then he got
tired of this slow repetition, and started singing
"They all ran after the farmer's wife," again and
again, rolling about in his seat, cannoning against

5

Frank and then rebounding against David. Long after Crowfoot had brought down the paper-knife among the ink-bottles he continued a sort of chanted rhapsody, " They all ran after the carving-knife, and she cut off their tails, did the farmer's wife. And the three blind mice had no tails for their life. So see how they run, with the farmer's wife and the three blind mice."

Mr. Crowfoot interrupted this rollicking impromptu by clearing his throat and uttering withering speech.

" We've finished eleven bars ago, Gepp," he said. " And now we'll have the next catch but three——"

" Blind mice," said A. G.

Crowfoot turned over the leaves of his book in a great hurry.

" Not at all," he said, and instantly began to sing, " ' London's burning, London's burning.' "

" Fire, fire ! " cried A. G.

" Certainly not," chanted Crowfoot. " ' Look yonder : look yonder ' comes first. Begin again, please. ' London's burning, London's burning. Look yonder, look yonder. Faar ! Faar ! Yes, that's better. Ho-o, bring me some water.' "

A. G. got tired of this before London had burned very seriously, and strolled across to the piano, where he improvised a singularly unsuccessful accompaniment, dabbing fortuitously at the keys.

" There was a delightful madrigal we used to sing," he said when London had finished burning, " but I can't quite remember the tune, though it was something like this, and I haven't got any recollection of the words. Ah, I believe I've got it."

Crowfoot, now trembling with unsuppressed pas-

sion at these interruptions to his glee-party, laughed
in a shrill, unkind manner, quite devoid of merriment.

"Extremely charming," he said; "but I don't
think we can attempt anything without words or
music. Page 32, 'Oh, who will o'er the downs so
free.'"

A. G. instantly began to pick out the air with one
finger. He got mixed up with some other tune.

"Are you ready?" said Crowfoot, to drown these
futile fragments. "On the fourth beat——"

The glee-book which he had propped up against
the ink-bottles slipped from its place and the dedicated pens skipped about.

"Oh, who will with me ride?" said A. G. "Nobody would ride with me for very long, because I
should undoubtedly fall off before I reached my
blooming bride. The noise would probably wake
the varlets, ha, ha! and they would all see the
greeting fair that passed there——"

"On the fourth beat," said Crowfoot in a strangled
voice.

This time the glee got resonantly started, and
Crowfoot, flushed with victory over A. G., whose
conversation and whose tinklings on the piano could
no longer be heard, never let his choir get below a
fortissimo. He brandished his paper-knife, he adjusted the lenses of his spectacles for large and
small print in rapid succession without the smallest
cause for so doing with one hand, and in trying to
turn over one leaf of the glee-book with the other,
turned over three or four, and found himself singing
"Mr. Speaker" again before he could stop himself.

Then in turning back he dropped his baton, and his spectacles slipped off his nose, but he picked them up with amazing agility, and beat time with them until he recovered the paper-knife. He beamed encouragement on his choristers, and dabbed Tommers on the end of the nose with his conducting-rod, which made Tommers sneeze. And all the time he kept on singing,

" ' The farlets, they were all asleep '—dear me, I beg your pardon, Tomlin—' and none was there to see '—I hope I didn't hurt you : do you feel the window ?—' the greeting fair that passed there '—a little rallentando—' between my love '—pause and wait for the beat—' and me ! ' "

The pause was embellished by a second sneeze from Tommers and a loud cracking hiccup from David, who, with ears again firmly stopped, had happened to look up at Mr. Crowfoot at the moment he was beating time with his spectacles, and had gallantly attempted, but vainly, to check an uncontrollable spasm of laughter. Nobody knew how long the pause was to be, as Mr. Crowfoot forgot to give the beat, and he sang " and me " all by himself, in a voice quivering with emotion. A. G. had not yet got quite so far, and added " and me " on his own account a few seconds later.

Crowfoot surveyed his choir with pride.

" Very good, really very good indeed," he said. " I don't believe we dropped half a tone. Just strike the note, Gepp, will you ?—oh no, that's no good, because I forget what note we began on. Very nice, though. We might rest and cool for a little. Won't anybody have some more Tintara, or another cigar ?

And some buns : the buns are in the fender, and I
hope I didn't hurt you, Tomlin. Now if we're all
rested, there's one more glee we might try. Will
you turn to page 221 ? Oh, there isn't any . . .
Of course, yes, that's in the second volume. I had
them split into two volumes to make them lighter to
hold, and what can I have done with all the second
volumes ? Aren't they on the piano, Gepp? Or
are you sitting on them ? No ? Now that's very
extraordinary, because I know I put them somewhere where they would be handy. Ah, I kicked
something ! Yes, here they are under the table.
How very droll ! Page 221 then in the second
volume. No ! I must cry *peccavi*. Page 41 in the
second volume, because I altered the paging when
I had made them into two volumes so that the
second volume should begin at page 1, instead of
page 180. There we are ! No, that doesn't seem to
be right. Where can the spotted snakes be ? "

He hunted rapidly backwards and forwards through
the second volume without finding anything of the
kind, and then luckily remembered that he had
detached the spotted snakes from the bound copies
altogether, in order to include them with some
further compositions by the same author. They
were soon discovered among Latin proses corrected
in green ink, in his gyp-cupboard along with wine
glasses. He lucidly explained how they had got
there.

"Most amusing," he said. "I put them there
myself, for I knew I should have to get some glasses
for our glee-singing, and so when I went to get the
glasses I should see the spotted snakes."

"Dear old Crowfoot," said A. G. "It sounds exactly like Delirium Tremens."

"Not at all. There would be the glasses and the glee ready for our singing all in one place, which would save me going to the gyp-cupboard for the glasses, and somewhere else, which I might easily forget, for the glee. There's nothing so wasteful of brain-power as to have several things to remember when one will serve. But then my gyp brought out the glasses for me, and so it slipped my memory where the spotted snakes were.

Crowfoot triumphantly dealt out the copies of "Ye spotted snakes" to his singers, and as they were mixed up with the Latin proses of last week (or perhaps the week before, for the ink was indeterminate), some people got spotted snakes and others pieces of Latin prose. But that was soon remedied and Crowfoot put the collected proses under the table-cloth, so as to be out of the way for the present, while, subsequently, the unusual excrescence on the flat surface of the table would instantly remind him where the Latin proses were. He was reminded of that, in fact, almost immediately, for he bounteously replenished Bags's glass with Tintara and set it down on the edge of the excrescence. It tipped up, and the rich purple flood was poured over the table-cloth. But that was soon absorbed by the application of sheets of blotting-paper, which were then put to dry in the fender beside the buttered buns. A heady ferruginous odour went up from the steaming sheets as the wine evaporated, and long before the glee was over they were quite dry, and mottled in the manner of marbled paper. In the secret re-

cesses of his ingenious brain Crowfoot conceived the
idea of pasting them, properly cut and trimmed, on
to the covers of other books that were worn with
use, thus renovating the binding. . . .

The spotted snakes proved to be teasers, and taxed
the utmost talent of the company. The newts and
blind-worms did a lot of harm by not coming in
right, and everyone got dreadfully muddled over
" Philomel with melody." But Crowfoot by no
means despaired of settling Philomel's hash at the
next meeting, and offered copies all round for private
practice. This was the final effort for the evening,
though A. G. was more than ready to impersonate
Dalua or a fairy again and sing any amount of the
Immortal Hour. But Crowfoot refrained from the
smallest encouragement, and after pressing more
wine and buttered buns and Borneo cigars on everybody, extended a general invitation, rather pointedly
withheld from A. G., to assemble again next Wednesday—no, Thursday, wasn't it, because it was the
winter term—for the same melodious purposes. They
clattered down with whistlings and musical reminiscences into the court, and as there was time yet for
further diversion, David, remembering that he had
not given Perpetua any treatment since morning,
proposed fetching the disgusting nymph and joining
Frank in his rooms for piquet or perhaps a little
work. Frank was not quite so sure that Perpetua
should be of the party.

" She stinks," he said. " Besides, I thought you
were going into training for the picked game and
giving Perpetua a rest."

David considered this.

"As regards the stink," he said. "Bags shall come too and bring Angelica. They neutralize each other."

Frank was firm about this.

"Bags shall come if he likes," he said, "but Angelica shall not."

"*Soit*," said Bags. "I mean right-oh," he added hastily, as he didn't want David to talk French.

"Just in time," said David, who was beginning to say, "s'il apporte Angelique." "And as regards the training, I'll run once round Court as hard as I can. I'll give you fifty yards start, Frank, and if I catch you I'll put you into the fountain——"

"Pooh!" said Frank.

"And Bags a hundred," said David.

"Swank," said Bags.

The effervescent A. G. had joined them, and entered enthusiastically into these arrangements.

"Awfully jolly," he said. "An Olympic race: how joyous and Hellenic! I will be the winning-post, and when the race is over I will be a bard, and write a Pindaric ode in honour of the victor. 'Best of all things is Tintara wine and spotted snakes, but it is your part, O my soul, to celebrate the ambrosial foot-race between Blaize the son of a Dean, and Crabtree the son of a baron, and Maddox the Bachelor of Arts round the royal quadrangle of King's, and crown with a garland of song and turnip-tops'—— Oh, are they off! Why didn't they wait till I started them? Fancy running like that after drinking Tintara wine and eating buns! See how they run! I wish I could run. I have not run since 1893, and that was only along a platform to catch a train which I missed. Why are we not all young Greeks in the morning of the world ? "

He forgot he was the winning-post and began strolling along to his rooms, as the race swept round the quadrangle, David going as if all the hounds of spring and all the Rugby three-quarters were after him. Bags ran with a high-stepping gait and was being rapidly overhauled, and as they came down the straight to where they had left their winning-post, David was not twenty yards behind the others who were abreast. Then a despairing cry was flung into the night by Frank, who was searching the darkness of the shadow below Fellows Buildings for the winning-post which was certainly not where they had left it.

" But the winning-post has gone," he shrieked. " Race is off, David. It isn't fair. Where's A. G. ? "

David began to laugh and lost the advantage that Frank's waste of wind would have given him.

" Thank God, there he is," said Frank, suddenly catching sight of him thirty yards away.

The three of them, all in a bunch, hurled themselves on the winning-post, which by sheer weight stood firm against the onrush. David cannoned into Bags, whose high action tripped him up and he rolled over like a shot rabbit on to the grass. Frank cannoned into Tommers and ricochetted into Bags. A. G. alone stood majestic and monumental.

" Ha, ha ! how awfully splendid and swift and beautiful and jolly," he said. " Why don't we have races and singing contests instead of lectures and that sort of rubbish ? Everyone seems to have won and everybody has fallen down. Awfully Homeric and idyllic and Theocritan."

David picked himself up and they all stood there panting and exhausted. Just above were the windows of the room where they had been singing, which Crowfoot had opened to let out the thickness of the tobacco-smoke and the fumes of the drying blotting paper. Tentative tinklings from the piano now floated out, and the unmistakable voice of their host diligently practising all by himself the difficult glee with which they had concluded. High and quavering came the notes on to the thin night air.

> " Beetles black, approach not here ;
> Worm and snai-hail do no offence !
> No offence ! no offence ! no offence ! "

There was a pause. There they all stood, Tommers and Bags and Frank and David all stricken into rapt attention, David supporting himself with one arm round Frank's neck and the other round Bags's, and beginning to squeak and mutter a little between his panting breaths. . . . There came a noise from above, exactly as if a book had fallen on to the piano keys (as no doubt it had) with a crash of notes, and they heard Crowfoot clear his throat. Then his voice began again :

> " Philome-hel with melodee."

He struck a chord on the piano and repeated this, phrasing it rather differently :

> " Philomel with mel-ho-ho-dee-ee."

David creaked and Frank stifled him by putting his arm across his mouth.

There was dead silence. Then Mr. Crowfoot struck a single note seven or eight times on the piano and echoed it with his voice. He began again, putting in far more dramatic expression, and declaiming the words in loud, indignant, prohibitive tones :

" BEETLES BLACK APPROACH NOT HERE ! "

He struck the note again,

" WORM AND SNA-HAIL DO NO OFFENCE !
NO OFFENCE. . . ."

David was shaking like a jelly, and muffled explosions came against Frank's sleeve.

David of King's V

DAVID's performance at the picked game was so deplorable that the Tooties, who for the first half-hour kept a keen professional eye on him whenever there was the least opportunity of his distinguishing himself, took no further interest in him whatever, nor ever again asked him to take part in their trial shows. Poor David was quite unable to do anything right on that sombre afternoon : if the ball was passed to him, he fumbled it ; when he wanted to pass, he carefully selected one of the opposing

side to bestow it on ; and when somebody made an
opening for him to run, he could neither get off
quickly nor show any of that speed which had
originally aroused the Tooties' fickle interest.

" Bungled every blooming chance I got," he said
to Frank, who dropped in to tea with him afterwards.
" Made a complete and utter ass of myself. And
though I say I hate Rugger, I wanted frightfully
to play decently. But I didn't. Couldn't pass ;
couldn't take a pass ; couldn't kick ; couldn't run.
Not even run ! What's the use of being able to
run like hell if when you want to run like hell you
can't ? Well, that is enough grousing. I say, do
be useful and make tea and toast things while I
have a bath and wash off the memory of—of this
Insolence ! "

David came back girt in a bath-towel, and wandered to and fro between his bedroom and his sitting-
room as he dressed, diverting his mind with pleasant
topics of the future rather than futile topics of the
past. . . . One of the cheerier lot was that he had
lately been elected to the Chitchat Society, which
met every Saturday evening in the rooms of its
members in rotation, the host reading a paper on
some subject connected with Literature or Art, or
something equally improving. The members consisted partly of dons, partly of undergraduates who
consorted together on terms of sociable equality, and
discussed each other's papers with engaging frank-
ness. There had been something of a flutter in this
studious and celibate dovecote last week, for Poet
Stapleton had read a passionate appreciation on
Swinburne's views on morality as deduced from

Poems and Ballads, which had been very exotic and embarrassing. A dead silence had succeeded his peroration, for discussion was really out of the question and Stapleton had sat very defiant and breathing through his nose. Eventually A. G., who of course belonged to this as to all other societies, said, " Dear old Stapleton, how awfully jolly and hectic. Now let's talk about something else." . . . To-night A. G. himself was to entertain his fellow-members, and David, warming his bare shins at the fire, looked at the card which gave notice of the meeting.

" A. G. on the Athletic Ideal," he said. " What on earth does that mean ? "

" Rugby football," said Frank promptly.

David laughed. It was better to do that than go on grousing.

" How to funk and when, by one who knows," he said. " Silly ass ! Is tea ready ? "

" Readier than you."

David had a shirt on after all, and he sat down in an arm-chair in front of the fire.

" I want tea more than trousers," he said. " Besides, tea gets full of tannin if you keep it waiting, and trousers never. I shall go to the Chitchat."

" A. G. told me he hadn't had time to write a paper," said Frank, who was secretary, " and was going to speak instead."

" Then we shan't get away this side of Sunday," said David. " And next week it's me. I hope nobody will come : I shall sink through the floor with nerves. It's awful cheek my reading my muck to all you savants, as Bags would say. But I suppose it's good for me ; it made me read Marlowe's

Faustus four or five times. Frank, why don't they teach us to read English before they try to make us write Latin and Greek? Why should I sweat at Latin prose and iambics when there's my own language to learn ? "

" Think of the unemployment among the classical dons," said Frank. " What would they do at their age ? "

David crossed one knee over the other and scratched the top one.

" Well, I'm jolly glad you suggested I should read Marlowe and try to jaw about it," he said. " But I wish you'd write my Chitchat paper for me. Then if I made any howlers, I could say ' Apply to the Hon. Sec.' . . . I wonder what makes some stuff so good, and other stuff such piffle. It isn't only the ripping language, and it isn't only the subject. There's something behind what a man writes which takes your breath away or only makes you yawn. No amount of style or splendid language makes you feel. That last speech of Faustus's, you know, when he's waiting for the clock to strike midnight and the devil to come for him. Sheer, stark terror."

Frank took David's cigarette out of his hand and lit his own at it. Then by mistake he threw David's into the fire.

" Doesn't matter," said David. " Just jaw to me ! "

Frank considered this point. David, he knew, took his views on intellectual questions as authentic gospel, and he had to try to make them something better than piffle.

" There's everything behind what a man actually

writes," he said. " Truth, you know, and red-hot
sincerity. Marlowe must have been in hell : that's
why he can make you sweat when he tells you what
Faustus felt like when he was waiting for it."

" Ha ! " said David.

" You can convey your truth badly or well," said
Frank ; " that's where words and style come in, but
they are only vehicles. You can only make people
feel by telling them what you know. Look at
Wuthering Heights : it's about as badly told as a
story can be, but that doesn't matter compared with
the fact that Emily Brontë *was* Heathcliff. . . . Or
take ' Violets dim, but sweeter than the lids of
Juno's eyes—— ' "

" Oh, ripping," said David. " And that was
because Shakespeare had buried his nose in a wet
bed of them ? "

" Yes. Lovely words there, too ; but he'd never
have found those words unless he knew. Or ' There's
pansies : that's for thoughts ! ' That came out of
knowing, as well as being aware that pansy meant
' thought ' in French. But when Milton talked of
a pansy, he called it ' freaked with jet.' "

" O Lord, did he really ? " said David. " How
frightfully rancid ! I hate Milton."

" Then you make a great mistake."

" But don't tell me to read *Paradise Lost*," said
David.

" Certainly I won't, because you wouldn't do it.
Don't skip about so."

" Me ? I'm sitting as still as—oh, I suppose you
mean my mind."

" Yes. Get back to Marlowe a minute. Imagine

yourself trying to write the last speech of Faustus. You'd cram it with red-hot pincers and boiling oil and gnashing of teeth, but there wouldn't be an ounce of damnation in it."

Frank paused a minute and changed the subject himself. " You know less about hell than anyone I've ever seen," he said.

David looked up in surprise.

" Why do you say that ? " he asked.

" Oh, it happens to be true. That's what I've always adored in you. When the nasty side of people comes up, you only see the funny part of it. You simply disregard the other, as if it wasn't there. I say, we're getting rather serious."

" Well, why shouldn't we ? " demanded David. " It's you and me, after all. About what you said just then. I can't help seeing the funny side of muck. When Bags told me about the gay cocoons——"

" The gay what ? " asked Frank.

" I mean *cocottes*, I could only think how priceless he must have looked with his arm round one fat wench and the other sitting on his knee, all stinking of musk, and smeared about with paint. Oh my ! How funny ! Fancy calling that love ! But I don't know that I should have done any better to be shocked. Bags would only have thought me a prig."

Frank laughed.

" What a blood ! " he said. " And of course you wouldn't have done any better to be shocked. Besides, it's your stunt not to be shocked, although you hate beastliness when it comes near you."

David was silent a moment, and the dancing light in his eyes at the thought of Bags and his cocoons died out, and they became quite serious. Some memory, long buried, stirred in his mind, and he covered it up again.

" There are such a lot of jollier things to do and think about," he said. " At least I think them jollier, which is all that concerns me. Interesting things, you know, funny things, and also quite serious things. Anyhow, I don't think it's got much to do with love to go sweating and mucking around with a cocoon. Love's something better than that. And I shouldn't wonder if mucking about in the way some fellows do rather spoils you for it. But, O Lord, how I love my friends : isn't that enough for a chap till he falls in love in the regular way ? If I'd *got* to kiss somebody I'd kiss one of them. You for choice, because I'm much fonder of you than the whole of the rest of them."

Frank burst out laughing at these surprising philosophies.

" Oh, David," he said, " there's no one like you. You always make me feel as if I had just had a bath with plenty of soap."

David flushed with pleasure.

" My word ! You couldn't have said anything nicer than that," he observed. " But them's my sentiments. No harm in telling you, though I guess you knew it."

David put down his large feet from the side of the fireplace where he had put them and held out his hands. " Pull me up," he said, and stood there a moment still rather serious.

6

" Good thing that God thought of inventing us,"
he said. " Which being so, I may as well dress.
. . . Gosh, I've never smoked Perpetua all day.
Fill her for me frightfully carefully while I put my
trousers on, and don't touch her smooth waxy
bottom with your blasted fingers."

The Chitchat assembled in Gepp's rooms that evening at nine, the members dropping in by degrees.
Frank arrived first with the minute-book and the
ceremonial snuff-box, and was soon followed by
David and Tommers. As Gepp had left lying about
the scarlet gown of a Doctor in Common Law
(of which he knew nothing whatever), David of
course was bound to put it on and get on a chair
in front of a mirror to see how he looked, and
(equally " of course ") a pepper-and-salt Scotch
don from Trinity arrived at that identical moment.
On which Frank amiably attempted to divert Mr.
Mackintosh's attention from the coy David by
plunging into conversation, but Mr. Mackintosh
totally disregarded him and continued to fix David
with a wooden and baleful eye, while he divested
himself of these insignia. Then he said, " Good
evening, Mr. Blaize ; I didn't see who you were
before," in a tone of withering sarcasm.

All this was slightly embarrassing and unsettling,
and it was a relief when other members, followed by
the host of the evening, drifted in. Gepp was full
of complacent apologies for his lateness : he had
been obliged to attend to an urgent trunk call on
the telephone from London, and his allusion to the
Prime Minister seemed to explain his complacence.

At this Mr. Mackintosh gave a short, hard cackle, for his sense of humour, which had not been stirred by David in a D.C.L. gown, was awakened by this, and remained, as they were all soon to find out, terribly alert. He took some coffee and the best chair.

The Chitchat, like all other honourable corporations, had its ritual. There was a large silver goblet filled with hock-cup which circulated round the members through the course of the reading, and before the reading began a snuff-box made a solemn tour, from which each member must take a pinch. Those who liked snuff and were not afraid of convulsive sneezing fits made a genuine dip into it, those who were made a ceremonial feint. Tommers thought he would have a go at it to-night, found it pleasantly aromatic, and took a second helping before he passed it on to Mackintosh, who laid a train of it up his forefinger and sniffed it into his nostrils with the mastery of custom. Then Frank, in his capacity as honorary secretary, read the minutes, which recorded the disastrous dissertation on Swinburne, and called on A. G. to address them on the subject of " The Athletic Ideal."

Gepp did not look very notably athletic, and seemed more the ideal of a *bon viveur* (as Bags would have said). But he evidently was intending to enjoy himself very much, and with a cigarette in one hand and a liqueur in the other he waddled to the hearth-rug, where, since this was to be a speech and not a reading, he took up his stand, a picture of genial repletion. This was just such an audience as he liked—half a dozen undergraduates to whom he felt

a brother, and three or four colleagues who would
have to listen to the biting reflections which he was
prepared to enunciate on their notions of education.
He still wore his collegiate cap and gown ; the former
was airily tilted on to the back of his head.

It was the athleticism of the mind, he began, which
was to be the subject of some remarks which he had
not had time to write down.   The tutorial body to
which he had the honour of belonging was hopelessly
unathletic ; it was sunk in indolent torpor instead
of being fit and active and bright-eyed and wiry
and lean.   In training, in fact.

The lecturer drank his liqueur, and forgetting that
he had one cigarette already, lit another at the
candle, by the light of which he consulted his notes.
It was so placed that it threw into strong relief his
enormous bulk. Mr. Mackintosh's eyes began to
twinkle.   He liked his friend Gepp talking about the
duty of being wiry.

" Sunk in indolent torpor," repeated A. G., leaning
against the chimney-piece.   " How are we to expect
to kindle the fire of intellectual activity in the bright
young minds committed to our care if we are content to be enclosed in the fatness of our antiquated
and conventional notions ?   Education, as understood in England generally and especially at her
Universities, consists in plunging our pupils into a
morass of sticky and useless facts.   There we all
are, embedded in the morass, most of us completely
submerged, and the few bubbles of ill-smelling gas
that rise to the surface represent our educational
efforts.   They flicker like will-o'-the-wisps and entice
our unfortunate pupils further into the slough.

There is nothing Athenian about us, nor joyous, nor Hellenic, no desire to learn and to impart some new thing. . . . My dear David, drink deep of that hock-cup and send it on its way. I am extremely thirsty."

" But we've got to get out of the morass ourselves," he continued, " before we cease to lure them into it. We've got to clean the mud of dry, uninteresting, and probably quite erroneous facts from our own bemired limbs, and make them swift and strong with exercise in the joyous sun and air and that sort of thing before we can hope to train the minds of others. History, for instance : the way we teach history is appalling. How can we convey the spirit of Greek culture by teaching the dates of Pericles and the Peloponnesian war and Pythagoras and Plato ? Five minutes' study of the Hermes at Olympia, even in a photograph or a cast, will teach you more about the greatest civilisation the world has ever seen than learning the whole twelve volumes of Grote's history by heart."

A. G.'s discourse began to stray a little from its advertised subject, for he found a difficulty in deciphering his notes, and he had no clear recollection of what he wanted to say about the athletic ideal of the mind beyond telling his colleagues how hopelessly incapable they were, and that he had now sufficiently impressed on them. Consequently his own mention of the Hermes of Olympia distracted him from his topic to the consideration of Greek statuary, on which he was perfectly competent to speak. He became discursive and far more characteristic, and called the attention of his audience to the statuette of the Medicean Venus which stood on a side-table and told them to look at it earnestly for three minutes if they wanted to realize the spirit of Greece. But before three seconds were up the Medicean Venus reminded him that he had once seen in the house of one of the most prominent leaders of society in New York a full-size bronze replica of the same with a clock let into its stomach. Ha, ha! From New York he took them to the falls of Niagara and his own lecture on Greek art at Montreal. That naturally led on to his return voyage across the Atlantic and quoit-playing on the steamer. He himself had proved an adept at the game, which was extremely good for the abdominal muscles, and was altogether awfully jolly. You stood balanced on your toes and then with a swing of the body and a sweep of your arm discharged your missile. The attitude, in fact, was very like that of the Discobolus of Myron (to get back to the athletic ideal), and he proceeded to adjust himself to the pose of that renowned statue. Of course it was difficult in clothes to show them the lithe tension of the figure ; they should see him naked. However, it was this sort of thing. . . . There came a muffled explosion from the region of his waist as of a button giving way under the unusual stress of this athletic posture, and his cap fell into the fender.

Mr. Mackintosh, sitting immediately in front of him, had been regarding the lecturer with an amazed and fascinated eye, and a mouth that had fallen open from sheer astonishment. At the moment when Gepp's cap fell off and his button burst, he was drinking the hock-cup which David had circulated,

and his self-control broke entirely down. He gave
one loud, lamentable cry of " Godsakes ! " and
hock-cup poured in torrents from his nose and mouth,
and seemed almost to stream from eyes and ears as
well. He set the goblet on the table, and with a
series of hard cackling noises snatched up his cap
and gown, and hurriedly left the room. He was
heard slipping and stumbling down the stairs outside and out into the court, from which yells of
demoniac laughter arose. They could hear him
slap his leg and roar again ; these noises became
mercifully fainter as he retreated. David, sitting in
the window-seat, saw his figure silhouetted against
the light from the porter's lodge, still doubled up
and writhing.

The other members of the Chitchat behaved with
the most admirable self-restraint. There were ominous
little creaks and shakings from various parts of the
room, and Tommers got so red in the face that he
looked as if he might burst into flame. Somebody
sneezed. Frank propped up his thoughtful brow with
his hand, and David could see his arm quivering.
Nobody spoke and nobody dared look up for fear of
catching somebody else's eye.

Gepp picked up his cap.

" I should like, Mr. Secretary," he said, " to move
that Mr. Mackintosh be requested to resign his membership of the Chitchat owing to his gross and un-
gentlemanly rudeness to his host. If he does not
take advantage of that clemency, I propose that he
should be expelled ; and if the Society do not agree
with me, I shall resign myself. He—he drank my
hock, and ate my anchovy-toast, and then thought

good to interrupt my lecture by wholly unmannerly
mirth. Will you please record that, and act on
it ? "

This was all very dreadful, and David could quite
safely take his tongue from between his teeth, where
he had firmly placed it to prevent his laughing.
Tommers's crimson face regained its natural hue
and Frank's arm ceased to quiver. A. G. consulted
his notes, and having succeeded in deciphering them,
went straight back to the point from which he had
bifurcated into the Hermes of Olympia and the
disastrous sequel. Indeed it was no laughing matter
any more, for the harmony of the Chitchat had
broken into wild and perilous discord.

The lecture proceeded, though shorn of its rich-
ness and exuberance, and at the end a serious discussion took place, to which all the members devoted
their best attention, partly to soothe A. G., partly
lest wandering thoughts should let them too vividly
recall the unique manner of Mr. Mackintosh's exit.
In spite of the urgent call for gravity, that remained just as hideously funny as ever, and David
wondered what would happen if they all let themselves go. Would the indignant lecturer move that
they should all be expelled and carry on the Chitchat by himself, or would he resign ? What indeed
would happen as it was ? It was quite impossible
to imagine the Chitchat without A. G., and it was
almost as difficult to suppose that the Society would
vote for the expulsion of Mackintosh. They were
all within an ace of doing what he had done. But
it really wouldn't do to recall that explosion, unique
in the annals of hock-cup ; it wasn't safe. . . .

Frank left the table as the discussion began to grow thin, and came and sat by him in the window-seat.

" I want to talk to you, David," he said.

David averted his eyes.

" All right, but do be careful," he said.

" Pull yourself together, you ass," said Frank. " We can laugh afterwards. Look here, this will never do. What's to be done ? "

David gave a gasp, and took control of himself.

" Get one of the dons to reason with him," he said. " Or get Mackintosh to apologize. But I don't suppose he will : a man don't apologize for what he absolutely can't help. Somebody had to laugh or we all would have. Mackintosh was just the scape-goat flooded with hock-cup."

" Absolutely no use getting a don to reason with A. G.," said Frank. " He wouldn't listen. He'd only boil over again, and we should have more rows."

" Well, let him cool down a bit first," said David.

" Rather. But if it comes your way, do blow on him. I say, I wish you'd stop behind when we all go, as we shall in a minute, and let him boil over to you, and then cool him."

" Lord, why me ? " asked David.

" Because you're such a kid, and you wouldn't put his back up again. And you're rather soothing if a man's in a bad temper. And A. G. thinks you a bright, joyous child."

" But what on earth am I to say ? " asked David, rather appalled by this prospect.

" Can't tell. Just whatever seems to you suit-able when the time comes. Pour oil."

Gepp had had his ruffled feathers rather smoothed by the seriousness of the discussion with which the members had received his address, and came rolling over to the window-seat. Frank got up.

" The athletic Blaizides," he said, instantly occupying Frank's seat. " Hasn't the athletic Blaizides any contribution to make to our symposium ? "

David laid himself out to be tactful.

" No ; I just sat and enjoyed it," he said " Frightfully interesting. Have you got a photograph of the Hermes ? "

Frank strolled away and picked up the minute-book and the snuff-box.

" Good night," he said to Gepp. " And thanks awfully."

" Good night. Please write to Mackintosh and inform him of my motion."

The others followed, but the obedient David did not move. It was evident that the outraged lecturer was on the boil still, and he waited for him to boil over. He did so.

" That ginger-haired, insufferable Scotchman ! " said A. G. " I have never been treated with such deliberate rudeness. It's perfectly evident that he and I cannot possibly remain members of the Chit-chat."

" Never saw anything like it," said David. " Beastly rude. But as regards the other, of course it must be him to go, if you feel like that. How on earth should we get on without you ? "

" Well, there it is. If he doesn't choose to resign, it's for the members to choose between us. Unless they expel him, I shall go."

David scratched his yellow head. A further repetition of his sentiments might not be a vain repetition.

"Naturally we're all on your side," he said. "We couldn't dream of losing you. We should collapse without you."

This seemed to have an excellent effect.

"Well, I think I may say I've done more for the Chitchat than anybody," said A. G. "I was one of the original founders of it, and if we're a flourishing institution now, I do take some little credit for it."

"Rather," said David. "All the credit."

"And I've been accustomed to consider it a gathering of gentlemen," said A. G. "Awfully jolly evenings we usually have."

"Ripping," said David. "I was frightfully pleased when I was elected. And rows are such rot ; they spoil everything. . . ." A bright idea struck him. "I think Mr. Mackintosh's rudeness was really an affront to all of us," he said. "You happened to be speaking—awfully interesting, too—but when a man is rude like that, he's rude to everybody."

"All the more reason why he should be expelled if he won't resign," said A. G.

"Yes, of course, in a way," pursued the artful David. "But I do think somehow that it would be more dignified, more like gentlemen, as you say, to take no notice whatever of it. That's only what I feel for myself, of course. I daresay the others will think that we ought to hoof him out. But a man who forgets his manners like that really hurts himself more than anybody else, don't you think, especially if they don't seem to notice, and that makes his rudeness fall so jolly flat."

David paused a moment.

" There'll be a good chance for more people to resign or be expelled next week," he said, " for I've got to read a paper, and I shall make the most awful hash of it.   You'll all laugh."

" Dear old Blaizides," said Gepp.   " I won't laugh at you."

David was quick as a lizard on to this, darting at a new opening.

" Oh, that's ripping," he said, " because that means you'll be there, and *that* means that you won't have resigned, whatever happens about old Gingery Mackintosh.   Of course the Chitchat would never allow you to resign, whatever happened, because they'd go phut without you.   We should have to make that impossible somehow or cease to be. But everything would be ever so much easier if you settled not to take any notice of what happened this evening.   And it would be an awful sell for him to find that nobody had noticed what he did."

This was rather sketchy and not strictly logical, but it served its purpose as a general cheerful medley of optimism.   A. G. was not cool yet ; he still simmered, but he didn't quite snuff out this optimism.

" What on earth he found to laugh at," he said, " is utterly beyond me, but I have long ceased to attempt to understand a Scotchman's idea of humour. I was talking about Greek statues, I believe.   I don't know that there is anything excruciatingly funny in that."

" Not a bit," said David eagerly.   " You were

just showing us the attitude of the Discobolus, and
—and then he burst.   But it's rather a feat to amuse
a Scotchman, I think.   Usually nothing does. . . .
I should like to see that statue.   It must be ripping.
Is there a cast of it in the museum ?   Mayn't I
come round with you one day and see it ? "

A. G. got up.

" Certainly, dear old boy," he said.   " I should
like to show it you.   The right arm is swung back,
and the body twisted round. . . ."

He began to illustrate this again.

" That was what I was doing," he said, " when
Mackintosh suddenly thought good to spew the
hock-cup about my room.   I don't see anything
extraordinarily comical about it.   Dear me, it's very
hard to maintain the pose."

" It must be," said the unwearied David.

A. G.'s face was beginning to beam again with
his usual good-nature, and David decided to rush
matters.

" And then your cap fell off in the fender," he
said.

" Ha, ha ! so it did," said A. G.   " And a button."

" Yes, I heard the button go," said David.

" Ha, ha !   Rather comical.   Yes.   Imagine poor
old Mackintosh showing us the pose of the Discobolus
and losing a button, and having his cap fall into the
fender.   I think perhaps I might have been amused,
though I hope I should not have made such a ridiculous exhibition of myself."

" O Lord !   Mr. Mackintosh in the attitude of the
Discobolus ! " said David.

This was a lucky thought.   David certainly could

not have remained grave much longer over this second illustration of the statue, but now he could laugh as much as he liked. There was A. G. open-mouthed and sonorous at this ridiculous picture and David could let himself writhe in his chair.

" Oh, I say, I haven't laughed so much for weeks," he said. " I must stop. It hurts. And then you know, it was devilish funny to see Mr. Mackintosh burst like that. I nearly laughed myself. And he kept stopping to slap his leg when he got out into the court. And the last I saw of him was all doubled up by the porter's lodge. It was he who was so frightfully funny all the time, and he didn't know it ! "

David pulled himself together.

" Oh, I'm so weak," he said. " May I have a drink ? And it's ripping to know there won't be any row. May I tell Frank that your motion's off ? "

The entire Society assembled at David's rooms the next week to hear him read on the subject of Mar-lowe's Faustus. As he had felt quite certain that not more than half of them would turn up, he had asked a guest or two as well, and now as there was not room for everybody in his small sitting-room, the overplus sat on his bed in the next room with the door open. His paper, over which he had taken immense trouble, was excellently written and deadly serious. He had put in a lot of interpolations after the first draft, on margins and between the lines, and sometimes in the middle of a most striking sen-tence he couldn't read these subsequent insertions.

There he sat underneath the electric light, twittering with nervousness, and looking quite absurdly young, with the grizzled, ginger-haired Mackintosh on one side of him, and A. G. on the other. He took rapid swigs at the hock-cup as it went on its rounds, and imprudently indulged in snuff as well. A sneezing fit seized him as he came to the most impressive passage, and he had to pause to blow his nose.

" The flame of the nethermost pit scorches us as we read," said David rather hoarsely. " Even from the first we realize that this is—can't read it : oh yes—that this is no imaginative effort of a student who has merely pictured to himself the horrors of ultimate damnation, but the authentic agony of one who has felt the flame itself——"

He took a sip at the hock-cup, and hurriedly passed it on to Mackintosh, jogging his elbow.

" Sorry, Mr. Mackintosh," he said. " From the first the spiritual horror begins to close in upon us ; the end is inherent in and inevitable from the beginning. The following passage, for instance, which occurs quite early in the play——"

David took up his Marlowe and couldn't find the place, but after turning backwards and forwards a little he got it. Tommers sneezed.

David read :

" *Faustus.* Where are you damned ? "

David had to stop. One more belated sneeze was coming, and he got it over. Then in a wheezy voice he began again.

" *Faustus.* Where are you damned ?

" *Mephistopheles.* In Hell. [Distant laughter from the bedroom.]

" *Faustus.* How comes it then that thou art out of it ? "

[More laughter from the bedroom, where presumably they felt out of it too.]

David gave a sort of despairing hiccup, but went on. " *Mephistopheles.* Why, this is Hell, nor am I out of it."

There was a snorting sound from the sofa, and a suppressed tremor went round the room. But suppression was impossible when, in the tense silence, Tommers sneezed again. The Chitchat was dissolved in laughter, and the reader was worse than anybody.

David wiped his eyes and collected himself again.

" There's some more," he said, " but it's frightfully serious. Hadn't I better stop ? "

" Eh, that's a nice lad," said Mr. Mackintosh. " No, Mr. Blaize, go on. We'll be grave. We want to hear what you've written. A jolly good paper— very well constructed."

And at that, audience and reader became perfectly serious. It wasn't only that it was bad luck to laugh at David, though it seemed to amuse him ; it was that what he had to say was very good stuff. For ten minutes more he read in silence, and came to his peroration.

" And he's lost, he's damned, and he knows it," said David, " and the gain of the whole world has not profited him in comparison with that. He sees where Christ's blood streams in the firmament, and knows that a drop of it would save his soul. But between him and it there is the great gulf fixed of his deliberate choice, the same gulf that severed Dives from Lazarus, who would have brought him a drop of water for the ease of his eternal torment. Faustus dare not call on Him, a drop of whose blood from that infinite stream that suffuses the firmament would save him, for by his own will and conscious choice he has betrayed and crucified Him, in that he has betrayed and bartered his own soul. His is the exceeding bitter cry, for the mess of pottage is finished and the birthright of his salvation forfeited."

David put down his manuscript, and looked deprecatingly round. He had done his best, and it was nice of them not to say " Piffle."

Mr. Mackintosh stretched out his hand for the sheets that David had read.

" A fine, thoughtful paper," he said, " well conceived, well expressed, and a great sincerity behind it all. For my part, I've no criticism to make on it, and no question to ask the reader. Admirable. But I should be glad to read it over to myself again, if you'd be so kind as to lend it to me. A paper that makes one want to think rather than talk."

" Awfully proud," said David, " if you really want to see it."

He got up, effacing himself from the limelight, and perched on the edge of Frank's chair.

" Well done, David," he said. " Jolly good."

" Oh, rot. You suggested the only decent idea in it," said David.

His audience began to circulate and relax ; there was no doubt that he had made them tense. . . . Someone had been thoughtful enough to hide Perpetua and it was only after considerable search that David

found her under his pillow.   Then came a movement
of departure among the dons, and Mackintosh found
an opportunity to corner A. G., who, up till now, had
been sublimely unconscious of his presence.

"I owe you an apology, Mr. Gepp," he said.
"Something overcame me at our meeting in your
rooms a week ago, and you know that though Scotch-
men seldom laugh, it's a terrible affair when they do.
I hope you'll overlook it."

Now, no one could be stuffier than Gepp, but on the
other hand no one could be breezier.

"Oh, that's all right," he said.   "Delighted to
have amused you.   I was quite wrong to have been
annoyed, as I confess I was.   I should have laughed
too, like that delightful boy just now, when we were
all so rude to him.   Not that you were rude.   Not
a bit.   Quite all right."

There was a loud squeal from the reader.   Frank
had twitched Perpetua out of his hand.

"But it's not fair," cried David.   "If Bags smokes
Angelica, I'm blowed if I won't smoke Perpetua.
Have some hock-cup ; have a cigarette ; have
anything you like.   But it's beyond a joke to lay
hands on my stinking nymph.   You'll be like
Faustus . . . ."

"I wish you would attend," said David. "It's really very interesting."

"I am attending," said Bags, turning the page of the book he was reading—Maupassant was wonderful at skating over the thinnest ice and never quite falling through.

"Well, there it is. Why is it that I can only run when I'm terrified, and not when I choose? If you've got the power, why can't you use it? I saw a book the other day, translated from the French, by a man called Coue——"

"Perhaps you mean Coué," said Bags.

"I don't think so. I fancy his name was Coue. He said that if you want to do anything or be anything, you've got to say it over to yourself twenty times before you go to sleep. I think I'll try that."

"Do," said Bags.

"I shall say to myself every night, 'I will run like lightning—I will run like lightning,' twenty times. But wouldn't it be awful if it took effect quite suddenly, like a pill, in the middle of chapel, and I began sprinting up and down the choir?"

David picked up the photograph of a girl that stood on the chimney-piece.

"Oh, I say — rather fetching!" he observed. "Is that one of the cocoons?"

"No; it's my sister," said Bags, shutting his book and getting up. It was no use trying to attend, and after all, the babbling David was just as amusing, though not quite in the same way.

David giggled in a silly manner.

" Sorry," he said. " I seem to have put my foot
in it. Let's change the subject. I believe I've
grown ; I can see over the top of your head. Golly,
you've got an Athenæum tie on, what a blood you
are, Bags. 'The tie that he's got's Athenæum.
And he'll take jolly good care that everybody should
see 'um.' Ha, ha ! Poetry. Can't think of any more
rhymes, at least only one, and that would not be quite
delicate. I'm so glad I'm genteel, aren't you?
About running, now. I'm going into training for
the Freshman's sports, I think. They come on in a
fortnight, and why shouldn't I run in the quarter ?
Hundred yards is no use to me. I can't start."

" Doesn't the pistol frighten you ? "

" Not a bit. If I could persuade myself that there
was a bullet in it just going to be discharged at my
hinder-parts, it might. What a splendid sensational
story you could write about a fellow who was
running in the hundred yards, and who had had a
row with the starter, by cutting him out with his
best girl. So the starter put a bullet in the pistol,
with the intention of shooting him in the middle of
the back—"

" Is that all ? " said Bags.

" No. He made a bad shot, and killed the best
girl, who had come to see Sebastian Maltravers—
that was his name—win the hundred yards. That's
all, and I should say it was about enough. Where's
Angelica ? "

" Sick," said Bags.

" Made you sick, I expect. So as it's a nice day
let's go down to Fenner's this afternoon, and we'll

borrow a pistol, and you shall see whether you can make me get off the mark within ten minutes of the time you fire it. Ten minutes, you know," said David argumentatively, " is a long time to remain at the start in a sprint. If you were in for a fifty-mile race, it wouldn't matter so much ; but I maintain that if you don't start in the hundred yards within ten minutes after the other fellows, you materially handicap your chance of winning. What a beautiful sentence. So come to Fenner's and everybody will see your tie, and everybody will see me with a blood."

" Right," said Bags. " Lunch with me first, if you like."

" I should like. But latish, as I'm playing tennis at twelve with Frank. And after Fenner's I'm going to a Turkish bath with Tommers, and there's Crowfoot's glee-singing this evening. A nice-ish sort of day. I wonder what else I can cram in ! "

David had determined not to sully the splendour of this nice day with work of any kind. He had been really very industrious lately, for Frank was studying hard for his archæological tripos, and that made an incentive to him, for it was natural to spend much of the day with Frank, and since he was working, to work too. But to-day some lure of the spring beckoned, making a boiling in his blood with which Demosthenes did not accord, and while he dressed, he had made up his mind to keep holiday. So having settled the disposition of the afternoon, and left no leisure for the temptation of books, he found some old golf-balls, and to fill up the morning, until it was time to go to play tennis, he went with them and a cleek into the meadow across the river, and practised lofting shots over it. The club was singularly ill-adapted for such an enterprise, and very soon all the balls but one had taken to the water. Thereupon the infuriated David took the survivor and recklessly drove it as hard as he could in the direction of Clare. Encouraged by the wind it developed a stupendous slice, and soared in the direction of the chapel. David watched the irretrievable with an awe-struck gaze. " Gosh ! " he said to himself—" all those pretty windows." But the slice was too great for such a destination, and soon it rattled pleasantly on the roof of Fellows Buildings. . . . As the Provost appeared at that moment out of the Lodge, David thrust the cleek down his trouser-leg, and walked chastely to his room with a pronounced limp.

Frank had insisted, as soon as David came up, that he should take up this game of "real" (opposed to " pat-ball ") tennis, which, according to his estimate, outshone all others. He himself had played second string for the University last year, and would probably play first string this year, unless by an event wholly unprecedented it was this amazing pupil of his who, after one year's acquaintance with the game, deprived him of that distinction. Some one particular form of ball-game " sets the genius " of most athletic and quick-eyed boys, and it was evident from the first that the king of games was what set David's. The stooping classical stroke which most find it so hard to acquire, came natural to him ; he cut the ball the first time he went into the court, and he learned the abstruse tactics as if they were a recollection to him, easily recalled. Half-way through his first term Frank could scarcely give him thirty ; by the end of that term the odds had been reduced to half-thirty ; and now they made a close match of it at fifteen. His rapidly acquired skill was really rather uncanny ; if A. G. was a reincarnation of Heliogabalus, David was that of a tennis-marker.

This morning, from sheer exuberance of the spring, and the desire to make perfect shots exactly one inch above the top of the net, David put the first eight services he received exactly one inch below the top of the net, and Frank won the first two games without a ball being returned at all.

" Oh, send something back soon," he observed ; " I'm getting awfully cold."

. . . . .

They had each of them won a set, and the third was left undecided at eight games all, when their hour was up, and limber with their game, they walked home along the Backs, where blackbirds were fluting in the college gardens.

" Wish I had an orange beak, and could sing like that," said David. " By the way, we sing this evening. You'll come to Crowfoot's glee-party, Frank ? "

" Can't ; I must work."

" Oh, come for an hour. I'm having an immortal day, entirely full of pleasure, and you're part of it. Besides, you must see Crowfoot's new dodge."

David began to walk with very small steps, adjusting imaginary sidelights on phantom spectacles and clearing his throat a great deal as he precisely reproduced Crowfoot's voice.

" Very well, take an ordinary wooden match-box,"

he said, " and first cut off the prepared surfaces on
the outside, on which you strike your matches, and
gum them on to the inside of the box. Or small
drawing-pins would do. Then there you are ! If
you're out in the rain, and want to get a light for your
cigarette—it applies equally to a pipe—you pull out
your match-box, and the striking-surface keeps as
dry as a bone. Then you strike your match on the
inside of the box, though of course you must take
great care that you don't set light to the heads of all
the other matches, because then you'd be worse off
than ever. Perhaps it would be prudent to practise
with empty match-boxes first. Stay ! I have it.
You could remedy that by having only one match
in each box, or if you didn't like that you might have
the other matches made of some non-inflammable
material. Or keep saccharine in your spare boxes,
or lozenges."

" All of which you made up," said Frank.

" No ; he is thinking of a dodge to strike matches
in the rain," said David. " Stand still a shake. . ."

With the aid of Frank's shoulder, David mounted
on to the low wooden rails that line the path and tried
to walk along them. He fell off at once, and began
talking in Crowfoot's voice again.

" Which shows that the rails ought to be ever so
much broader," he said. " Or better still, have the
path entirely covered with wooden rails, so that you
wouldn't tread on the newts and blind-worms. Or
you could have no rails at all, which perhaps would
be the most convenient plan, since then you couldn't
fall off them in any circumstances. . . . Oh, Lord,
the spring's got into my head. So do come to

glee-singing for an hour. What a ripping game we
had ! I am glad you made me take up tennis."

" I'm not sure it wasn't very unwise of me," said
Frank. " I believe you'll be beating me level before
the 'Varsity ties next term."

" Rot ! It was only a fluke I won a set this
morning at fifteen. I had all the luck right away
through; you can give me fifteen and knock my head
off five times out of six."

" I can't. If you win to-morrow, we'll play at
half-fifteen for the future."

" Stay ! " said David, still Crowfooting. " Half-
fifteen is seven and a half. Therefore if I ever got to
forty, I should be forty-seven-and-a-half. So if you
say that forty-five is game, very well, it's my game.
But if fifty's the game, or fifty-five——"

" David, you're daft," said Frank.

" I am. It's the spring, I tell you. I woke tipsy
with it, and swore a vow not to do a stroke of work all
day, but give it to idleness, like Wordsworth, who
never did a stroke of work in his life. To-morrow
I'll be sober. I say, there's two o'clock striking,
and I'm lunching with Bags. After that we go to
Fenner's, and I shall probably be sick if I try to run,
because I shall have eaten too much rich and luxurious
food."

David spent a desultory afternoon of mixed
athletics. He filched a pistol from the pavilion at
Fenner's, and practised starting for the hundred
yards without much success. The pistol missed fire
a good deal, and once springing forward from a
complicated attitude of expectancy, he hit his nose a
severe punch with his knee. The quarter of a mile

with Bags, who held the pistol, as time-keeper, went better, and David came storming down the straight to the finish with huge strides, catching up and passing a rather fancied runner thirty yards from the post. But as Bags had forgotten to set the stop-watch going, the only conclusion to be drawn from it was that David had run the quarter in so small a fraction of a second that it was totally unrecorded. . . . A little high-jumping forced him to resign himself to the fact that, even at the cost of a stitch in his side, he could not clear more than two feet six inches, which did not seem up to any known standard except that of small children and elderly ladies. One leg jumped magnificently, but the other wouldn't go ; or the other went like a rocket, after the first had knocked the lath down. Then Bags tried to put the weight, and narrowly escaped dropping it on his own toe, and at the second attempt split the buttonhole of his collar and dislocated his new Athenæum tie. A little research in the matter of hammer-throwing followed, and David, wildly whirling and shouting " But I can't let go," fell in a heap as the hammer flew high in the air and came to earth again at the measured distance of seventeen yards. This performance brought on them the baleful attention of a young gentleman like a beetle, with very short shorts and hairy knees, who proved to be the President of the Cambridge University Athletic Club, and constantly ran three miles for fun. He asked David, clearly with sarcastic intent, if he was throwing the hammer with a view to entering for that event in the University Sports, and David with a cowed but propitiating demeanour said that he was

only ragging. Upon which the withering Beetle said
" So I perceived."

They strolled back to King's again in a mellow,
windy sunset, and David, quite unwearied, picked
up Tommers to go to a Turkish bath. Tommers,
being of a fleshy habit, was an habitual bather, but
his bath always made him feel so hungry afterwards
that he ate a Gargantuan dinner, which undid all the
good that the profuse action of the skin might have
done him. . . . A loud crooning noise welcomed them
as they went into the hot-room, and there, lying on a
stone-slab in the corner, was a large pink jelly, which
turned out to be A. G. He was singing vague melodies
to himself, in a dripping kind of trance, and looked
even less like the Discobolus than usual. So absorbed
was he in sweating and song that he did not notice
their entrance till he rolled over on his side. Whether
lying on his back or on his side, he looked the same
shape.

" Why, it's David and Tomlin," he said. " How
awfully jolly ! I came here in order to feel like a
Sultan with the gorgeous East in fee, but the gorgeous
East will demand fees instead of paying them.
Turkish baths ought to be supplied gratis to any
member of the University ; indeed, they ought to
be compulsory instead of Greek. David, your
shoulders are the most Praxitelean things I have
ever seen. Ha, ha ! How awfully jolly to be
Praxitelean."

He struggled to a sitting position on his couch.

" I shall never be Praxitelean," he most truthfully
remarked. " If I took Turkish baths from morning
till night, and tricycled all the rest of the time, I

should never become truly statuesque. 'Spreading,'
as dear old Gilbert said, 'is the taper-waist!' I
fancy that I suggested that very lyrical outburst.
Thickly spread, in fact, like bread and butter. But
I felt quite lithe and sinuous till I saw you. Why
should age be attended with obesity, as well as all its
other disadvantages? Where is my shampooer?
Oh, there you are, Dickie; I am ready for you: I
am a dem'd moist, unpleasant body, like Mr. Mantilini.
Awfully jolly being pinched and poked and pommelled."

He walked majestically into the shampooing-room,
and poured out an incessant monologue, interspersed
with little squeals and shrieks as Dickie stroked and
squeezed his fat ribs, and presently there was a loud
splash heard (accompanied, so David swore, with a
hissing noise as of a red-hot substance being plunged
into cold water) as he fell into the tank. Then
swathed in toga-like towels, he retired to the cooling-
room with a cup of tea and a vermouth and a
cigarette. . . . Somehow, there was an autumnal
touch about him as of a rich, red, ripe October,
strangely unlike David's vernal idiocy.

Despite the lure of Crowfoot's wet-weather match-
box and any other similar dodges, Frank resisted the
joys of glee-singing after Hall, and applied himself to
the study of the cult of Asclepius, certain that when
David had drank his fill of spotted snakes and Tintara
wine he would come to disperse his industry. . . .
And really the subject was enthralling. Asclepius
was only a human doctor, it appeared, in Homeric
times, with his two sons both in the business, the one a

surgeon, the other a general practitioner. Then, as people began to think more about their health, he was deified, and took his place among the hierarchy of authentic gods, as the son of Apollo, and instead of calling in the doctor when they were ill, the Greeks went to the sanctuaries of the divine physician and slept in his sacred precinct. Sometimes the god cured them as they slept (palpable faith-healing), sometimes they dreamed in curious ways about their diseases, and in the morning they recounted their dreams to the priest, who interpreted them into the terms of a treatment. There were hydropathic establishments in the sanctuaries, and inclined planes up the steps of the temple, so that cripples might be wheeled up in their bath-chairs. Many patients were confirmed hypochondriacs, who clung to their ailments, and kept experiencing new and interesting symptoms, till the god got fairly fed up with them and exhibited signs of impatience. To one such he ordered a mustard-plaster all over his body, to give him something real to think about, and the unfortunate patient, thus drastically cured, or at any rate not desirous of any further prescription of the kind, put up an inscription in honour of the god, and said that the mustard-plaster smarted very much. What was wrong with another patient was that he had not got enough to do, and wanted occupation for his mind; the god told him to go away from the sanctuary at once, and write a poem in his honour, and make it as long as he could. . . . How completely modern the whole thing was: just so, nowadays, some people were ill because they had not enough to do, and others felt that if only the medicine they were given

to take were nasty enough, it would do them good, and
therefore it probably did. . . .

There was the charm of archæology : as soon as you
began to dig into it, you unearthed something
completely modern. It was only if you confined
yourself to scrutinizing the surface that you found
yourself exploring a dead world, grown cold like the
extinct volcanoes in the moon to which A. G. so
dithyrambically objected. But the moment you got
below the surface, you came upon human nature again,
which was as old as time and as young as this spring
day, upon people of the twentieth century, with all
their queernesses and oddities, their pathetic pursuit
of happiness, and their insatiable love of beauty.

He got up to light a pipe, and sitting down again
forgot to take up his book. . . . What was happiness,
anyhow ? Was it getting what you wanted, or did
it really consist in wanting ? Or did it consist not in
either of these, but in consciously abandoning all
thought of either, and just merging yourself in all that
was not yourself ? Instantly the immense contrast
between himself and David jumped into his mind.
Did he himself, he wondered, really like people
because they were people, or was he not rather
critically observant in them in order to see what
absurdities they presented ? There was A. G. with
his colossal egoistic fatuity ; there was Bags with his
riding-breeches and his cocoons ; there was Gowles
with his golf, Crowfoot with his Tintara. Such
ridiculous or contemptible points in them all formed
to him their main characteristics. How utterly
different was David's scrutiny from his ! Nobody
saw people's rich absurdities with so perceptive an

eye, but David, cackling with laughter, loved them on that account as individuals. He started by assuming that they were all delightful, until (or rather long after) there was indubitable evidence that they were not. He shut his eyes to their most gross and blatant blemishes, till some such was brandished in his face, and even then he blinked and looked away and said, " Oh Lord, I don't want to know ! " Instead of marking it up against them, he found some excuse, or else he only saw the funny side of it, or chose to forget about it ; whereas Frank knew that he himself would have said, " Oh, the fellow's a sweep or an ass. Don't have anything to do with him." And David's tolerance of bores and pompous people was really colossal ; indeed, no one ever succeeded in boring David, for, like a hungry chicken, he picked up from the driest dust grains of palatable stuff and enjoyed them, and that appreciation of his bucked up the bore, and he became far more tolerable. David, wherever he was, always raised the level of enjoyment, because he found so much to like.

And all that was only the public David ; Bags, A. G., any Tom, Dick, or Harry, could see that (and to do them justice, they did, even as they could not help seeing his dancing eyes and his strong brown hands and his sky-scraping spirits. But there was a private David, ever so wise and serious, who sat in a shy quietude far below his bubbling nonsense and his ready laughter. And yet even he was not the complete and entire David ; some day the real David would manifest himself in the ways of a man with a maid, and, in a certain sense, the private David would be accessible to him no longer.

Frank knew that he was far more to David than any other friend had ever been or ever would be. As far as David was aware of his own heart, that heart was his, open to him and beating for him in that sexless surrender which boys make to boys and girls to girls. But there was a chamber there of which neither he nor even David himself had the key, which was dangling round the unheeding neck of some girl unknown. She with the glance of an eye and the twist of her finger would unlock it, and the David never yet seen by friend, however intimate, would stand on the threshold, and jubilantly take her in, and the door would be shut on the two of them. And David, all the time, hardly suspected that there was that locked chamber in him ; he had not, at any rate, the sense of an empty space unaccounted for. No girl, except in one brief flash of remote summer lightning, had revealed it to him as yet. David thought of girls as amiable, inefficient creatures, slightly terrifying and enigmatical at close quarters, but easily avoided by the wise. There was a certain daughter of a don, for instance, who doted on him, and David, very polite but with a scared eye, ran from her like a hare and escaped, slightly breathless, to less embarrassing companionship. But one day, instead of running like a hare from some similar situation he would prance up like a neighing horse, and when Frank whistled to him he would give him no more than an ear laid back in irritation at the interruption. And when the wooing and the winning were done, they would all be great friends, and everything would be completely changed. Perhaps he himself would marry too. . . .

Well, this was a long way from Asclepius, and Frank

with a shrug that expressed not what he felt, but what
a sensible person would feel, took up his book again,
for since he had absented himself from glee-singing
with David in order to work, he might as well have
something to show for it. On this mild February
night he had opened his window, drawing the blind
down over it, and from the corner of the court where
the songsters were assembled there came fragments
of Mr. Speaker and spotted snakes. He could pick
out, now and then, the shrill, quavering tenor of
Crowfoot, and then the lower voices joined in, amongst
whose no doubt was David's, who sat heavily frowning
with his ears stopped against the intrusion of distracting parts. " Philomel with melody." . . . Oh,
confound Philomel ! David would be here presently
and he had not done a half-hour's solid work yet.
He would send David away, saying that he really
wanted to get on with his Asclepius, and David, if he
thought that he meant it, would go like a lamb. But
Frank knew that he would not say anything of
the kind. Or should he, just to see how David would
take it ? Or should he, out of some indefinable
bitterness, be ill-tempered and silent, just to make
David wonder what he had done to vex him ?

A. G.'s fat laugh sounded somewhere in the court
outside, and there was certainly David's voice. Steps
crackled on the gravel, and, as they came nearer,
words were audible through the open window.

" Come up to my room, Blaizides," said A. G.,
" and while you drink a whisky and soda, I will speak
of the moon and the joy of existence and that sort
of thing. Bring your Jonathan Maddox up with
you, for you're never happy without him, and we'll

8

'tell sad stories of the death of Kings.' King's is expiring ; there's no life left in it except you."

There was a perceptible pause, and Frank listened with held breath for what David would say.

"Oh, thanks awfully," he replied. "But I'm afraid I can't. I haven't done a stroke of work all day, and I must put in a couple of hours before I go to bed."

"Ha, ha ! The model, industrious Blaizides ! Well, good-night then ! "

Heavy footsteps, accompanied by crooning noises, sounded in one direction ; light ones and a whistle in another. Frank did not quite believe that David had gone to his room without looking in. . . . Then, after a couple of minutes, there was a stealthy tread outside, and the door opened very quietly.

"And so Ananias escaped," said David. "Gepp suggested that I should bring you up to his rooms, but I said I was going to work. You have to lie, you know, on occasions, and this was one of them. Lord, such an evening—ripping good fun ! Never was such a sing-song ! "

Frank slowly rose to the surface, but kept his finger marking a line half-way down his page.

"Oh ! so glad ! " he said. " I heard you singing," and he looked back at his book again.

David cocked his head, full of intelligence.

" I say, Frank, I believe you want to go on working, don't you ? "he said. " Shall I go away ? "

Frank continued to simulate the morose and disturbed student.

"Oh no. Do stop—er—stop ten minutes ! "

David went towards the door.

" Think I won't," he said. " I'll go and do some sap, too. I know how beastly it is to be interrupted if you're keen on something. Rather ! Good-night."

Frank threw his book in the air. It came down on the floor with crumpled leaves.

" Caught you that time," he said.

David wavered.

" Sure you don't want to work ? " he said.

" Absolutely."

David laughed.

" Ass ! " he said. " But you did catch me ; you did it jolly well. I really thought you wanted to sap."

" You lamb ! " said Frank.

" Well, if you wanted to sap, I didn't want to be a nuisance. But if you don't——"

" Well, if I don't ? "

" We might sit and jaw for a bit. Or piquet ? Or come and stroll down to the bridge, and then you can look in on me, and I'll give you a drink. Spring-night, you know. You can almost hear the things growing."

" And when we get to the bridge ? " asked Frank.

" Throw matches into the river. Or rag. Or anything."

" Selfish devil," said Frank, " you always want to have everything your own way."

David did not rise to this.

" Of course I do," he said. " Come on ! "

MAY had come in like a cold fish (not a lamb) and had
turned to a salamander, and David on this baking
morning was proceeding very slowly down Trinity
Street on his way to King's with his straw hat on the
back of his head and no waistcoat anywhere. There
were some nice little things happening to beguile
a leisurely wayfarer, for two dons, one coming up
Trinity Lane and the other walking very fast down
Trinity Street ran into each other at the corner, and
the cap of one fell off and the other dropped a quantity
of papers. It was pleasant that they should both be
very stout and very red in the face, and look so deeply
offended with each other. Then a playful Irish
terrier pretended that these shed papers were rats,
and pounced upon one and worried it. Its owner
(the reddest of the dons) gave a shrill cry, which
encouraged the dog, and a boy on a bicycle ran into it
from behind. So it sat down and howled till it found
out that it wasn't hurt at all, and its mistress came up
and smacked it soundly, to restore it to a sense of
reality.

A loud clattering of hoofs on the asphalte diverted
David's rapt attention, and a tall, truculent chestnut
horse, with Bags rather imperfectly attached to it,
trotted swiftly by. Bags was wonderfully smart,
and so was the chestnut, but they seemed to disagree
about the matter that jointly concerned them, for
Bags was sawing at its mouth, and the horse, with
determination in its eye, was trotting relentlessly on.
Then Bags, evidently without intention, touched its

side with a bright beautiful spur, and the horse broke
into a sprawling canter. Then, almost best of all,
Mr. Crowfoot, walking very fast and with all his lenses
adjusted for the smallest print, charged into the Irish
terrier, which was shaking itself after its smacking,
and became extremely unpopular with it. It made
short runs at him, snapping at his heels, and Mr. Crowfoot whirled round and round, nervously ejaculating
"Good doggie," and good doggie's mistress caught
it a whack over the head with her umbrella. Upon
which it cowered in the road, and another bicycle
from the opposite direction ran into it. It was having
an eventful though a miserable morning.

David finished laughing, and felt rather miserable
too. His cricket, which throughout the term was to
have been the aim and the glory of existence, had
gone completely wrong, and he had disappointed
Frank and himself, and everybody else who enter-
tained the slightest regard for him. He had come up
from school with the reputation of being the deadliest
left-hand bowler seen for ten years, and he had utterly
failed to come off. He had done nothing in the
Freshman's match, and in spite of that, had been
tried twice for the University, and the sum of his
achievements there had been to miss an important
catch. As for his batting—but it was not kind to
talk about his batting. In the less distinguished
field of College cricket he had been every bit as useless;
all that he could do to wickets was to lose his own, and
never once had he justified his existence. Lately,
and quite properly, he had not even been asked to
play for his college, which was a fine fate for a boy who
had been expected to make havoc with the Oxford

batsmen. The weather, it is true, had been against him, for all the term there had been slow easy wickets and David wanted hard baked pitches, off which his slow bowling kicked and bucked in the most unexpected manner. And now, quite at the end of the term, when for all practical purposes he had ceased to exist as a cricketer, there came the weather he had been starving for.

Tennis had been an alleviation to these disasters, but even tennis threatened to-day to prove Janus-faced. David had gone on improving enormously (here was the smiling countenance), and had got through the challenge rounds of the University ties without losing a set. Frank, as he had played for Cambridge last year as second string (the first string having gone down), was not called upon to play through these ties, and would meet the winner in the challenge round. If he won, he would play first string against Oxford ; if he lost, he would be challenged by the loser in the final tie of the preliminary rounds, to determine who should play second string. And this afternoon David would meet Frank to decide who would play first string for the University.

It all sounded very nice and noble. If David was beaten, he would still play second string for Cambridge ; if he won, he would play first. It was un-heard-of that a Freshman should represent the University at all, and considered in the abstract the glory of it would have almost atoned for his failure at cricket. But, unfortunately, the matter, however glorious in the abstract, was complicated in the concrete by considerations which made his heart sink. It was Frank who had taught him his tennis, and

Frank, as David knew, put tennis, as an achievement, above even cricket, and would sooner, as he had said, play first string for Cambridge, and beat the Oxford man, than make a century at Lord's. It sounded quite incredible, but so it was : tennis, according to Frank's notions, was the king of all games, and now the person who perhaps was going to stand in the way of the attainment of his ambition was David himself. Modest as he was about his own accomplishments, David could not help knowing that he had more than a decent chance of winning. Frank, all this term, had been working very hard at his archæological tripos, and he certainly had not been playing up to his best form ; whereas David, who had no such occupation or preoccupation, and had had his cricketing ambitions so soundly thwarted, had thrown himself, brain and limb alike, into this delectable sport, and was at his very best. Only a few days ago he had been playing Frank in a friendly game on level terms, and had taken three straight sets off him. It was true that Frank had only just come out of the final paper of his tripos, and no doubt his eye was a little out after three hours of short focussing on his paper ; but with all allowance made for that, he should not have lost three sets right off the reel.

But what made the gloom in David's mind was the way Frank took it : the approaching crisis had certainly come between them. It made an embarrassment, and for some weeks past they had not talked about tennis, and, if David alluded to it, the subject was changed. Nor, indeed, had they played together with the old frequency, for David had had his ties to get through, and Frank had been grimly practising with the marker, getting coached in his weaknesses, and being very diligent with the abhorred American service. One day, previous to playing himself, David had watched one of these encounters for a few minutes, and had airily mocked from the dedans.

" You'll see how I'll make hay of that," he observed gaily when Frank had served a couple of dead nicks. But Frank had not been airy or gay at all.

" I daresay I shall," he observed with withering dryness.

David, with that quiet comprehension of his, was sure that he knew exactly how Frank felt. The idea of being beaten and not playing first string for Cambridge had got on his mind and soured it, and he could not bear to talk about it, especially to his possible executioner. Of course, below such silly things as balls and racquets, their friendship, David assured himself, was all serene, but balls and racquets were assuming a nightmare aspect. It was Frank's last chance, too, of playing first string for Cambridge (that made it so much the worse for him), whereas whatever happened this year, it was as certain as anything could be that next year and the next David would realize the ambition that the other so much coveted. David would thankfully have scratched to him ; he would have welcomed any mischance that would have enabled Frank to win ; but nothing was in the least likely to happen between now and three o'clock that afternoon. But something in Frank's awful aloof attitude and the fact that all chatter about tennis had ceased between them made it impossible for David to tell him that.

He knew perfectly well that Frank, with his nerves thoroughly on edge about the whole thing, would make some rasping rejoinder which would not have mended matters. Of course he was taking it all wrong : David could not conceive behaving like that himself . . . wretched it must be for him, feeling like that.

" Wish I'd never gone inside a court," thought David as he turned into King's. . . . And the very next moment he was picturing himself volleying a service that looked as if it was going to make a nick and laying down a slow, short, sticky chase that wouldn't allow his opponent to get at it. " Mustn't snatch at the service," he thought. " Just play it quietly with lots of cut . . ."

He passed below Frank's window. There he was in the window-seat, reading the paper.

" Hullo ! " said David.

Frank looked up and then down at his paper again.

" Hullo ! " he said.

" Jolly hot," said David rather pathetically.

" Yes. Three o'clock this afternoon, isn't it ? "

David assented and paused a moment.

" Won't you have lunch with me ? " he asked.

" Oh, thanks. But mine's just come. I was just going to eat it now."

" Right-oh," said David, and passed on.

David heard himself hailed. Bags had got rid of the relentless chestnut, or the relentless chestnut had got rid of Bags, and he waited for him at the corner of Fellows Buildings.

" Feeling fit ? " asked Bags.

David wanted to say, " No, you blasted fool," or something of the sort, but, after all, these complications were not Bags's fault.

" Lord, yes—fit as a fiddle," he said. " I saw you just now in Trinity Street. Your gee-gee looked a shade too fit for you. Get a nice rocking-horse, Bags, all red inside the nostrils, and smelling of paint, and have done with those fiery animals."

" Funny," said Bags with dignity. " I'm coming up to see you play this afternoon, and I'll give you a topping dinner if you win."

David took Bags's arm. Despite his cocoons and his swank Bags was a very reliable and affectionate person. He sounded silly, but he understood.

" Well, I hope you won't," he said. " Oh, Bags, it's all so rotten. Frank wants to win so awfully, and he's got the jumps about it, and is as cross as two sticks."

" That's pretty small of him," said Bags.

David instantly had to defend him.

" It isn't a bit," he said. " It's just got on his nerves and he can't help it. I hope to God he will win."

Bags pondered this.

" That's rather like you," he said. " You've been living for tennis, and now you'd rather die than win. What an ass you are, David ! "

" I suppose I am. But we all are, you know. If I wanted a thing madly, like that, and you stood in my way, you'd efface yourself. Proving yourself just as much an ass as me."

" Well, it's only a game," said Bags with the intention of infuriating David, and bucking him up.

" Oh, do shut it ! " shouted David. " Only a game, indeed ! What more do you want ? It isn't worth while playing any game, unless you think it's the most important thing in the world."

" Copy-book," said Bags. " Whatever's worth doing is worth doing well."

" Wrong again ! " said David. " There are lots of things worth doing rather badly, but games aren't among them. But what's the use of arguing ? Let's go into hall and have lunch. No, I don't think I want any lunch."

" Needle," said Bags.

" I know. One part of me is mad keen to win, and that part's nearly sick with nervousness. And the other part wants to be beaten. I shall be ; I shan't be able to hit a ball. That's what I want most."

" Well, I want lunch," said Bags. " Come on. And I think I shall order dinner, too. I'm sure you'll win. By Jove, I'll ask Frank, too."

" Oh, for heaven's sake don't. It'll be the most awful frost."

Bags burst out laughing.

" One minute you say you know for certain you'll be beaten," he said, " and the next you tell me not to ask Frank, because it would be a frost. It wouldn't be a frost if he won."

" Oh, don't be logical," said David with a faint grin.

The hours went on, and by three o'clock David was changed and in the court. The dedans was crammed with spectators, and the side-galleries also, for apart from the fact that this was the challenge round, the circumstances of a Freshman being matched against one of last year's representatives who was also a cricket-blue was a sufficient draw. Frank was not ready yet ; just as David finished changing, he looked into his dressing-room, and said, " Sorry : I'm afraid I'm late," and instead of changing and chatting there, went next door. So David had five minutes alone in the court and hit balls on the wood of his racquet, and put others into the net, and got on the wrong leg, and mistimed everything, being, in fact, a bundle of exasperated nerves. And why had Frank behaved like that, as if they were total strangers ? Putrid behaviour. . . . Then, thank goodness, the time of waiting was over, for here was Frank. They spun for the choice of sides, and David crossed over to receive the service.

It looked at first as if he need have been under no apprehension that he would win. He could neither attack nor defend, while Frank, playing at the top of his form, kept piling up the games, two love, three love, four love. And as he kept David dancing from side to side of the court, and worrying him with his service, and placing the ball precisely where he did not expect it, the jangle of his nerves that had made him so bleak and beastly began to evaporate. He knew perfectly well with what whole-heartedness David would rejoice in the victory that now seemed so probable ; he knew, too, that the thought that David might beat him had so blackened his own mind that, if David won, he felt that he could hardly speak to him or give him a word of congratulation. Now he could judge and condemn his own churlishness. As they passed each other, changing sides, he had not yet once looked at David, nor given him a single word, but soon out of the corner of his eye he saw David's troubled face, and knew that it was not lack of form alone that caused that. David too . . . he knew that if it had been anybody else at all with whom he had to play off this tie he would have been polite and pleasant. But just because it was David, it seemed, he had to behave like a cad—just because it was David. . . .

Meantime a sort of desperation had come over David. He would have been genuinely delighted for Frank to win, but it wasn't this he meant, namely that Frank should go on scoring simply because he himself couldn't hit a single ball correctly. And then Frank's victorious progress wasn't making Frank cheerful or human again. He was winning as fast as David could put balls into the net, but he still wore that filthy flinty face, withering as an east wind. Frank's general attitude, his snappishness, his aloofness, had put him off altogether, and he could neither concentrate on the game nor capture that breezy enjoyment which always characterized his play. A love set had already gone against him, and Frank had won two games of the next. . . . Well, it would be over soon, and he only hoped he would be able to stifle his own disgust at himself sufficiently to make him genial when the last point was lost, and to congratulate Frank on his victory with some semblance of sincerity. At all costs, he mustn't behave as Frank had been behaving for weeks. And what was to happen afterwards ? Somehow he must expunge from his mind all Frank's behaviour, as well as his own wretched performance in this nightmare of a match.

As they crossed over, David saw that his shoe-lace was untied, and he bent down in the marker's box by the net to remedy that. And then he was aware that Frank, instead of walking grimly by, had stopped by him, and then came his voice.

" I say, David, I'm a rotter," he said. " I'm awfully sorry."

For one second the devil took possession of David. It would serve Frank right to say, " Oh, don't mention it," in the sort of voice that Frank had been using lately, and to proceed to lose the match as soon as possible. That would take off the edge of Frank's pleasure in winning, and well he deserved it. . . . But the next moment all that was swept out of his mind. It was Frank who was sorry, so what did it matter what he had done ?

But it was useless to pretend not to know what Frank meant : that would only make another false situation. And so he was perfectly natural. He looked up at him.

" Oh, nonsense," he said. " That's all right."

" But I am a rotter. Apologies."

David finished with his shoe-lace and straightened himself. And the ready laughter bubbled on his lips.

" Oh, Frank, what nonsense ! " he said again.

But Frank still lingered. He laid his hand on David's arm.

" David, do buck up," he said. " It's all my fault. For God's sake pull yourself together, and take the stuffing out of me. You can. Knock my silly head off."

This was elixir to David. He pranced out into the court again, for whatever happened now, all was right between him and Frank.

" I'll have a jolly good try ! " he said. " Look out ! "

The relief of it ! To David the match, already half lost, became a game again, instead of being a mute, miserable quarrel. He could not fight against that demon of jealousy and ill-temper which had possessed his friend, but that was exorcised now, and paralysed him no longer. As he went to the dedans to get a couple of balls for his service, he heard someone say, " Match as good as over," and that heartened him even further. Over, was it ? . . .

Frank made a fine return from David's service, which, two minutes ago, David would have failed to get to at all, or, having got to it would have put it into the net. Now, with taut wrist and his weight behind his racquet, he sent it quite firmly into the grille. Luscious stroke. . . . All his gaiety and con-fidence poured back on him as from behind some pent-up sluice, and whereas, before, Frank had only got to return the ball anyhow once or twice for David to make some childish misjudgment and pre-sent him with the point, now he had to fight for it. Already he had got a long lead in the second net, but the wily David played carefully and well within himself till he caught him up, and then went all out, beating him in attack and defence and everything else, and won the set. . . . One all, and who'd have thought it ?

And then began a grim and delightful contest.

With the withdrawal of Frank's black mood, and his apology for it, the wholesome sun of sport came out again from the obscuring clouds, and they both played their best, enjoying instead of hating the fact that they were pitted against each other. All Frank's essential " decency " rejoiced in the fact that this young devil to whom he had taught the game, and who was showing himself pupil no longer, but master, was David, and that moral change in him, infectious as influenza, gave the young devil a positive seizure of uncanny skill. The paralysis of his induced depression had passed, and here were he and Frank unhampered again by the ill-temper of the one and the consequent trouble of the other. Never before in all their friendly games had they been so unmitigatedly bloodthirsty, and the rivalry now was no snarling contention, but something bright-eyed and breezy, and gay in its fierceness. No longer did David fret over the possible tragedy of victory, nor Frank over the bitterness of defeat. What mattered only was by swiftness or masked cunning, or force or quiet skill, to win this point and that, to defend or to attack, and with all the combined assault of brain and muscle to thwart and discomfort the adversary.

David won this set, making him two to one, and in what proved to be the final one he turned on full horse-power, no longer playing a little inside himself, and cautiously allowing a little margin for error, but taking all risks in order to turn Frank's attack into defence. He was not content with getting back a difficult return and preparing to be attacked again, but at all costs and without delay he kept converting a losing position into a winning one. If Frank forced hard for the dedans, he no longer stopped it only, just lobbing it back, but attempted some vainglorious shot into the grille, or with a dragging cut, tried to make his return expire at the foot of the tambour. He made plenty of mistakes, but to cancel them there were a brilliance and a pace that left his adversary always labouring and hustled. Halfway through the set Frank was mopping and crimson ; as for David, his face almost threw a red light on to the wall like a signal lamp. They were both fighting for all they knew, but Frank was fighting desperately countering attacks, whereas David was delivering them.

At this pace one of them seemed bound to crash, which was a pity, . . . David had sent for a drink of some sort, and as they crossed over, Frank leaned against the post of the net, immensely glad of a pause. He wanted to win just as much as ever, but not in the stuffy, sultry manner which had been his, and though he meant to fight every point to the end, doggedly and with set teeth, something at the back of his brain could contemplate, without dismay, what it would feel like to be beaten. . . .

He poked David in the ribs with the butt-end of his racquet, as David buried his nose in a lemon-squash, and this, according to plan, made him splutter.

" Oh, shut it ! " cried he. " If you only knew how I wanted a drink."

"I like to see that, it'll put you right off. David, I can't keep this pace up, nor can you. Which of us is going to crack first ? "

9

David finished his drink, and turned the glass upside-down so that the lump of ice slid into his mouth.

" You, of course," he said.

And then came the end. David got five games to four, and proceeded to lose the first three points of the next game, with three of the feeblest shots seen for years. Then just to show he had not cracked, he sent two expresses into the dedans and laid down a yard chase, which he defended with an untakable service, at which Frank could only dab in the manner of someone trying to hit a troublesome fly. He then got to advantage, and put the easiest possible return which would have given him game, set and match, not into the top of the net, or even the bottom of the net, but on to the floor, not far from where he was himself standing.

" Great and merciful God ! " said he very loudly, and gave a hiccup of unquenchable laughter. . . . Once more he defeated himself out of pure idiocy, got to advantage again, and then made no mistake. The ball, heavily cut, hissed over the middle of the net with two inches to spare, hit the floor below the grille, then the side wall and lay down stone dead off the back wall. Never was a ball so classically killed.

Frank threw his racquet into the air and caught it by the handle.

" You beast ! " he called out. " Well played, David ! "

The appreciative gallery crowded and congratulated. Though only four sets had been played there could not, in their opinion, have been a better fight, but then nobody among them knew of the fiercer battle which the vanquished had won over himself. A. G. came rolling out of the dedans and explained what a magnificent player he had been in the days of his youth, and nobody believed a single word of it. Bags was there with a rather supercilious blood, and Poet Stapleton, in whose romantic brain a short ode to David in *vers libre* was already seething. But by degrees they melted away, and David, after a prolonged wallow in a cold bath, strolled nakedly, in answer to Frank's call, into the bathroom next door, where he was sitting on the floor in the draught from the window to cool by evaporation.

"The tennis-blue," said Frank, rudely—"The blooming, swaggering, indecent blue."

David sat down on the edge of the bath.

"I know; it's awful cheek," he said. "I want a cigarette."

Frank nodded towards his clothes.

"Coat-pocket," he said. "And give me one."

David rummaged.

"O Lord, there's only one," he said.

"Pinch it in half, then. If they aren't equal, give me the largest half."

They lit their fragments; Frank inhaled three full breaths of the smoke, and threw the end out of the window.

"What a game!" he said. "I wish I could have taken you to the five sets. But I don't believe I could have lasted out another. I was done to a turn as it was."

"Rot! I should have gone to bits first. My word, those two I missed in the last game!"

"Yes; shocking bad. But a decent one for the end."

He got off the floor where he was sitting. It was their way to be curt and telegraphic when there was emotion about, but the situation demanded just a word or two. He took hold of David's shoulders.

" I *was* a tragic ass," he said. " Sorry, David."

He pressed his hands down on the boy's shoulders a moment, then slapped him right and left on the ribs.

" That's over," he said. " What about dressing ? "

" Right-oh," said David. " Altogether right-oh. I say, I do feel such a beast."

" Oh, don't make me sick," shouted Frank, " or I'll spank you."

" Oh, spanking is it ? " said David. " And what about me ? "

He sprang up ; Frank closed with him, and David, trying to step back to get free, was blocked by the edge of the bath and fell backwards into it. So he had to dry himself for the second time, and then dressed.

Frank had still a week of waiting for the publication of the lists concerning his archæological Tripos, and David was able with a very small effort to persuade himself that the duty of a sympathetic friend was to shut his ears (as at glee-singing) to all frigid calls on his own industry and studiousness, and devote himself to the sharing and lightening of those empty hours. Frank had still to meet David's last victim in the preliminary rounds to determine who should play second string for the University, but the match was not productive of the smallest excitement, and now the two of them had to practise the antiquated (though possibly noble) double game which formed part of the event against Oxford. That occasionally filled up a couple of hours in the afternoon, but there happened to be no University cricket on, which would have occupied Frank (though it would have provided no occupation for David), and the two were perfectly content to loaf the days of waiting away, the important thing being that they should be together. For once the climate (which is responsible for so much industry) permitted the idle to be happy, for day succeeded day in windless and unclouded sunshine, and how was it possible to be lazier in a thoroughly satisfactory manner than on the upper river in a Canadian canoe which neither of them had the smallest idea of handling? But Canadian canoes are mild domestic craft, which conform to the intentions of their occupants, however clumsily expressed, and seldom upset. There were materials for lunch or tea on board, a kettle with a spirit-lamp, towels for bathing, cigarettes for smoking, and books to be abstained from. Usually something was forgotten and they then managed perfectly well without it.

To-day it was towels that had been left behind, so, when they had bathed in Byron's pool, it was necessary to lie in the sun till they got dry again. But the kettle could be put on to boil in this interval, and David, having (as he thought) lit the spirit-lamp, threw the match into the dry crop of the hayfield by the river's edge and certainly set light to the county of Cambridge. A sort of Molochian ritual had to be then performed, and putting on their shoes they trod and stamped on the fire till it was extinguished, and then found that the spirit-lamp had not caught fire at all.

"So like life," said David bitterly. "With the intention of lighting it and nothing else, I set fire to everything except it. Gosh, what a smell of singed india-rubber. What a pity one of us doesn't faint, and then it would bring him round. Or is it feathers?"

"Feathers," said Frank firmly.

"'Feather, said the Sheep,'" quoted David from Alice.

"I'm not a sheep," said Frank.

"Never said you were. But surely the Sheep may say 'feather' as well as you. You haven't a monopoly of saying 'feather.' . . . I think the country-side is extinguished."

David curled himself round the kettle to shield it from the breeze.

"I could go on loafing and messing about like this for ever," he said. "Why should I work? Why shouldn't we go on picnicking till we're old men with grey beards and one if not two feet in the grave?"

"How about the winter?" asked Frank.

"Go to Egypt for the winter, or go to bed."

The lamp was prospering now, and he lay back on the grass with eyes closed against the glare.

"O—oh, the sun!" he said. "If it can behave like this at all, why can't it do it always? Why doesn't it clean itself up? Why doesn't it stay still? Then there wouldn't be any to-morrow. Oh, that's the earth, but the principle's the same."

"But there is to-morrow," said Frank, "and it's lists at ten o'clock. I may get a second, but that's

the most. And I do want to get a first so frightfully.
That means I shall stop up here and work for a fellowship. Otherwise, I shall have to go down, and enter
my uncle's office. Solicitor, you know. Middle of
London. Muck!"

"Can't be done," said David. "You must stop
up another year. What's to happen to me otherwise?
How selfish you are! Tell your uncle I said so.
Say that I wish it. Tell him not to be a blasted
tyrant. Tell him not in mournful numbers——
What on earth's tickling so frightfully?"

David rolled over and rubbed his back. He gave a
wild scream when he looked at the hand that rubbed
it.

"Covered with ants," he shrieked, "millions of
ants," and made a bolt of it into the water again.

Frank moved his clothes to a less populous place,
and presently he came out again; rolled in the
hayfield, and began to dress.

"You've got to be a passive-resister," he said.
"Kind but firm. Of course you will get a first, but
if you don't, you've got to take a ticket for Cambridge, just an ordinary ticket, when the October
term begins, and merely come here. Smile and look
idiotic. Pretend you're deaf and can't hear a word
they say. Shake your head and smile and count
your fingers over and over again like the village idiot.
Say you've got a wife and child whom you must
support by archæology. Say—— Hurrah! the
kettle's boiling."

"I shan't go and hear the lists read out," said
Frank.

"I shall. You may expect me back at two minutes

past ten with a crown of cabbages for you. Blow it, there's some hay in my trousers. Life seems entirely to consist of dressing and undressing."

David had to take them off and turn them inside out to brush off spiky grass-seeds and pieces of vegetable débris. Then he must convince himself that no ants remained in the small of his back and that the bumble-bee which had been fussing about and had unaccountably vanished was not making a nest in his socks. But presently peace and plenty of tea descended, and between speech and silence they sat on until the sun began to do its evening stunt. The light grew suffused with crimson, and the level ray shining through the tall grasses set the hayfield afire again, and the trees by the river glowed in the molten conflagration. High in the air in screeching circles the swifts went a-hunting ; rooks returned from their patrol of the pastures, and a heron winged heavily by. Above the red of the west the sun made rosy the feathery wisps of strayed cloudlets, and set them adrift in a pale-green sea. Then he allowed a star, just one, but a good one, to be lit there, and himself illuminated the gilded crescent of the moon. He spread a curtain of clear shadow as of deep and dusky water below the trees, and so slid behind a bank of remote cloud. . . .When they thought his stunt was over, he cleared the cloud away, and emerged redder than ever and absurdly magnified, balanced on the edge of the flat horizon.

" Positively his last appearance," said David. " Rather theatrical, but not sloshy . . ."

Frank got up—the thought of the impending lists clearly weighed on his mind—and began throwing

the cushions into the canoe. There was half a bun
left over from their tea, and David with due cere-
mony made a burnt-offering of it, and examined
the entrails with augur-like solemnity. They were
doughy, but propitious, and an unconsumed raisin
indubitably pointed to an archæological success. He
contrived, without apparent effort, to be fatuous all
the way home, and Frank lost the sense of impending
calamity.

The burnt bun was right. At five minutes past
ten next morning David, with his cap and gown over
his great coat, below which were pyjamas and no
socks (for he had not fully awoke till ten minutes to
ten and was only just in time to get to the Senate
House for lists), burst into Frank's room with a woe-
begone face.

" You're ploughed," he said. " No mention of
your name at all. A fellow called F. Maddox of
King's took a first. . . . O Lord, how ripping ! I
told you so, and so did the bowels of the bun. Give
me some breakfast at once. I feel rather sick with
running on an empty stomach. Bad luck on your
City-Uncle."

Second Year

DAVID had been spending ten days in London during the Christmas vacation, staying with Frank and his mother. To-day Mrs. Maddox had gone out of town for the week-end, leaving the house to the two friends, and on Monday Frank was starting for Athens, there to spend the next four months. He had annexed a Craven travelling studentship, and, with a view to a dissertation for his Fellowship, was to study at the English archæological school there. He would therefore not be at Cambridge during either of the next two terms, which was rather a dismal prospect, and it was clearly proper that the two should have a final fling together before the separation. Mrs. Maddox therefore had openly lamented that she was obliged to pay this visit, and would not see the last of Frank, but as a matter of fact she had carefully arranged it. Frank was devoted to her, but she was aware that he would really much sooner get David to himself for these last two days, at ease and uninterrupted, than have her muddling and messing (so she put it to herself) about the house. So with many laments about this tiresome visit which could not be put off, she left them in possession.

David was an absolute stranger to London, for with his father, first Archdeacon of Baxminster, and now Dean of Truro in the remote diocese of Cornwall, his holidays had always been spent in the country, and probably he had not passed more than a few weeks in town, all told, since he was born.

Their days therefore hitherto had been spent in a wild orgie of sight-seeing and theatres. The Zoo, the Houses of Parliament, the Museums, the Tower of London, were all new amazements to him, and had solidly filled in the interstices of time between music-halls, theatres, and football matches. He was seeing everything with fresh eyes and vivid perceptions, and at one moment he wanted to be an actor, at another a professional football player, at another a taxi-driver who was paid, actually paid, for the treat of whirling about these fascinating streets. Best of all, perhaps, would it be to be the policeman at Hyde Park Corner and hold up all the roaring traffic precisely as he pleased by walking into the middle of the street, with a large hand extended, and standing with his back to the panting vehicles, superbly conscious that none of the awe-stricken huddle of 'buses and motors would dare to butt into him. He was like a lion-tamer who, without even the spell of the human eye (for he turned his back on it), cowed and controlled the roaring monster of traffic. Or like Orpheus with his lute. . . . David had even on one wet afternoon, when Frank was being overhauled by a dentist, made the complete inner circle of the Underground, starting at Sloane Square, and taking a ticket only as far as South Kensington, but continuing in the train till it reached South Kensington the second time. There was the joy, too, about this of indirectly swindling the shareholders in the company, in having made so long a journey for so small a copper coin. David, in fact, had been just twelve years old all these days. . . .

But this Underground excursion was an hour of

abnormal juvenility, and by Sunday he was getting satiated, and could manage to sit and smoke after breakfast without wanting to go out in a very thick London fog, to see what happened. But the fog, peering in blackly at the windows, was thoroughly delightful with its kaleidoscope of varying degrees of gloom, and gave him the sense of being warm and secure deep down in some very comfortable rabbit-burrow. . . . But to-day was the last : to-morrow the other rabbit would have gone.

" Oh, Frank, I do hate your going away to-morrow," he said. " We shan't do anything more together till God knows when."

" I know when, too," said Frank with dignity. " I shall come straight up to Cambridge when I get back from abroad, and spend the last fortnight of the May term there. It isn't such a secret ! "

" Talking scraps of modern Greek, like Bags and his French, and I shan't understand a single word you say. And on Wednesday I go back to Cambridge, and it'll be rotten without you. . . . I say, do you think your mother can really bear me till then alone ? It was awfully kind of her to ask me to stop on, but I can perfectly well go back to-morrow."

" She's resigned to it. In fact she likes it. Besides, I thought you and she were going to marry, so that you'd be my stepfather."

David laughed.

" So we were. Gosh, I'll keep you in order. . . . But I should like to stop if I shan't be a nuisance. You see, Bags has been staying at the Savoy all this time with some of his people, and I haven't set eyes on him yet. Simply not been time. But he's asked

me to go to some show with him to-morrow night :
Phyllis in Philistia."

" Ho ! Hot stuff ! " said Frank. " Bags will be
Lotharian."

" I know. I shall yell. I'm to join him there,
and we're to have supper afterwards at somewhere
awfully gay."

" Giddy night. I shall be roaring across France.
Damn ! "

" Whaffor ? "

" General survey of the situation. I say, the fog's
thicker than ever. What are we to do ? "

" Nothing," said David. " Just sit."

" And after that ? "

" Lunch. And then some more nothing. Then
dinner. Ripping day, I call it."

This thrilling programme was duly carried out.
Never for a moment did the fog lift, and there was
no telling when the day was over. They tried an
acrostic from a Sunday-paper and could only solve
it (and that not very successfully) by the use of
such words as no respectable acrostic-editor would
have sullied his page with. They ate large lunches
and went to sleep ; they woke up again and had
tea, and going up to Frank's bedroom turned all his
clothes out of the drawers and put on the bed what
he wanted to be packed and put back in the drawers
all that he didn't. About half-way through they
got mixed as to which dump was to be packed and
which left behind, and David put all his handker-
chiefs into a drawer, and his skates on to the bed.
Before all this was rectified, it was dinner-time, and
then there were piquet, soon abandoned, and talk

and silence. Finally came a retarded bedtime with
the consciousness of a last day wonderfully well
spent, for, after all, they had been together with
nobody to interrupt and nothing to do, and friends
cannot have better pastime than that.

David walked back along Buckingham Palace Road
and across the Park, when, next morning, he had
seen the train slide out of the station, feeling that
the light of London had waned, and passing the
sentries outside the Palace without any desperate
sense of envy. It would be fun to be a sentry in
one box if Frank was sentry in the next, so that
when they took their stiff little walks to and fro
they could cut each other or make faces at each
other, but it would be dreary work if the next sentry
was anybody else. It was a dreary morning, too:
the limes were weeping their last sodden, sooty
leaves to the ground, and the air smelt grimy from
yesterday's fog. There was just as much to do as
there had been throughout this blissful week, but
there was no one to do it with. At least not the
right person, and anybody else was as bad as
nobody. Probably the best thing to do was to
buck up.

David had lately joined the Bath Club as an undergraduate member, and now he pulled himself together to make his first entry into it, which somehow
seemed to him a terribly formidable undertaking.
His trials began on the very threshold, for a polite
attendant blocked his way and asked him whom
he wanted.

" I don't want anybody, thank you," said David, feeling himself an object of suspicion.

" This is the Bath Club, sir," said the man.

" I know that," said David, rather testily and suddenly beginning to stammer, as he did sometimes in embarrassing or exciting situations. " That's wh-wh-why I c-came here."

Then the light began to break.

" Oh, I'm a new member, if that's what your driving at," he said. " Blaize. Quite all right. Don't mention it."

He hung up his hat and coat and washed his hands, not because they needed it, but because the soap and the nail-brush partly belonged to him, and he might as well use them. He went through into the smoking-room, and again a waiter, after a prolonged hover in his neighbourhood, asked him whom he was looking for, and David explained the position with unruffled patience. " But you might tell the others," he added. . . . Then he settled himself in an arm-chair in the window and read a paper, because that was the way people behaved in clubs. That very soon palled, and with a view to using some more of his property, he wrote a wholly unnecessary note to Bags, on black-edged paper. Then a small weak gentleman like a moth put a lily-white hand on his shoulder and said " Hullo, Horace ! " and retired with a wan smile when he saw it was somebody else, and David added a postscript to Bags saying, " They call me ' Horace' here." . . . That seemed to exhaust the experiences to be gained from the smoking-room, for nothing more happened after that, and exploring further he discovered the swimming-bath filled with pale green water and surrounded with header boards and athletic apparatus. A row of rings on ropes stretched from one end of the bath to the other, and these (being more of his property) seemed well worth investigation. If only Frank had been here what a joyous morning they could have spent; but even in his absence, swimming and messing about with rings and dumb-bells were clearly more exhilarating than sitting in a chair and reading a paper, and after supplying the stale news that he was Blaize, a new member, to the bath attendant, he undressed, and pommelled a ball and experimented with dumb-bells in order to get hot before his bathe. Then there were the rings over the bath: you swung forward, holding on to one, so he gathered, and caught hold of the next; got up momentum by swinging on the two, and letting go of the first, advanced to the third. This acted beautifully, and he was about halfway down the bath when his hand slipped, and he fell with a shriek and a loud splash into the pale-green water.

This was all pleasant enough, and as he rose to the surface again from his ducking he observed near him a large round pink object, clearly a piece of some further submerged body. David's eyes were dim and choked with water, and at that first glance it might have been the top of a bald head, or a section of a round stomach or some other circumferential part of a man. But before he noticed more than this, an instantaneous conviction flashed into his head, like some telepathic brain-wave, that it must belong to A. G.: nobody else in the Bath Club or in the whole world could be so orbicular. Then it

heaved itself up, and he saw he was right; it was
A. G.'s head.

The imperial face came out of the water, and he
began to talk so immediately that it seemed as if
he must have been talking under water and was
only going on with what he was saying.

" Hullo, it's Blaizides," he said. " How awfully
jolly ! I've been having a Turkish bath and dived
in for a swim. The athletic and amphibious
David—ha ! ha !—David the son of Jesse, fair and
of a ruddy countenance. Can you really stand
there ? I have to swim. Let us move a little
farther down to the shallow end, where I can stand
too. We're always meeting in Turkish baths, and
if not a Turkish bath, a glee-singing party. You
must come and have lunch with me presently."

A. G. paddled into shallower water, and sat down
on some steps leading into the bath.

" One of my most intimate friends is lunching with
me," he said: " Prince Bumniowsky. We will be a
party of three. He lost all his possessions in the
Russian revolution, except rather over a million
pounds, which he had invested in English funds, and
he says he's ruined. How awfully jolly to be ruined
like that ! What are you doing in this modern
Babylon, David ? Washing off the grime and squalor
of Cambridge in its lascivious and sparkling flood ?
Cambridge stifles me: I can only breathe in the
atmosphere of London and Paris and Rome. You
must soak yourself in the frivolity and corruption
of London. We are all like cheese-mites and only
flourish in the midst of decay. Or else lead a simple
and artistic life (it comes to much the same thing) like

10

me. I went to *Phyllis of Philistia* on Saturday, an exquisite idyll out of Theocritus with all the modern improvements, and had supper in my flat just opposite Marlborough House, and then read the Phædrus of Plato, translating it to dear old Boris Bumniowsky till three in the morning. He is the most exquisite flower of that barbaric and cultured Russian civilisation, and was engaged to an equally exquisite Princess of the Imperial House, and nobody knows where she is. I wrote my name at Buckingham Palace, yesterday, and made a blot. I should have been sent to Siberia if I had done that in Russia. I am learning Russian. Let us swim."

A. G. launched himself into the water again, and continued to pour out amazing pieces of information as he paddled along so slowly that David had to swim in circles round him in order to keep within earshot, and by degrees they progressed to the end of the bath, where A. G.'s Italian servant was waiting for him with a towel and an orange dressing-gown of floss silk with a hood to it, and matches and cigarettes and a pair of crimson leather slippers. He stood on the edge of the bath, talking all the time while his servant took off his bathing-dress and wiped him down, and put on his dressing-gown for him, and thrust his feet into his slippers and a cigarette into his mouth and lit it for him. With his hood over head he looked like some preposterous cross between an Emperor, a monk, and a Turk.

"Never do for yourself what other people can do for you," he said, as he sat down on a small camp-stool which his servant had brought for him. "Thank you, Antonio. What should I do without you?

I suppose I should do all the things you do for me.
Just go and see if there are any letters for me, old boy,
and bring me a cocktail, no, two cocktails—you must
have a cocktail, David—and pay for them with the
money in my trouser-pocket, and put my studs in my
shirt, and get my clothes ready, and bring me the
menu from the dining-room for me to order lunch.
Go on swimming, David, till your cocktail comes—I
like to see people swimming. And you might take a
running header from that board ; you would look
delightful flying through the air. Why aren't there
some Nymphs paddling about in the water ? You
would make a delicious group with a nymph, and I
would sing ' Sabrina fair ' to her."

He rubbed his head dry (Antonio had forgotten to
do this for him) and put down his hood.

" But the nymphs have the Turkish bath and the
swimming-bath to themselves three mornings in the
week," he said, " and I can never recollect which
those mornings are. They are either Monday,
Wednesday, and Friday, or Tuesday, Thursday, and
Saturday, and it is useless to try to remember which.
Some day you should escape observation, and steal in
here on a nymphs' morning. There would be little
shrieks of dismay and the rustle of white feet, and
you would find yourself like Actæon surrounded by
cohorts of the most delightful but indignant Dianas.
Horns would sprout from your head, David. You
would look extraordinarily classical with two small
horns just above your temples at the edge of your
curly hair, and the Pekinese dogs of the infuriated
Dianas would tear you limb from limb. Why should
we not have mixed bathing at the club ? It is the

height of prurience and Puritanism not to allow it.   I shall put down a notice in the book about it.   We would bathe and sing madrigals, and I would bring a camera and photograph everybody.   I imagine it must have leaked out among women by now that men have arms and legs, so why should they not face in the concrete what they know in the abstract to be true ?   You must come to my flat after lunch, David, and dear old Boris Bumniowsky shall sing us some wild Russian melodies which always make me feel as if somebody was being murdered in a snowstorm, while Cossacks were telling fairy-stories round the fire on the steppes as they supped on caviare and samovars and astrackhan.   How delightful to be a Russian with a million pounds and a tenor voice and all those generations of barbaric splendour beating in your blood !   Here are the cocktails with a preserved cherry impaled on a toothpick.   Thank you, Antonio. Antonio, will you ring up his Highness Prince Bumniowsky—no, I will do it myself and practise talking Russian."

David, like the man who saw a giraffe for the first time, found it difficult to believe in Prince Bumniowsky, so highly improbable did he appear. He had a round white face like a plate, with crimson lips and yellow eyes like an Angora cat, and ate more than you could imagine was possible.   Though A. G.'s flat was a bare quarter of a mile away, they all got into a prodigious motor-car after lunch, and were immersed in sable rugs while they made the transit at the rate of about sixty miles an hour.   He was absolutely unable to understand A. G.'s Russian conversation, and politely explained this (in excellent

English) by telling him that he had not talked Russian for a long time and had forgotten it. However beautifully he may have been able to sing, he did not attempt to do so, but went fast asleep in an arm-chair, waking up at intervals to light another cigarette from the one that had begun to burn his crimson lips. So A. G. sang instead, which did not appear to disturb him in the least. When he woke up for another cigarette he said " Bis " and went to sleep again. David left them about four o'clock, feeling feverish.

He dined at Mrs. Maddox's house, where Bags had sent his ticket in case he himself might be late, and went to that very up-to-date theatre " Red Ridinghood," where Phyllis was in Philistia. He arrived there a good deal too early, and since it was a dull employment to sit among empty stalls with only the curtain to look at, he made his way to the bar, which was far from dull. There were a large number of young ladies there, dressed in the most dazzling fashion with low dresses and large hats, and fraternizing in the friendliest way with comparative if not complete strangers. David had hardly lit a cigarette when one of them, who looked like a full-blown peony and whose person would have been described in an inquest as " the body of a well-nourished female," came and sat extremely close to him, breathed heavily through her nose, and said " Good evening, dearie."

" Lord, it's a cocoon," thought David to himself. " I wish Bags would come."

" Good evening," he said politely.

" Feelin' a bit lonely, dearie ? " she asked. " So'm I."

This was priceless, but David felt he must be firm.

" No, thank you—I'm not a bit lonely," he said.

" Well, that's nice," said this communicative lady ; " and I'm not neither, now I've got you to talk to. Such a headache as I've got this evening. I know what would do it good."

" That's all right, then," said David.

" Well, you are a funny boy ! " said she. " A glass of port would take it away at once. Not a large one, mind. Been to see this show before ? There's a waiter."

David gave orders for a glass of port. It was rather a large one to the ordinary man, being a brimming claret-glass.

" It's not what I call a narse show," she said, " and if the girls weren't to wear more than half a dozen stitches between the lot of them, they ought to have chosen them with a bit of plumpness about them. Who wants to see twenty pairs of drumsticks dancing ? But then I know what you men are."

The headache seemed to get better as the port waned in the glass.

" My, you're not drinking with me," she said as she turned it upside-down to get the last possible drop. " You must have a glass of port. Pals should drink together. I call that real unfriendly, I do. Here, waiter, get this gentleman friend of mine a glass of port, and look slippy."

He looked so slippy that he was gone before David could tell him that it wasn't wanted, and returned with a brimming glass. It appeared that the unfriendliness of his refusal to drink it could be easily mitigated by her doing so.

" Pity to wiste it," she said. " You haven't got a cigarette, have you ? I don't usually smoke in public ; bad form, I call it, but just for once to please you, dearie."

Quite suddenly David, who, according to his admirable habit, was seeing and enjoying the comedy of this preposterous lady, felt frankly sick. The comic side was that he was supposed to be succumbing to the irresistible allurements of this peony. This great full-blown siren, with her glasses of port, and her powdered face, her flowery hat, her fat arms, her heaving bosom, and her hopefulness that they were getting on nicely, was a huge joke, funnier than anything that he had imagined about cocoons. Presently, if he played up at all, she would tell him that she shared a nice flat with a lady friend, and they both often brought a pal home in the evening for a bit of a chat. He bubbled with laughter as he thought of it, but even as his ribs shook, he felt nauseated. . . . And what nauseated him most was the knowledge that something in himself, even while he laughed, responded not to her indeed but to what she stood for. If it had been not she, but that slim girl over there with the narrow eyes and the tired mouth who had sat down beside him, he would have felt a need that clamoured dangerously. He would have seen nothing comic in it, nothing grotesque and incredible. . . .

Just as she lit her cigarette at his, Bags appeared in the doorway, evidently looking for him. He jumped up.

" There's a friend of mine," he said.

" Right-oh, dearie. See you again afterwards

perhaps," and she finished her port and began looking
out for somebody else.

David hurried across to Bags, and chucked out of
his mind everything but the comedy.

" Bags, take me away," he said. " I've been
drinking port with an enormous red cocoon, at least
she drank it all. She was perfectly killing. I say,
this is awful fun. I haven't seen you for ages. Let's
go in : the show's started."

Their stalls were right up at the front of the house,
and they had a perfect sight of all the pairs of drumsticks which had excited the peony's contempt. The
piece had no particular plot, and no relation to its
title, except that there was a young lady called
Phyllis who lived in a restaurant with a beautiful
garden at the back full of Chinese lanterns and
drumsticks. There lived there also a young naval
officer with a comic admiral who kissed all the
waitresses and an elderly comic waiter by mistake, and
sat down first at one table and then at another and
called for empty bottles of champagne which he
distributed with impartial liberality. His wife, Lady
Sophonisba Vereker, had heard apparently of these
goings on, and took him away from time to time, but
he always came back, and instructed the young
naval officer to make love to her, so as to give her
something nice to think about. . . . So in the second
act, which took place on the deck of the admiral's
battleship at Portsmouth, Phyllis, for no particular
reason, dressed up as the young naval officer, and
the admiral's wife thought it was the other one, and
ran about after him. There was a ball on the battleship, and half of the drumsticks appeared as midship-

men, and danced with the other half who were guests.
The comic admiral then got drunk and tried to sing
" Rule Britannia," but sang " Rule Philistia "
instead, with a chorus of guests and midshipmen.
Meantime Phyllis had changed her naval uniform for a
ravishing costume made of pearls and diamonds, and
got engaged to the young naval officer. . . .

Bags had early singled out the most voluptuous
midshipman, and kept smiling in her direction.

" Dam' fine girl," he said, " I should chuck Cambridge and enter the navy if I thought I could hit off
that lot of middies."

" Rather ! " said David cordially. " But what's
it all about ? "

" I don't know. You never know what a revue is
about. It's just a revue ; not about anything. I
vote we go round to the stage-door afterwards. I'm
sure she smiled at me then. I wonder if she'd come
round to supper. In Paris——"

This might or might not have been swank on Bags's
part, but David thought that the middy's presence at
supper would be extremely embarrassing. He had
not been aware that she had smiled at Bags at all,
for she seemed intent on sending volleys of nods and
smiles and grins to someone in a box at the side.
Bags was extremely short-sighted, and had probably
seen one of them still lingering on her face, and
thought it was meant for him.

" Oh no, don't," he said. " Besides, she's smiling
like anything at some chap in that box there."

A little observation proved that this was certainly
the case, and Bags, abandoning all thought of the
stage-door, became critical.

" I don't think much of them," he said. " Rather a weedy lot ; they'd be hooted off the stage in Paris. That's the end. Let's nip away before the crowd comes out. We're going to have supper at the El Dorado just round the corner. There are sure to be some smart bits there."

They had only to cross the street, and entered through the glass doors of the restaurant. The place was crowded and brilliantly lit, a band was playing in a gallery at the end, and up and down the narrow gangways between the table, couples were dancing, leaving their supper while their plates were being changed, and putting down their cigarettes when they returned for the next course. At some of the tables were seated large parties, at others there would be a couple only, and here and there a man or a woman supped solitarily. Waiters dashed about with dishes and ice-pails holding champagne bottles, and the startling kaleidoscope of colours was dizzily reflected in the mirrors which lined the walls between pilasters of yellow scagliola. The air was thick and hot with the smell of flowers and scent and food, and charged with some ferment of gaiety. Wherever you looked you saw white shoulders and eager faces thrown into relief against the black coats of the men ; the place tingled with the insouciant spell of the festive hour.

Of all that in London had seemed so new and entrancing to David, this was the most seductive. His face glowed with the rippling fire of it.

" Oh, I say, top-hole," he said to Bags. " I've never been to a place like this before. Frank and I used to go home after the theatre and eat sandwiches."

Bags felt wonderfully superior. He was always a little jealous of David's devotion to Frank, and it was pleasant to exhibit a touch of airy contempt.

" No, I don't suppose it's much in Frank's line," he said. " Ah! there's my waiter; I told him to keep a table for me in case I looked in. *Bon soir,* Charles."

Bags conducted a solemn conversation in French, and David was impressed rather than amused. There was good reason for using that language to a Frenchman, and really it was jolly clever of Bags to be able to reel it off like that, without apparently devoting his mind to the construction of sentences, and to be able to understand what was said without concentration. Soup, quails, and an ice were decided on, and Bags was very firm about the precise length of the time that the champagne should be allowed to nestle in the ice-pail. That being fluently concluded, he had another dab at Frank.

" He's gone off to-day, hasn't he," he said, " on his mouldy archæological stunt ? I daresay he'll enjoy it : I only know I shouldn't. Of course he's an awfully decent chap."

David flared for a moment over this, and then laughed.

" Jolly condescending of you," he said. " I'll tell him you said so."

" Well, don't be stuffy. I only said he was awfully decent. But he doesn't think about anything except sap and games, and makes you do the same. Bit narrow. Oh, let's have some coffee afterwards and a liqueur. They've got a topping old brandy here, st. . . . , *garçon.*" . . .

David completely abandoned himself to the spell of the place and the hour. It was no use arguing with Bags about Frank, for he could not argue about Frank with anybody since there was nothing to be said about him except that he was Frank. Besides, argumentativeness was not a graceful attitude for a guest who was being treated to this gorgeous hospitality. A guest's duty was to enjoy, and he had every inclination to do so. He wasn't exactly hungry, but this exciting atmosphere and the delicious food made it natural to eat, and Bags was assiduous in filling his glass the moment there was room for any addition to its contents. Pretty girls with their partners, moving rhythmically to the band, swept by them ; now and then the floating lace of a sleeve or a flying riband brushed David's head, and he looked up with a smile and apologies for being in the way. He got several delightful smiles back in return, too, which, after all, was not the least to be wondered at. Once a girl said to her partner, " Who's that awfully handsome boy ? " in a voice that he could not help hearing.

" You gave him the glad eye," said the man.

She laughed, and they twirled away. David, pink with a pleasant confusion, turned to Bags.

" And you've been here three nights running, did you say ? " he asked.

" Three or four."

" You are a gay dog," said David, " and it's awfully good of you to ask me. Oh, I say, the salad's made of grapes and apples, I believe. Ripping ! I'm going back to Cambridge on Wednesday. I thought of going to-day, but I'm glad I didn't.

There'd have been hardly anyone up, and I should have been yawning in my rooms all evening. Look here, you're giving me much more than my share of the champagne—I must have drunk nearly a bottle."

" Well, there's lots more," said Bags ; " they don't run short of fizz here. Finish that up, and we'll have some more. Here, *garçon*."

" No, I swear I don't want any more," said David. " I've had lots. I say, did you get a good look at that fat old hag who came and sat next me in the bar at the theatre ? It was really awfully funny."

David marvellously reproduced her cockney intonation, thought no more about champagne, and had two goes of ice. And then suddenly, as he inhaled the first whiff of a fresh cigarette, an awful qualm overtook him. He became aware that it was difficult to fix his eyes on any given spot. If he looked, for instance, at the edge of the mirror opposite, which surely should have been firm and stationary, it gave a little jerk and sidled away a foot or two. If he looked at Bags, Bags did exactly the same thing. This curious effect came as a complete surprise to him ; he had just been drinking champagne without another thought than that it was delightfully cold and bubbly, and harmonised excellently with his surroundings.

The discovery pulled him up with a jerk. It was annoying, for he had only been enjoying himself without a thought that alcohol, steadily imbibed, produces precisely the same effect as intoxication.

" I say, Bags," he said solemnly, " if I drink any more I shall be drunk. What beastly rot ! "

" Nonsense ; you're miles off being drunk," said Bags. " You're talking all right."

" But I'm not seeing all right," said David carefully. " Things slip about, and you look misty."

Bags was conscious of having drunk enough himself, but that had happened several times to him lately. He felt perfectly clear-headed, but extraordinarily hospitable and very clever.

" Every man in the world has been drunk once," he said. " If a man tells you he hasn't, it means that he often gets drunk. And if he says he's a teetotaller, it means he's drunk now. That's rather cynical and well put. Take your hand away from your glass, and let me fill it."

" I'd rather not," said David. " Absolute waste of jolly good fizz."

" I was rather screwed last night," said Bags, " and I felt frightfully fit this morning. That shows I couldn't have been screwed. It must have been a hall—hallucination. There ! Well, if you won't——"

He filled up his own glass, drank it, and quite suddenly became rather mournful.

" I meant you to have such a jolly evening," he said, " and I planned it all carefully, but I'm afraid you're not enjoying it much. I expect you miss Frank. You don't really care about anybody but him. I've always been devoted to you, David, but you never really liked me. You always laugh at me. Luckily, there are one or two girls in the world who don't think so badly of me."

David gave a sort of hiccuping giggle.

" Oh, don't make me laugh," he said. " If I

began to laugh now I should never stop. I'm in a precarious state, Bags."

" I don't know that there's anything particularly comic in what I've been saying," said Bags.

" But there is—take my word for it. And if you get any worse you'll burst into tears, and I shall howl with laughter. That would never do ; we should be making awful asses of ourselves. As for getting drunk once—I say, you put all that awfully smartly—I'm going to keep that for another occasion. Do be sensible, Bags ! Let's go away. Much better."

Bags looked up at that jolly, handsome face, which he knew he loved so much better than any cocoon's. He still felt sad and inclined to be reproachful, but he was aware that this was due not to anything David had done, but to what he had drunk.

" But what about the coffee and the liqueur ? " he asked. " I'm afraid I haven't given you a supper you like."

" All A1," said David. " Never had such a good supper. But counter-order the coffee and liqueurs. I know I should be sick if I tried to drink old brandy. Mustn't be sick in the El Dorado. They'd hate it. And I've had an awfully jolly evening, and it's been ripping seeing you again. I don't want to spoil it."

Bags rose.

" Right-oh," he said. " Good old chap, David ! Legs all right ? "

" Lovely ! " said David, taking a tentative step or two. " Just a little care, you know. No harm in being careful." . .

THE Lent term was dribbling along in its own un-
eventful fashion. David's performances in the Freshman's sports last year had not encouraged him to
pursue distinction on the track. It was no use,
from a competitive point of view, being able to run
extremely fast when frightened, because plenty of
other people could do that without being frightened,
and took their talent seriously, and trained and went
to bed early and didn't smoke. He had once intended to take up running, and learn how to use his
pace at will, but the idea had become no more than
one of the many enthusiasms which glittered on the
surface of his mind like sparkles of sunlight on
water. To see anybody performing almost any feat
with ease and neatness always made David instantly
want to do it too, and he would throw himself with
ardour into the new accomplishment for about two
minutes and a quarter. It was not that he was in
the least harebrained, for no one could more steadily
apply himself, when his mind was set as his had been
on tennis. That was a serious pursuit; so too,
disastrously, were cricket, and friendship, and the
fascinating things that could be done with words
(which is literature). Outside that inner orbit re-
volved similar brightnesses, all those things in fact
which other people did delightfully and which he
must instantly try to do too. To play the piano was
one of these, and his neighbours wished it hadn't
been. The one pursuit constantly practised at Cam-

bridge which never had the slightest allurement for him was rowing.

Tommers this year had dropped Rugby football altogether in despair of ever attaining excellence himself, or of the college team doing so. He was very big, and much stronger than most horses, but awkward and without dexterity, and had violently taken up this lugubrious form of aquatic exercise. He was rowing in the King's Lent boat, and had induced David this afternoon, when they were rowing a full course, to come down to the river and see if that inspiriting spectacle did not kindle in him the lust of imitation. David had been bored stiff, to say nothing of the sheets of rain that swept the towing-path where he cowered to see Tommers go by in his boat, and had trotted home without waiting for him. An hour afterwards he was arguing about it with him over a comfortable tea.

" Can't see it," he said. " Torrents of rain : I hate rain——"

" The rain's got nothing to do with it," said Tommers. " It just happened to be raining. I might just as well say that cricket's a rotten game, because there was a thunderstorm."

" But the rain's got lots to do with it," said David. " It nearly swamped you, you told me, to begin with. But when it rains at cricket, we go into the pavilion."

" If that's all you've got to say against rowing——" began Tommers.

" But it isn't. I haven't begun yet. I was just sketching the thing out, starting with the background, which was rain, to give you the atmosphere. Rain seemed to come into the foreground too. But don't

argue till I've given you something to argue about.
You can't dispute the local colour, which was rain.
Have a muffin."

"Muffin!" said Tommers with infinite contempt.
"I thought I told you I was in training. You might
as well offer me a pound of suet."

David took a large buttery bite, and sucked his
fingers one after the other.

"Well, there's a pretty good argument against
rowing out of your own mouth," he said. "I say,
that's rather neat. The muffin: out of your own
mouth, not in your own mouth. See? No, you
don't, but never mind that. Listen! You can't
eat muffins because you're in training. What's the
good of a game that prevents your enjoying the pleasures of life?"

"Well, you dropped smoking Perpetua when you
were trying to play cricket last summer," said
Tommers brutally. "Lot of good it did you."

"I hoped you'd say that. Not smoking Perpetua
was adding to the pleasure of life, or rather deduct-
ing from its pains," said David ingeniously. "That's
one to me; fifteen love. Let's get on. What's rowing about? You sit in a frail, tremulous bark——"

"Well, you used to go in a canoe," said Tommers.
"That was tremulous enough when you were in it."

"That may be. But it was *about* something. I
wanted to get to Byron's pool and bathe and picnic.
Unless I'd gone in a canoe, I should have had to walk
carrying a tea-kettle and a spirit-lamp and a book
and a towel and milk and sugar and buns. I wish
you wouldn't interrupt in the middle of a sentence.
I'm going to write an article about rowing to the

Cambridge Review, and I thought out the sentence about 'frail, tremulous bark' as I was coming up from that mouldy river. Now I've forgotten it."

"Bad luck on the *Cambridge Review*. Not that they'd have put it in."

"I don't see why not. They put in the University sermon every week, and that's mournful reading. By the way, my father's preaching it next Sunday, and I shall have to go."

"And lead the applause and laughter. What Bags would call clack."

David scratched his head.

"Lemme think," he said. "Frail tremulous bark . . . No, I can't remember it : what a bore you are ! Anyhow, you step into it, taking great care where you put your hoof, because otherwise you would crash through. And then you have to sit down very carefully, because this ripping game has given you boils, and they push you out into that dirty ditch entirely full of the drains of Cambridge, holding on to a handle. Then you paddle down to the start, and sit and shiver with cold and cold feet till somebody fires a pistol, and you shove your oar into the water, give a great hoick, and pull it out again. Eight silly asses sitting in a row, and looking at each other's backs—no, let's be accurate : stroke looks at Bilton's face, and I'd sooner look at anybody's back than Bilton's face ; it's like a face in a spoon—eight silly asses, I was saying, shove their oars into the water, and pull them out again as fast as ever they can, twenty-three million times. They can't see where they're going, and it wouldn't be much of a prospect if they did ; they just look at the next man's back, and pull that handle like hell. I hate going backwards anyhow. I can't bear it even in a comfortable corner-seat in a train. And when it's all over, and you've been bumped by somebody else—oh yes, I forgot that : you can see the next boat gaining on you all the time to keep your spirits up—when you've been bumped, you all fall sideways and collapse and pant and roll your eyes. And when you're better and have been beaten, you paddle back to exactly the same place as you've started from."

David hurriedly ate another muffin, holding up his hand the while to show Tommers he hadn't finished. The last piece stuck in his throat, and he hastily swallowed some tea to wash it downwards.

" And where's the sport of it ? " he asked. " It can't be fun doing it. It's just a question of which set of asses can pull a handle quickest for a quarter of an hour without dying."

" Rot ! " shouted Tommers. " It isn't a question of ' quickest.' There are all the things that make up the stroke, smoothness and rhythm and getting your weight into it, and leg-drive and——"

David stopped his ears as he did at glee-singing, to shut out this rude, angry voice, and continued :

" Mere races aren't games at all," he said. " I've thought it all out. What's the fun of seeing who can get to a place first, unless there's some object in getting there ? There is when you've got to get to your crease before the ball, or else you'll be run out. Or getting your racquet in the way before the ball gets into the dedans."

He saw that Tommers had finished speaking and unblocked his ears again.

" There's some point in that sort of getting there first," he said. " But at rowing, when you've paddled down to Ditton or Ely or wherever it is, and nearly burst yourselves with getting back, you haven't done anything but arrive at the place you started from."

" Yes, but the point is to get there before the other fellows," said Tommers. " You might as well say that cricket is no fun because, when the bowler has delivered a ball which gets hit for four, it only comes back eventually to his hand from which it started."

That was rather ingenious, an unexpected agility of mind on the part of Tommers. He must be led away by quibbles, thought David.

" Not at all," he said. " If it's the last ball of the over, it doesn't go back to his hand, but to the other bowler's hand."

Tommers stuck to it.

" That's so about the last ball of the over," he said. " But then all the other balls of the over are piffle——"

" Depends who bowls them," said David.

Tommers held his mouth open to go on exactly where he left off :

. . . " and it's only when the ball is returned to somebody else's hand that there's any sport in it," he said. " That's what your argument comes to."

David sighed. Of course Tommers had scored, but that couldn't be acknowledged.

" I don't know what we're talking about," he said.

" I haven't the slightest idea," said Tommers.

"Very well, we'll scrap that," said David hurriedly, "and get back to what I was saying before, when you interrupted me. It's a mean pursuit to go on pulling at an oar, doing exactly the same thing over and over again. You might as well stand with a basket of balls at the net in a tennis-court, and hit them at the other fellow, and call it a game."

"Sounds a pretty good one," said Tommers appreciatively. " I'll hit a basket of balls at you as quick as I can, and as hard as I can—that's what you do in rowing—any day, and I promise to enjoy it awfully."

"Then I hit them back at you," began David.

"No, you don't, because you'll be dead long before I've finished.   And rowing's frightfully good exercise. I've gained two inches round the chest this term."

"This term ! " said David scornfully. "Why, I've gained two inches round the stomach this afternoon by eating muffins. But I don't swank about that. As for exercise, who cares for exercise ? It would be good exercise to run up and down these stairs a hundred times, but awful poor fun."

Tommers' eyes fell on David's piano.

"Well, it's awful poor fun for everybody else when you do your exercises on that foul tea-kettle," he said.

David strolled across to the foul tea-kettle, played an octave of a scale very laboriously, and pounced on the top and bottom notes of the piano.

"That comes in Chopin," he said. "And besides, I want to be able to play. I don't think there's anything I want to do so much just now. Fancy being able to rattle off the Polonaise in P or anything you pleased, just to amuse yourself. I've known my notes ever since I was a kid——"

" We all know them now," said Tommers.

". . . so it isn't as if I was beginning fresh. Solid foundations. Have a firm knowledge of your notes and then you'll get on. Hymn-tunes even : you've no idea how different a perfectly ordinary hymn-tune sounds if you play it yourself. ' The Church's one Foundation,' for instance. Perfectly melting ! Do listen ! So rich ! "

David with a corrugated brow, and the tip of his tongue sticking out of the corner of his mouth, forced his laborious way through this melody.

" It may be rich," said Tommers, " and it certainly sounds quite different."

" I shall get it in time," said David hopefully, beginning again.

" Oh, for Heaven's sake don't try to get it this time," said Tommers. " We've been having it all morning."

" I know ; and I shouldn't wonder if you had it most of the evening."

" But you're getting an awful bore——" began Tommers.

" I don't mind that a bit," said David. " I've got absolutely used to it. Aren't they rich oily chords— blast, that's B natural—if you play them slowly ? I'm getting on with that, don't you think ? "

It was impossible to be angry with David, thought Tommers ; you had to laugh. But a neighbour apparently could manage it, for there came a tapping on David's wall, and an exasperated though muffled

shout of " Shut up, Blazes, you ass ! " from next
door. . . .

David instantly opened the top of the piano, and
put his foot firmly on what is known as the " loud "
pedal.

" I hate rudeness," he said : " it never pays," and
he played slowly and emphatically through the tune
again, and added a fortissimo " Amen."

" I'm not sure I don't like the Polonaise in
P Minor better than that," said Tommers.

" How nice of you ! " said David.   " I'll play them
both, shall I, and then you can judge."

" No, I didn't mean you to do that," said Tommers.
" I'm sure I like the Polonaise best——"

" Then you don't appreciate ' The Church's one.'
I'll just——"

" No, I like ' The Church's one ' best," said
Tommers.   " Or I like the Polonaise in P best.   Have
it your own way.   Only stop."

David began playing a quantity of notes with each
hand in opposite directions, in the manner of an
arpeggio.

" The Polonaise in P Minor and a great many sharps
and flats," he said.   " It's by Me.   I'm not sure that
it isn't a rhapsody.   You play anything as quickly
as you can with both hands.   Like that.   You have
to lift your hands very high, with a good deal of
action——"

Just as he lifted his hands very high, Tommers came
swiftly up behind, closed the lid of the piano and sat
on it.   David continued to play on the lid.   Then
Tommers sat on one of his hands, and David flipped
his nose with the other, and there might have been a

rag, but Bags came in. He grasped the situation, and sat on David's other hand. So there they were, the baffled composer pinioned, with two firm people sitting on his hands on the lid of the closed piano.

" Of course I'm helpless if you do that," he said in an injured voice.

" Yes, that's the idea," said Tommers. " Bright of you."

" All right. I won't play any more. Pax to the Polonaise in P. Hullo, Bags ! Been riding ? Been kicked off ? Now, what's the point of riding ? You climb up on a horse and it kicks you off. And then you climb up again, and if you're lucky it doesn't kick you off. So you get back to Cambridge, and pat its bottom, and feel its fetlock or its forelock, and say to your groom, ' Nice quarters, but a shade sickle-hocked. Give it a rub down and a warm spavin, and bring it round about the same time to-morrow for me to be kicked off again.' I shall write a story about a mare that could throw a splint further than anybody else."

" What's he talking about ? " asked Bags.

" He doesn't quite know," said David. " But he's been down to the river to see a torpid——O Lord, I nearly forgot, I've found a glorious story by Ouida, which describes a boat-race. King's were rowing Third Trinity, and the Third Trinity stroke was the hero. And then she says, ' They all rowed fast in the Third Trinity boat that afternoon, but nobody rowed as fast as stroke.' "

Tommers, who had become serious again the moment rowing was mentioned, gave a contemptuous snort.

" Drivel ! " he said. " That's quite impossible. Stroke sets the time for the rest of the crew. Whether it's a fast stroke or a slow one, they all row the same pace."

David gave the ghost of a wink to Bags. Like the Tooties and Rugby football, Tommers could never admit anything that bordered on humour to approach the sacred subject of boats.

" I don't see why they shouldn't row at different paces," said David gravely. " It stands to reason that a boat will go its fastest, when everyone in it is rowing as fast as he can. I don't pretend to know much about rowing myself, but Ouida's probably right about it. You seem to think that nobody knows anything about rowing but you. What's wrong with it ? "

Tommers made a scornful noise.

" It's utterly impossible," he said. " If they all row their own pace the oars would get all muddled up together. Look here, suppose you're sitting behind me, close behind, and Bags behind you——"

David gave a crack of laughter, and the light began to dawn on Tommers. . . . .

David wanted his cigarettes, so instead of walking round the end of the sofa he jumped over the back. Then he tried to jump back again, tripped on the edge of it, and fell on to the seat.

" What's that for ? " asked Bags.

" Nothing. Just energy. What a pity it is you can't save energy, store it in a dynamo, you know, for future use. Probably the energy I expended over

that would have run the electric light in my room for
five minutes.   As it is, I've only barked my shin, and
Nature will have to expend some more energy in
repairing it.   At least I hope she will.   Rather a good
subject for the Chitchat."

" You're like Crowfoot," said Tommers.   " Go
on."

" Well, there it is.   Probably you and Bags and I
have got enough energy to run the whole University
or support large families.   But nothing happens :
we don't employ it, and it just dribbles away.   There's
Bags, who's going into Parliament.   By the time he
gets into the Cabinet, he'll be a weary old battered
old dog, without any energy left in his derelict
carcase.   Whereas if he had the energy he's got now
he would gallop along with the whole caboodle on
his shoulders, and disrupt the British Empire without
winking.   There's Tommers, who by that time may
know how to row and win every Diamond scull in
existence, and he'll be too gross to lift himself out of
his arm-chair except to go to dinner——"

" It's all been said before and much more shortly,"
said Bags.   " All it comes to is ' Si jeunesse savait '
——"

" Savvy be blowed," said David.   " What I'm
telling you is that when we're young we're pifflers,
and when we're old we're poops.   I want to write
books ; I could sit up day and night writing books,
but I don't know how yet.   And by the time I've
learned my trade, I shall only want to toddle down to
the club and write a letter in a boiling rage to the
papers about the state of the London streets.   And
when I've done that I shall sit in the window with a

shiny bald head and snooze. It's a rotten arrangement, and as for my piano-playing——"

Tommers got quietly up with an abstracted air and
sat on the lid again.

" No, I wasn't going to play," said David. " But
by the time I can play like Paderewski, I shall have
knotted rheumatic fingers——"

" Before," said Tommers.

" Right you are : before. I felt a bit stiff this
morning. Then there's Crowfoot. Long before he's
really perfected his scheme of shutting the window
at the far end of the room before he gets out of bed,
he'll be past any need for keeping off the draught
when he's dressing. Yet somehow he has kept going,
though he must be quite old : forty at least. I
think it must be the pursuit of the impossible which
has kept him frisky. He's always planning to do
what can't possibly be done. ' The Pursuit of the
Impossible.' That's rather a good title."

" I should call it ' The Rape of the Highly Improbable,' " said Bags.

David laughed.

" Oh, ripping : well done, Bags," he said. " That'll
whip up the members of the Chitchat. They'll
think it's something about you and the sweet young
thing at the tobacconist's. Lord, it was funny ;
the other day, Tommers, I went in there, and there
was Bags sitting on the counter with the fingers of
the sweet young thing coyly nestling—yes, ' coyly
nestling' is the word—in his strong manly hand.
That's where Bags's energy goes. Oh my ! Such
lovely little fingers, like—like coral, and an ear like
a pink shell peeping out from the tendrils of her

hair, and a mouth like a Cupid's bow, and little feet—let's see what are they like ?—Oh yes, like mice that pop in and out from her skirt. Ickle Tootsicums! And eyes like stars, and a face like a small ham."

" Rather a flapper for the Honourable Crabtree," said Tommers. " He usually likes something mature and pillowy."

" Full-blown," said David.

" After all," said Bags, " I've seen David giving port and cigarettes to the full-blownest old hag in Piccadilly."

" So you did," said David. " We're all in the same boat, and Tomlin shall row us. By Jove, how she creaked when she breathed ! "

" Did you snatch a chaste salute, David ? " asked Tommers.

" No. I'd as soon have kissed the hind-parts of an elephant."

Tommers left the lid of the piano.

" I say, let's have Pax with Paderewski till Hall," he said. " I've got a Greek prose I must do, and ' The Church's one ' makes it absolutely impossible to think. I vote we play bridge directly after Hall. You, Bags, I——"

" Can't," said Bags.

" The tobacconist's daughter of Cambridge town," said Tommers.

" Raise two others, Tommers," said David.

" Right," and he went thumping downstairs.

Bags wandered aimlessly about the room. There was evidently something simmering in his mind, and

David waited for it to boil over. Eventually Bags came to anchor on the sofa.

" I can't understand you, David," he said. " You're simply dripping with energy, and yet you never dream of going after a girl. It seems to me absolutely unnatural. You don't even want to."

" Hullo, it's the gay Lothario," said David encouragingly.

" Not a bit. It's just an ordinary usual person. Your not wanting to is what beats me."

David looked up. It was evident that Bags was not Lotharian at all, but perfectly serious, for he wore the worried expression that always made him look like an anxious nanny-goat.

" And you're quite sure I never want to, are you ? " he said.

" Well, it's pretty obvious. Isn't it ? "

David had opened a book, now he shut it with a bang. It was quite a good plan, he thought, to rag and chaff Bags about his amorous temperament, because he made it ridiculous ; but, given the opportunity, it was an equally good plan to be serious.

" Obvious ? " he said. " I'm jolly glad it appears to be obvious, because that's what it's meant to appear. But it isn't. I want frightfully sometimes."

" Rot ! "

" It's nothing of the sort," said David. " You think that because I don't go messing about with girls I don't want to. But I do, if you care to know."

" But you never talk about them, and you're always ragging me about them," said Bags. " And you always say they're stinkers."

" I know I do. But what's the good of talking about a thing you don't mean to be mixed up in ? And what's the good of thinking about a thing if you don't intend to do it ? It only makes you worse."

" But, confound it all, you're twenty," said Bags.

" I know I am, and I've never kissed a girl yet, let alone the other thing. And as I don't mean to at present, it would be dam' silly always to be thinking and talking about it. Like saying you don't mean to drink, and putting a bottle of whisky on the table. But as we are talking about it——"

David had really not known how strongly or how clearly he felt on this subject till he began to discuss it seriously. It was a topic that he always consistently banished from his mind, except when he was ragging Bags on the subject.

" To begin with, look at the fellows who go messing about with women," he said. " They're an awful measly lot. You don't really belong to them, so I'm not being particularly personal. And what makes me laugh is that they think they're being manly. Absolute error ! It isn't manly to cuddle a girl, or soak your mind in beastliness and probably your body as well. It's far more manly not to. Oh, Bags, you do rather belong to that class sometimes, and then you make me sick, so I laugh at you instead. But that's what I think about it if you want to know."

Bags was profoundly amazed at these revelations.

" Good Lord, I thought you never looked at a girl, let alone wanting one. When did it begin with you ? "

" I can tell you that to a day. It was when we went to that play, and I gave port to the large peony."

David laughed.

" No, I didn't want the peony," he said. " But there was a girl there, o-oh . . . don't let's think about it. But there it is. The f-fact is " (he began to stammer) " that when the time comes that I see a girl I really want, and ask her to m-marry me, I mean to go to her clean. It's just a fad of mine—call it that, or call it pi and p-priggish. You may call it anything you please."

" But——" began Bags.

" I know what you're going to say," cried David, cracking his fingers with a sudden inspiration. " You're going to say it's good for the health or some piffle of that sort. It isn't anything of the kind. Of course if you let your imagination run riot with you, and think about nothing else and then don't do it, you'll get jumpy and nervy and *that* will be bad for your health. But that is a very different thing. So I don't choose to think about it. I think about every other blessed thing under the sun. Of course, if I went mooning about and looking at cocoons, and squeezing their hands and pinching their fat places, and fiddling with them, I should be done. Done in the eye. Couldn't stand it."

David leapt from his seat with a sort of whinny, and pawed the ground with his foot.

" That's what you're doing all day," he said, " and that's what I won't do. If I began, I don't believe I should ever stop. So, as I don't mean to begin, I keep my mind off it. But as for its being

bad for the health to lead a clean life, I never heard
such rot. And you were going to say that, Bags,
weren't you ? "

" Yes, I was," said Bags.

" Jolly good shot of mine. But don't you believe
it. Look at me, my amorous Bags, and tell me
whether I really look debilitated and nervy. Do I
want a rest-cure or a woman or a tonic ? Course I
don't. If you're right about it, and if you are such
hot stuff as you want us all to think, you must be
in the most marvellous state of health owing to your
amours—French word—so let's go to an impartial
doctor and ask him which of us is the fittest."

" Well, I'm not so bad as you think," began
Bags.

David interrupted him with a yell of laughter.

" O Lord, you make me howl," he said. " I daresay you're not what you call bad at all. I'm sure
I don't know. You may only be bluffing. But
you've got into your head that it's rather fine to
have the air of an old buck-rabbit. 'Tisn't fine really ;
any old buck-rabbit can do it. Besides, you miss
such a lot of pleasures. To-night, for instance, we
might have a ripping game of bridge, but you want
to sit on a counter in a fuggy shop, and squeeze that
girl's podgy hand, and look ever such an ass if any
decent chap comes in. If you want to know, I should
like to do it too—and I'd cut you out in two shakes
with that girl—only I won't do it. And as I won't
do it, I say podgy hand and fuggy shop and that
sort of thing. Oh, Honourable Crabtree, I wish
you'd drop all that smelling about."

Honourable Crabtree considered this.

" But if I thought I wasn't going to kiss a girl or
—or that sort of thing till, say, the end of the term,"
he said, " I should—no, I shouldn't cut my throat,
but I should feel infernally flat."

" But nobody wants you to think anything of the
sort," said the artful David. " Why look forward
like that ? If I thought I was going to shave every
morning till the end of my life, I *should* cut my
throat instead. I couldn't face shaving so many
times. But don't think to-night what's to happen
or not to happen to-morrow or next week. Just
confine yourself to to-night. Come and have a
hectic rubber with Tommers and me and somebody.
Let that suffice for the present. You'll enjoy it
awfully. . . . Good Lord, I never knew I could
preach so fine. Shall I take orders ? Or do you
think they'll let me preach the 'Varsity sermon next
Sunday instead of my father ? Leave the licentious
wench alone, and come round after Hall and play
bridge. Do ! "

David paused a moment, looking frightfully gay
and attractive.

" Oh, do," he said.

" Right you are ! "

" Ripping," said David.

He went to the window and shouted " Tommers !
Tommers ! Tomlin, Tomtit . . . Tommy-rot . . . "
until the window below was opened.

" Well ? " said Tommers rather acidly. " What's
the row ? "

" Oh, I say, Bags will play bridge all right,"
shouted David. " Just get one more, Tommers.
And have some clean cards."

David shut the window and pranced back into the room, where Bags was already looking irresolute.

" But really I don't know if I can," he said. " Get someone else, David. I promised I'd go round there after Hall. She'll be——"

" Poor little devil ! " said David. " She'll cry. She'll have a sleepless night. She'll find somebody else. She'll drown herself. She'll meander about Cambridge wailing ' Where's my Honourable Crabtree ? ' She'll talk Scotch like the people in Stevenson, and say, ' Where's my ain ain laddie, my ain, ain Bags ? ' She'll dye her petticoats black——"

" David, you're the greatest ass I've ever seen," said Bags.

" Stale news ! " said David. " And the greatest prig. Rather ! But we'll rook Tommers after Hall."

David of King's   X

DAVID's father was a notable commentator on the obscurities in the epistles of St. Paul, and his erudite work on that to the Galatians was so difficult of comprehension that the most advanced ecclesiastical scholars of the day had been known to turn back with a sense of relaxation to the text of the epistle after a study of his exposition of it, for nothing that St. Paul wrote could possibly be so hard to understand as Dean Blaize's explanation of it. He always gave

David a copy of his works as they appeared, and with a humorous smile was kind enough to cut the leaves for him, before he presented him with them. "For you will never do it yourself, David," he observed, "and it would hurt my self-esteem to find them uncut."

David had certainly inherited his zest for life from this admirable parent, for apart from this melancholy habit of making St. Paul's epistles even more difficult than they were already, Dean Blaize was the most youthfully exuberant of men with a delightful passion for entering into the life of any place and people at or among which he happened to find himself. This habit, when David was at a private school, and his father paid a visit to it, had been deeply embarrassing to his son, for the Dean bowled with small boys at cricket-nets, made the most awful comments on the game, bathed in the swimming-pond, where he took loud, flat headers, and generally disgraced him. But now David's attitude was completely changed; he delighted in his father's youthful spirits as being "jolly sporting," loved him and laughed at him, and looked forward to his advent to preach the University sermon with (apart from the necessity of attending it) the keenest satisfaction. The only thing which seemed at all likely to jar the harmony of their meeting was the consideration, which must be talked about, of what David was to do in life after he had left the University. His father would certainly have liked him to be a clergyman, but it was so obvious that David wouldn't like it at all, that this project might be considered as abandoned. Till lately, David's own mind had been an absolute blank with regard to any alternative, but now he had begun to make up his mind for himself, and intended to talk it over with his father. It would rather worry him, he was afraid : the vague idea of " writing " for a livelihood would be likely to seem Bohemian to the parental view.

David bicycled up to the station to meet him on Saturday morning, and it was quite obvious that his father would vastly prefer to bicycle down himself, leaving David to follow with his luggage in a taxi, rather than the other way about. David jumped to this at once and was guileful.

" I think I'll put the bicycle on the top and drive down with you," he said. " And then we'll leave your luggage at the Provost's lodge, and you'll come and lunch with me in my rooms."

The Dean's kind little eyes dwelt on the bicycle.

" My dear, I should so much enjoy riding down myself," he said, " if you don't want to."

" Sure ? " said David.

" Yes, I should like it. But as for lunch, oughtn't I to lunch at the Provost's, as I'm staying there ? "

" Oh no, don't," said David. " Because if you do, the Provost will probably ask me as well, and I'm dining there this evening. It'll be much more fun in my rooms. Besides, we shan't be able to get away early, and I want you to come and play squash with me directly afterwards."

" Squash ? Well, I should like a game of squash," said his father. " I brought some flannels in case you suggested it. So let's do that. I'll just look in at the Provost's, and shake hands and come and join you ! You dear fellow, what fun we'll have. I wish you'd stop growing, David."

David collected the luggage and gave his father the
bicycle.   The saddle was some inches too high for
him, but he refused to have it altered, saying that it
was exactly right (which was odd, as David was some
five inches taller than his father), and he rode off in
his gaiters and stringed hat, with the tips of his toes
just touching the pedals when fully extended.

"Rum old gent," said the porter to David.

David turned and withered him.

"Oh, that's your opinion, is it?" he said.   "There's
a shilling for you for being such an ass!"

"No offence, sir," said the porter.

"Not an atom," said David.   "Shut the door."

The two had a wonderful game of squash.   David
stood quite still in the centre of the court, and sent very
easy shots first down one side and then down the other,
while his parent dashed to right and left, and bumped
himself against the walls.   When he seemed very
much out of breath, David either put one below the
line, or sent him something round the corner which he
couldn't get near.   This brought the rally to an end,
and the exhausted commentator had a moment's
respite.

"But you don't run about, David," he gasped.
"Why can't I make you bustle?"

"You will, and no mistake, when you've warmed
up a bit," said David.

So David gradually changed his tactics to suit his
father's ideas: he rushed after balls into the corners
of the court instead of waiting where he was for them
to come out to him off the back wall; he began
misjudging them and letting them get out of reach,

then wildly flying after them; he served with a great
deal of action and ran aimlessly across the court and
back again, producing generally the effect of a prodigious hurry and exertion. The point of all this, of
course, was that his father should think that, as he
" warmed up," the struggle became tremendously
tough, and the boy had to exercise infinite tact and
cunning (for if he played as he ordinarily would have
done, the Dean would never have got a point at all)
in order to produce the impression that he was having
his work cut out for him if he wanted to win. So he
ruffled his hair and mopped his face, and with great
care hit a quantity of balls just below the line. That
wanted some doing : they had to be beautiful shots
just a shade too low.

David did his best to make his father win, but
unfortunately at the end of the third game, in attempt-
ing to put the ball just below the line, he made four
superb shots just above it, and so won the game. His
father, dripping and dishevelled and enjoying himself
enormously, had to lean against the wall for a little
while to recover. David did the same, and absorbed
in his pleasant drama, failed to see a certain twinkle
in his father's eye.

The Dean recovered his wind.

" One more game ? " he asked faintly. He felt as if
he was made of wet paper, and would shortly die of
accelerated heart-beat. But he wanted another game.

" Couldn't," said David. " I'm absolutely done.
What a wind you've got ! "

They dressed and went back to David's room for
tea. They were dining with the Provost to-night,
and to-morrow his father was coming to the weekly

dinner of the Sunday Club with A. G.'s Sunday
evening at-home to follow. So they were to have this
hour, David had arranged, to themselves for private
talk, and he had warned any who might be expected
to stroll into his rooms for purposes of general
sociability to keep away.

" Now, that's jolly," said the Dean as they settled
themselves. " Gracious me, how stiff I shall be
to-morrow ! But there's nothing nicer than being
stiff from exercise. No, I won't have a cigarette.
You can't give me a pipe to smoke, can you ? "

" There's only Perpetua," said David. " You're
welcome to her, but I'm not sure she'll be welcome to
you."

" Perpetua, Virgin and Martyr ? " he asked.
" Let's have a look. Why Perpetua ? . . . . Ah,
a meerschaum, I see. No, my dear boy, I think I
won't. Precious things are meerschaums. Now,
how goes it all, David ? "

" Oh, rippingly, all but Frank's being away. He's
at Athens, you know."

" Yes, you told me. But you're working hard, I
hope, and playing your games hard. While you're
young, my dear, do everything as hard as you can.
There'll be time to do things quietly when you get
older."

" Well, I might do a little more work if I tried,"
said David.

" Have a try, then. I must call on your tutor, by
the way, and see if he agrees with you."

" He will," said David.

" Highly likely. And have you got any clearness
yet about what you want to do when you go down ? "

David had filled Perpetua for himself, as his father did not care to assist at the burning of the " Virgin and Martyr." He made a few bubbly squeaks and groans before he answered.

" I want above all things to write," he said. " Literary gent, father ! "

" What do you mean exactly ? Newspaper work, novels, research ? "

" Anything, so long as it's writing," said David. " I like writing so much better than anything else."

His father nodded.

" Well, come now," he said. " It's something to know the sort of thing you want. Up till now you've only been clear as to the sort of thing you didn't want. My dear boy, surely that's a remarkably foul pipe, isn't it ? "

" Yes, horrid," said David. " Think I'll stop."

" Don't mind me," said his father. " But you really can't enjoy it much, can you ? "

" I don't. I only want to make her black," said David, putting it down. " I say, Dad, do you dislike the idea of my taking to writing ? I see such lots of things that interest me and amuse me, and whenever I do, I always want to describe them."

" Well, that sounds like a vocation. We'll go into that. As for disliking it, I hope I should never dislike anything on which your heart was set. It's part of you, David, and up till the present, I don't dislike anything that I know of you very particularly. Now, where are we ? Yes, I remember that you once showed me an essay you had written on Marlowe's *Faustus*. It was well written, and lucid too, which the critics always tell me I am not.

I remember thinking that you seemed to have thought out what you wanted to say, and then to have gone and said it. That's certainly the way to write."

He put one plump gaitered leg over the other, and quickly took it off again. The stiffness . . .

" It isn't what I should have chosen for you," he said ; " but then, as you might remind me, it isn't for me to choose. Now, whether you can do it or not, so as to succeed, we don't know, and we can't know unless you try. But apart from that, it's a chancy profession : there are few prizes, and many blanks even for the industrious and the competent, though I don't say that that is the main consideration in any choice. If you'd said, for instance, that you wanted to enter the Stock Exchange, I should have disliked that very much indeed. Now let's take another point. Unless you get a post on a paper, reviewing or what not, there's no salary attached to the profession of letters. That again is not everything, but it's something. I'm not a rich man, David, but even if I was, I should want you to be earning money on your own account. To be able to support yourself and make an income of your own is by no means a sordid consideration. Money-making is not a bad test of a man's character up to a certain point. It implies industry and application and self-reliance, as well as ability—all good things. Do you follow me ? "

" Rather. And agree with you."

" You won't presently, I expect," said his father. " Now, when you say that you see such lots of interesting and amusing things and want to describe them, what class of subject interests you most ? "

" Oh, people, any day," said David.

" Now we're getting a bit more definite. That points to fiction, novel-writing. I don't deal much in that branch of literature myself, but to write a fine novel is to do a fine thing. But how many people in the world can write a fine novel ? And what's the chance of your being one of them ? Of course you don't know till you've tried, not once or twice, but till you've sweated and bled over it. However, that's what you want."

" I want it awfully," said David.

His father laughed.

" You needn't say that," he remarked. " Whenever you want anything at all, you want it awfully. That's one of the things I thoroughly like about you, David."

" Got it from you," said David.

" Heavens, how polite we are ! What compliments ! Now, if you want a thing awfully, you must be prepared to make sacrifices for it."

David's face fell. He anticipated a suggestion of his leaving Cambridge, and acquiring experience of writing and books in some newspaper's or publisher's office.

" Yes ? " he asked.

" Well, the sacrifice I propose and expect of you is this. I want you to work extremely hard at your Latin and Greek. Really hard and regularly. You would, of course, much sooner be reading English and practising writing it. You probably think it a great waste of time, with the literary profession in front of you, to be doing Latin proses and Greek iambics, and to be devoting all your energies,

which I ask you to do, to learning to write and
translate in obsolete dead tongues, instead of working
at your own.   Don't you think so ? "

" I do," said David.

" I thought you would not be agreeing with me
before we got much further in our talk.   But here I
want you to do as you're told.   I daresay you won't
believe me, but I tell you that to translate Greek
accurately and well into English, and to put English
with precision and economy into Greek, gives you a
mastery in expression that is the prime essential to
good writing.   You've got to grasp a thought firmly
and fully, and to prove you've grasped it by expressing it in another medium.   Moreover, it's drudgery,
and drudgery is extremely good for you, my dear,
because you do things easily.   And it's gymnastics
to make your mind-muscles strong.   See ? "

" I understand, if you mean that, Dad," said
David.   " I don't agree."

" I don't want you to ; I don't ask you to.   I
want you just to take the medicine I suggest, and
perhaps in a year's time you may agree that it has
done you good.   But it doesn't matter really whether
you agree even then.   It will have done you good,
if you've taken it regularly.   That is the one condi-
tion I insist on, if you want me to accept your choice,
and to think you're serious about it."

" Right," said David.

His father got up.

" Well, you've given me a jolly tea," he said,
" and we've had a jolly talk—at least I have ; but
I've not quite done yet.   There's a thing more important than all brains and intellect and success put

together, dear David, and that's character. You're a handsome boy and an attractive one, and there are hundreds of temptations round you all day, which we needn't talk about because you know what I mean every bit as well as I do. Walk warily and walk boldly, my darling boy, and God bless you."

He laid his hands on David's head a moment, looking him in the face both earnestly and merrily. What he saw there gave him a full heart.

" You were but a little chap when your mother was taken from us," he said. " If she'd lived, she'd have been proud of you, David."

He paused a moment, patting his shoulder.

" I am too," he said, " and that's all I need tell you. I must be off now to see your tutor. And you were very kind to me over that game of squash. I saw through you."

" Saw through me ? " said David. " What do you mean ? "

" Now you've got to answer me faithfully. Do you or don't you know that you could give me twelve points in a game ? "

David burst out laughing.

" Yes, about twelve," he said.

" Very well. What an old ass you must have thought me, if you really believed I didn't see through you. But you meant it kindly. Walk with me as far as your tutor's."

David attended his father's discourse at the University Church next day, and took Bags with him. It lasted a full hour, was totally unintelligible, and they both went peacefully to sleep. But the Sunday evening supper was a great success, and the Dean enjoyed himself enormously. He was wonderfully young, younger than anyone there except David, and he sat down on Perpetua, breaking her into stinking smithereens. David begged him not to send him a new meerschaum, but gracefully accepted the cash equivalent.

He left early next morning, in order to get down into Cornwall that night, and popped into David's room to wish him good-bye. David's sitting-room was tidy and empty, and as there was no sign of breakfast there, he most mistakenly concluded that David had already had it, and in pursuance of the industry they had talked about was already at a lecture or at work with his coach. As a matter of fact there was no sign of David's breakfast, not because it had been cleared away, but because he had ordered it for ten o'clock, and it had not yet come. So his father left a note on his table, bidding him farewell, and expressing his gratification at this early rising.

The noise of the shutting of the door roused David from his pleasant sleep. He had meant to see his father off and breakfast afterwards, and seeing that he had overslept himself, he dressed in a great hurry, and found that laudatory note on the table in his sitting-room.

" Oh, this'll never do," he said, and rushed to the station on his bicycle. The train was on the point of starting, but he found his father in the corner of a third-class carriage smoking his pipe and reading his Bible.

" Just caught you," he cried. " I say, father, I wasn't out at a lecture at all. I was fast asleep. . . . Not had breakfast yet. But I will get up earlier. I *have* enjoyed your visit. Perfectly ripping ! . . ."

David of King's   XI

MR. CROWFOOT was walking very quickly along the broad gravel path that led past the Provost's Lodge to the bridge over the river at the back of King's. He put down each foot directly in front of the other, instead of slightly to the side as is the habit of most people, on an ingenious theory (which he was perfectly willing to prove to you, if you had time, by means of a contraption of weights and string and pulleys which invariably got into a sad tangle) that the pedestrian thus ensured a more stable equilibrium with less fatigue. The foot in process of advance had to be swung in a slight curve, otherwise it kicked the heel of the foot that was on the ground. That occasionally happened when he forgot about the curve, and then the equilibrium lost something of its matchless stability. As the sun was extremely powerful, Mr. Crowfoot wore a black bowler hat (for black thwarted the action of the actinic ray, which produced sunstroke), a thick sweater underneath his coat (for on these very hot days it was easy to catch cold unless you were care-

ful), and flannel trousers which hung in festoons
over his shoes (for they were sure to shrink in the
wash and would then be exactly the right length).
He carried a croquet mallet of peculiar construction
under his arm: this had a hinge half-way up the
handle with a catch to it, so that when you were
carrying it you could slip the catch and fold it up for
convenience of transport, and there you were. Sometimes when he was making a very vigorous stroke the
catch came undone by accident, and the mallet
head swinging round caught him a smart blow on
the shoulder, and swinging back again pinched his
finger in the hinge, but this was a comparatively rare
occurrence.

He also carried a string net for lawn-tennis balls:
this had a hole in it other than those involved in its
construction, but a piece of newspaper spread inside
it prevented the balls from falling out. In his other
hand he had a small travelling-bag of shiny black
leather covered with labels, containing all the various
things which he might possibly require during the
afternoon, and under his arm was a lawn-tennis
racquet with a metal disc on each side of the centre-
piece. This was a most ingenious dodge: it had a
circular clock-like face on which, instead of hours,
were the figures " 15," " 30," " 40," and " advantage," and you twirled round the pointer in accor-
dance with your score. The second disc on the
other side of the racquet was precisely similar, and
on it you recorded the score of your adversaries.
So if there was any dispute about the score, as so
often happened, you could refer to these discs as to
a court of appeal.

Mr. Crowfoot came underneath David's window in the buildings by the river, and after clearing his throat, shouted " Blaize " in a bell-like voice.

David had forgotten that Crowfoot refused to recognise summer-time, and as he had said that he would call for him at two, had been expecting him for the last hour. Crowfoot maintained that the time that won the battle of Trafalgar was good enough for him, and he referred to it as God's time, as if on one of the days of Creation, God had said, " Let there be a watch," and there was a watch which He had wound up and set going. . . .

David hurried downstairs.

" I've been waiting for you," he said. " I thought you told me you would come for me at two."

Crowfoot laughed delightedly and cleared his throat.

" Caught you there," he said. " You forgot my principles about summer-time. . . . Oh, dear me ! "

The piece of newspaper in the string net for lawn-tennis balls got displaced, and all the balls fell out and bounced on the gravel walk. Two of them rolled swiftly down the grass slope to the river. Some were brown, some black, some green with length of service.

" How very tiresome ! " said Crowfoot. " Save them, Blaize, save them ! Oh dear me ! "

David bounded down the grass slope in time to intercept one of the balls ; the other trickled into the river.

" And that was the best one," said Crowfoot, adjusting his spectacles to get a good look at it " But wait a minute, I've got a dodge."

13

He hurriedly put down his black bag and his tennis racquet, adjusted the catch of the croquet mallet, and looped the string bag on to the end of the handle, like a landing net.

" That's awfully ingenious," said David. " Shall I fish it out ? "

" No, let me," said Crowfoot in the pride of invention. " But you might catch hold of my coat-tails. Better run no risks."

The string bag thereupon fell off the end of the croquet mallet into the river, and it looked as if they were worse off than ever. But as David could reach both it and the tennis-ball quite easily with his hand, all the floating property was recovered, dripping but intact.

" I can soon set that right," said Crowfoot, greatly pleased.

He opened his black bag (the leather one covered with labels) and took out a small towel, with which he dried the ball. David had one intoxicating glance at the rest of the contents, and knew he would get no real peace of mind till he had a good look at all its treasures. That one glimpse had showed him such miscellaneous articles as a shoe-horn, pieces of notepaper, a small wooden mallet, and a bottle with a red label of " Poison " on it.

Meantime the piece of newspaper which had so dismally failed in its office of stopping up the hole in the string-net had blown away on to the lawn, where it was trundling along under the hot breeze. David sped after it, but by the time he had retrieved it and returned, Crowfoot had put the tennis-balls into the black bag. But a piece of newspaper might easily come in useful before the afternoon was over, so he folded it up and put it in too.

" We're sure to want it," he said, and even as the words were on his lips, he added, " In fact we want it already," and opening the bag again, he wrapped up the damp lawn-tennis ball in it. . . . Thrilling though all this was, they had at present only got as far as the bridge over the river, but now Mr. Crowfoot, having packed everything up again, looked at his watch, and began to walk very briskly.

" Just half past three," he said, " by this new-fangled time. Stapleton and Gepp are coming down presently, so we might have a single first or a game of croquet. What do you say to a short game of croquet, Blaize ? Why shouldn't we play with one ball, and hit it in turns ? You might make a very diverting game out of that idea. Then, you see, whoever got through the last hoop first would become a rover and put the other ball out. Stay ! That wouldn't work, because there wouldn't be another ball."

He appeared lost in thought over this complicated notion, and David incautiously said that it was a fine day. He thought that could not lead to argument, and was completely wrong.

" That all depends what you mean by a fine day," said Crowfoot eagerly. " I daresay that when a fish says it's a fine day it means an extremely wet one."

" I meant an ordinary fine day on land," said David, beginning to feel his head whirl.

" Very well ; but then I say ' fish,' " said Crowfoot, " which means just the reverse. So where are you then ? "

David hadn't the slightest idea where he was, but they had arrived (in the feeble literal sense) at the croquet lawn, and Crowfoot began trying all the hoops like a dentist feeling a patient's teeth, and found that one was loose.

" I suspected as much," he said delightedly, " and I've come prepared for it. Would you mind giving me the wooden mallet that you'll find in my bag, Blaize ? I'll stop here by the hoop, otherwise we might forget which it was, and have to try them all again."

David's opportunity had come, and he opened the black bag which Crowfoot had left in the summer-house and pretended not to see the mallet until he had noted the other contents. There was the shoe-horn and the notepaper and the bottle labelled " Poison " which he had seen before, and now he found some cigars in an old envelope, with the address crossed out and " Cigars " written in, several copies of a glee, a quantity of pieces of string, some sticking-plaster, an ash-tray, several tram-tickets, and a small shagreen case, which flew open and disclosed a set of false teeth. Then there were a nail-brush, a half-bottle of Tintara, with a wine-glass without a stem, and a watch. There were some other things as well, but there was not time for a systematic survey, and he went back to Crowfoot with the wooden mallet.

" Lucky I brought it," said Crowfoot, and proceeded to deal prodigious blows at the hoop. The third of these struck him on the foot, and at the next the mallet flew in half like Siegfried's anvil.

" Very fortunate it didn't break before," he said, as he stood on one foot, and rubbed his injured toes, " but now the hoop's as tight as tight. Better not

throw the pieces away ; we might hit upon something
to do with them. Now for our croquet. Oh dear,
the boundary line isn't marked out, and I haven't got
any whitewash. I must remember that another day.
As it is, let's play without boundaries. It makes
a very pleasant game. Will you have a small
cigar ? "

David declined the cigar, and while Crowfoot was
adjusting the hinge of his patent mallet, fetched an
ordinary one for himself and the balls. They then
croquetted each other into thickets and flower-beds,
and Crowfoot, who had adjusted the side lenses of his
spectacles in order to focus the balls with distinctness,
dropped them off his nose into a dense bed of forget-
me-nots, where David had sent his ball, and in looking
for them got stung by a bee. But the bottle of
" Poison " had been brought for that extreme con-
tingency (it was equally good for the bites of gnats),
and he rubbed it on his neck with such satisfaction that
it was clear he would much sooner have been stung
than not. Then resuming, he captured David's
ball, and in making a prodigious swipe at it, he must
have pressed the catch in the handle of his mallet.
The head did not hit the ball but flew like a shell
from a howitzer into the bushes. He retrieved
it, and made it safe, by wrapping round the socket
the newspaper which should have prevented the
tennis balls from falling out of the string bag.

The game did not last so long as might have been
expected, for one of David's balls got interned among
the roots of an elm-tree, and he could only hit it on
the top, which, if anything, made it tighter than ever.
He wanted to lift it, but Crowfoot assured him that

no such privilege was allowed in the rules, of which he had a copy in his bag.

" But then it doesn't allow for elm-trees being on the ground," said David.

" There you are then ! " said Crowfoot. " You mustn't do anything it doesn't say you may. Otherwise you might put your ball by hand through the hoops."

Crowfoot therefore had two turns to David's one, for it was not worth while to go to the elm-tree and hit the yellow ball on the top each time it had to play, and black and blue proceeded merrily. When the game was over, he uncorked the half-bottle of Tintara, and they drank from the stemless wine-glass draughts of that tepid but generous wine.

" Very refreshing," said Crowfoot, " and now won't you have a small cigar ? "

By an unaccountable oversight he had forgotten to bring any matches.

" Really, very extraordinary," he said, turning the contents of the bag over. " Here they are—no— that's only tintacks. Stay ; here's a burning-glass. We shall manage it yet."

Crowfoot made a memorandum of this omission on the note-paper he had brought down, but had not got farther with the lighting of a cigar than burning a small hole in the knee of his flannel trousers, when Gepp and Stapleton appeared.

" Ha, ha, Blaizides," said A. G. " How awfully jolly ! You and I will play together, and you shall take everything. But are these the balls we're to play with ? They're all black and brown and green."

" They're very good balls indeed," said Crowfoot snappishly. He had not asked A. G. to play at all, but A. G. had heard him unsuccessfully asking someone else, and had merely said that he would do so. . . . Besides, there had been high words between them at a Fellows' meeting that morning on the subject of a mowing machine for the lawn. Crowfoot had objected to the purchase of a green one, because it would be hard to see it against the grass ; you might easily stumble over it and get a bad fall.

" But we shan't see them against the grass, like your mowing-machine," said A. G.

" That's perfectly different," began Crowfoot.

David intervened in the cause of peace, for Crowfoot was winking his eyes with incredible rapidity, as he always did when he was annoyed.

" They bounce beautifully," he said, hurling one on to the grass. . . . .

The game was no dull or stereotyped one. A. G. stood quite still in the middle of the court, talking all the time, and dabbing with his racquet at any ball that threatened to hit him as if it had been some troublesome fly, while David, with the perspiration streaming off the end of his nose, dashed from side to side of the court, and sent the ball whizzing past his partner's majestic immobility. He knew nothing whatever about lawn-tennis, and played the real tennis stroke with great enjoyment but little effect. Crowfoot, with his bowler-hat fixed firmly on his forehead and his eyes gleaming with angry passions, pattered about with extraordinary nimbleness, and seemed bent on hitting Gepp in the stomach. His racquet was about as tight as a landing-net and he

did not so much hit the ball as receive it in the
landing-net, and then with a sharp turn of his wrist
sling it back again with paralysing speed.   He was
not very accurate, but if it did not go into the net or
far beyond the backline, it was most difficult to return
as it shot along the ground.   Stapleton, on the other
hand, made no effort at attack, but was content to
send the ball back very slow and high, and in an absent
manner, because he was thinking about an erotic
rhapsody in *vers libre.*

There was considerable difference of opinion about
the score, for A. G. mixed up in his agreeable conversation any scoring numerals that came into his
head, and Crowfoot, though he marked something
up on the dials on his racquet at the conclusion of
every rally, was not always sure which dial recorded
his own score and which that of his adversaries.   This
uncertainty he remedied by writing " Us " on one
dial in purple indelible pencil which came off
on his fingers, and " Them " on the other.   But
A. G.'s random assertions confused him, and the
pointer of " Them " got loose and kept on record-
ing " Advantage " to Them, while his own score
was nothing, and this was clearly an impossible
state for the game to be in.   But through all these
agitations A. G.'s voice went serenely on.

" Ha, ha, well played, Blaizides," he said.   " Forty
love.   That one very nearly hit me.   The ball is as
invisible as dear old Crowfoot's mowing machine.
How awfully jolly it all is !   Thirty.   I used to play
lawn tennis on the Golden Horn with the Grand
Vizier of Abdul Hamid and one of his wives in a yash-
mak, at the time of the Armenian massacres.   Such a

charming woman. I think he had her strangled. Where has Stapleton sent that ball? I saw it go up, but it never came down. Probably it has—advantage to us—become a satellite of the earth. I think I shall go and bathe afterwards, if you will be awfully kind and go and fetch my towels for me. I would send Antonio, but he has got a bad headache. Love all! How very Biblical and Christian that sounds —or are we fifteen? I don't believe you are more than fifteen, my dear David. You are an imperishable child. How delightful to be able to run like that and not mind. I was at Athens once when the Olympic games were being celebrated, and they wanted me to go in for the lawn tennis champion- ship and King George gave away the prizes and we had tea afterwards. Let's have tea afterwards to- day, and that will be a most remarkable coincidence. Forty love!"

"It isn't anything of the kind," said Crowfoot, referring first to one dial and then the other. "It's thirty fifteen; no, it seems to be thirty advantage, or advantage thirty, but the pointer has slipped. It's thirty anyhow."

"It's thirty all," said Stapleton firmly. "At least it was just now, because I heard you say so. I served four faults, and then they put two into the net."

"Very likely, but lots of things have happened since then," said Crowfoot. "Let me recollect. There was that high one, and then Gepp didn't take—"

"Dear old Crowfoot," said Gepp, "you talk about me as if I had just been vaccinated. The smallpox was very bad in Athens that year—— No, do that again, Stapleton. I wasn't ready; you were all talking."

" But you tried it," said Crowfoot excitedly. " Forty thirty."

" I always try everything," said A. G. " There is no pleasure, however subtle, that I haven't tried. Dear me, my shoelace is undone. It would be awfully jolly of you, David, if you would tie it for me. My doctor has told me never to stoop even to conquer : all good doctors tell you never to do what you have no intention whatever of doing. They tell you never to touch baked blue-bottles. Thanks so much, my dear boy. How is your father ? I wish I was a Dean and lived in gaiters and Gothic coolness. Now I'm ready, Poet Stapleton. ' Stand still, true poet that you are,' as Browning said, and serve to me. Where has it gone ? Up somewhere out of sight above the moon. ' O moon of my delight that knows no wane ! ' Dear old Fitzgerald !—he used often to read Omar Khayyám to Tennyson and me."

This ceaseless flow of preposterous monologue was madly irritating to Crowfoot, and David heard him murmur, " I don't believe a word of it," in an acid voice.

" There is the ball again," continued A. G. without pause. " It has come down again. Take it, David— or was it served to me ? Get out of my way, then. Awfully sorry, Stapleton, but I forget whether it was served to me between the time it left the earth and returned to it. Send me another—Deuce ! "

" ' Advantage,' " said Crowfoot, twirling his pointer round.

David thought that this divergence of opinion had yet to be talked out, so when Stapleton sent him another high one, he merely caught it and threw it back.

" Good service," said Crowfoot. " That makes us game. Three love, or is it three all ? Three love, I think. Gepp's service."

A. G.'s technique in service was to stroll about well inside the court, sending balls casually over the net and into it. If he thought the first was not going over or was defective in any way, he instantly served another before the first had declared itself. He sent two thus to Crowfoot, who returned them both raspingly out of court and cried :

" Foot-fault ! love fifteen."

" Crowfoot and his Mormonisms ! " said A. G. " Thirty love."

" No ; love fifteen," reiterated Crowfoot.

" But you've just sent two out of the court. Thirty love. Give me another ball, David. Feed me with balls ; comfort me with racquets, as the Song of Solomon says."

" But-it-was-a-foot-fault," said Crowfoot, all in one word.

" I haven't the slightest idea what you're talking about," said A. G. " Ha ! ha ! that was out."

" No, it wasn't ; I saw the whitewash jump," said Crowfoot. " Love thirty."

" Forty love," said A. G., lighting a cigarette. " Fair, fat, and forty."

" This is a farce," exclaimed Crowfoot. " And that was another foot-fault."

A. G. paid not the slightest attention to this, but

he thought he had served enough for the present on this hot day, and hit the rest of his balls over to the other side.   Crowfoot missed the first, but sent the second smartly back again, and his hat fell off.   The ball hit A. G. in the stomach with a hollow sound.

David, who up till this moment had been behaving with ascetic self-restraint, suddenly gave out, and burst into hoots of laughter long overdue.   Crowfoot, already much exasperated, thought he was laughing at the fall of his hat (which was true), A. G. at the severe impact of the ball (which was true also), and they both turned flinty faces towards him.   But he laughed on, and as they looked, the creases of justifiable annoyance were expunged from their faces; it was impossible to be angry with anybody while the boy laughed like that.   A. G. joined in first, and a moment afterwards Crowfoot.

Crowfoot picked up his hat, and cleared his throat.

" Really very humorous," he said.

Stapleton alone remained grave and lost in thought.

" Have we finished the set ? "   he asked.   " Is that all ? "

This caused a fresh paroxysm; when it had subsided, David wiped his eyes.

" O Lord, how it hurts ! "   he said.   " Sorry for laughing, but I couldn't help it.   Where are we ? . . . Let's go on. . . . Let it all happen again."

" Very comical," said Crowfoot.   " I hope I didn't hurt you, Gepp."

" Not a bit, old chap.   How's your hat ? "

" If that's all, I shall go away," said Stapleton.

Nobody felt inclined to sing the glees which Crowfoot had put in his bag, and after a while David strolled up to the real tennis court, leaving Crowfoot trying to tighten the pointers of his scoring disks with a hair-pin. Every now and then his mouth broke into merriment as he recalled the really wonderful events of the afternoon, but presently he settled down into a general beaming content with existence. The term had been thoroughly delightful and prosperous; he had done a most creditable amount of work, according to the bargain struck with his father; Bags, though still Lotharian at heart, had changed his tobacconist for one over whose counter there was no temptation to linger; and David could not only read hymn-tunes on the piano without any overpowering efforts at concentration, but was playing cricket for the University eleven. The dry crumbly wickets suited him, and though in the last match he had taken no wickets whatever, and had probably established a record by having more boundaries hit off him in a short space of time than had ever been hit off anybody, he had established another record by going in eighth wicket down and hitting eleven fours in succession off the Middlesex bowlers. He was then caught off a no-ball and completed his fifty with come careful singles. . . . In fact he had won the match for his side when it appeared to have been lost, and nobody had been more surprised than himself. But it was clearly useful to have somebody on the side who had been bowling in the most devastating manner (and might therefore do so again) and who could do impertinent and unlooked-for things like that against good bowling. In the deep field he could, by virtue of

the astonishing way in which he could get over the
ground, save runs as nobody else could, and if no
catches came his way, he was wonderfully useful.
He usually dropped catches, because he thought he
was going to, and no recital of M. Coué's formula ever
made him think otherwise. . . . Then there was his
tennis, the challenge round of which was to be played
to-morrow, but unlike last year, he had no divided
mind as to whether he wanted to win or not. The
challenger was an odious young gentleman, about
whom even David had been unable to discover any
good points, except his tennis, and he didn't think
very much of that. He wore a green shade on his
forehead, disputed the rulings of the marker, and it
was impossible not to believe that he did not try
to put you off by clattering with his feet while
waiting for the ball to be returned. He didn't play
games like ordinary people, but when he had a court,
he had basketfuls of balls cut over to him, and hot
forces sent for him to stop. David intended to give
him some of these to-morrow.

But it was not retrospect only, nor indeed retrospect mainly that conduced to David's content this
afternoon. To-night, if Frank had caught his connexion in Paris, he would arrive here by half past
nine ; if he had failed to do so, he would get here
to-morrow morning. Probably not a day had passed
since his departure for Athens on which David had
not consciously missed him, but there would be no
more such days for the present. Would he ever, he
wondered, come to the end of the things he had got to
tell him and talk over ? Yet what was there worth
telling ? Frank would burst into his room and say

"Hullo!" and David would say "Hullo!" and
they would be back again precisely at the point where
they left off, and probably begin to rag or contradict
each other. . . .

David caught sight of a figure walking very airily
ahead of him. Such tittuping gait and such riding-
breeches could not possibly belong to anybody but
Bags. So he concealed himself behind a couple of
men who were between him and Bags and were
walking the same way, so that if Bags looked round
he would not see him. When he had come quite
close, David darted out of his ambush, took hold
of him firmly by the shoulders, and ran behind him,
pushing him swiftly along, and bending down behind
his back, so that Bags could not see who it was that
so strongly propelled him. For some fifty yards
they progressed like this, Bags uselessly resisting.
Then by a violent effort he disengaged himself and
disclosed to David the face of a perfect stranger
with an awful squint.

David, very hot already, turned to the most remarkable crimson.

"Oh, I'm awfully sorry," he said. "I thought
you were a man I know."

The stranger chattering with rage said, "I'm glad
you don't."

"It was awfully rotten of me," said David.

"Awfully," said the stranger, and waited for
David to go in front.

David turned into the gate of the tennis court,
his knees trembling with terror at this severity.

There was no one else up at the court, and he had
a couple of sets with the marker, but then abandoned

the game, for a dense bank of cloud had come up in
the west, and the light grew too bad to go on.   The
clear baking heat of the afternoon had become vastly
more oppressive, and when he came out again, it
was like stepping into some airless vapour-bath.
Not a breath of breeze stirred, the towers of full-
foliaged elms stood motionless as if cast in iron, and
the outlines of trees and buildings, though veiled in
this premature and gloomy twilight, were of a curious
hard distinctness, as if seen through a telescope.
Right across the sky, from the west and already
reaching nearly to the zenith, there had built itself
up a rampart of cloud, with black blotted edges,
and tinged within some with stale coppery light
against which the grey pinnacles of the chapels showed
chalky-white.   Now and then some furnace-hot eddy
in the air made a sudden commotion in the trees;
the leaves were tossed and displayed their pale
under-sides, and as he crossed the bridge, the surface
of the river, smooth as ice and dark as asphalte, was
momentarily corrugated, and the long sprays of the
weeping willow lashed themselves against the coping.
Once, very remotely, there was some mutter of
thunder from the far base of that tremendous bastion
of blackness which now, reared up over more than half
the sky, was hard-edged like masonry, and a couple
of raindrops plopped on the stone parapet of the
bridge, and instantly evaporated from the hot surface. . . . It was all rather exciting and ominous,
and David as he passed by the willow, which after
its sudden wild commotion was absolutely still again,
found himself noting the signals of the approaching
storm.

" Everything dark and distinct," he said to himself. " Looks like something in a dream. Not real,
but terrifying, like a dream of the end of the world.
One gap in that monstrous cloud with pale green
showing through. Dead still, but with hot eddies,
whirling madly. . . . River like marble. Hullo.
Tommers ! "

Tommers strolled limply out of the court by the
river.

" Something's going to happen," said David.
" There's such a storm coming up as never was.
Probably the judgment day. Well, I'm glad I've
had a ripping afternoon for the last. I've been
playing croquet and lawn tennis and real tennis and
drinking Tintara. Crowfoot had a small bottle
of it with some false teeth in a black bag. It
was exactly like the mad tea-party in *Alice in
Wonderland.* Have some more wine ? What's the
matter ? "

Tommers had collapsed on the grass.

" Nothing. I'm only dead," he said.

" How awfully jolly and peaceful ! " said David
in A. G.'s voice. " One ball hit A. G. in the middle
of the stomach. I love a thunderstorm. It makes
me feel excited, and my hair stands on end."

" It always does," said Tommers.

" Liar ! It usually only sits up. You feel ill
before a storm, Tommers, because you're fat and
wicked. It's the grossness of your vile body which
trembles and quakes. I take no notice——"

A tattered streamer of lightning flicked across the
sky ; in the clear darkness it was like a sudden
beam from a bull's-eye lantern. David ducked his

head, as if it had been aimed at him and had narrowly missed him, and Tommers gurgled.

" As for you, you take no notice of it," he observed.

" But it shouldn't have done that," said David in
an injured tone. " It should have begun gradually.
Now they're pouring out bagfuls of marbles on a
wooden floor. Come on ; it's close on hall-time.
Isn't it frightfully interesting ? "

Though it was still not yet the hour of sunset
(even by the time that won the battle of Trafalgar),
the darkness, when they came out of hall, was that
of night, thick and hot and of windless and menacing
tranquillity. There had just been that one vivid
discharge of lightning and no more, nor any further
drop of rain beyond such as had steamed and dried
on the parapet of the bridge, and heaven and earth
waited, finger on lip, for the storm to break. Groups
stood about at the entrance of staircases to get a
breath of air and watch for the crash of the unloosed forces. Then in the stillness there came the
loud hiss of the rain from just beyond the river,
and David bolted at top-speed for his rooms. Before
he got there, the sluices directly overhead were
opened, and he was soaked through during the last
thirty yards of his run. He stripped off his wet
things and, for the sake of coolness in the sultry
swelter, put on pyjamas.

The kitchen had already sent in the supper for
two that he had ordered, for Frank would have had
but a hurried dinner in town, and if one thing in
the world was certain, it was that immediately on
arrival he would come round to David's rooms and

demand to be fed. Till then there was a couple of
hours to be got through, and he rather wished that
his flight down here had not been so precipitate, for
apparently nobody else had come down but had fled
to rooms more neighbourly, and he seemed to be
quite alone in the buildings. " Mr. David Blaize,"
he thought to himself, " at home. ' Thunder and
lightning ' in the bottom left-hand corner," and he
sat down in the window to observe.

The rain came down in point-blank volleys, strip-
ping the leaves from the trees. His electric light
made an illuminated square outside, and from time
to time some white rod of rain sparkled with a flash
of prismatic colour. Then, as if by the brisk turn-
ing-off of a tap, the rain ceased altogether and the
dead wall of blackness, now that his light had nothing
to shine upon, moved close up to the window. The
trees dripped, and the charged gutters gurgled in
the stillness, but his eyes, peer as they might, could
see nothing whatever. Then along the gravel path
came the shuffling footsteps of half a dozen fellows
who had taken advantage of this lull to get back
to their rooms, and David heard some voice say,
" Black as pitch. Where on earth is anything ? "
And someone answered, " Hold on ; I've got a
match ! "

There was no need for a match, nor indeed for the
light of moon or sun, for at that moment the pall
of that gross darkness was whisked away by a terrific
illumination. Right down the centre of the sky, as
if the heavens had split with the crack of doom,
leapt a riband of blinding light, and David's eyes
still blinked with it when the crash of the thunder

followed, no roll or rumble among echoing clouds, but sharp and appalling. Straight on the heels of that came another blaze, intense and violent, and the floodgates were opened again.

For near on two hours David knelt on his window-seat, with elbows on the sash, entranced by the wild tumult, and his mind seething with words to express it. One storm had broken directly over-head, and in the pauses of that he could hear that another was coming up from the east. Sometimes the whole foreground was lit as by an instantaneous noonday that showed the yellow flush of buttercups in the meadow beyond the river and cast black shadows of the trees in front on to the grass below his window, and sometimes from some flare out of the other quarter the shadow of the building in which he sat was imprinted on the lawn and every leaf of the dripping trees was green and distinct. It was in vain that he attempted to occupy himself with work, vain even was it to amuse himself with his piano, for everything, himself included, was dwarfed and puny compared with this spectacle. But as the hour for Frank's arrival came and passed, and still the minutes ticked on without sign of him, David began to wonder what had happened to stop him. Of course there were a hundred explanations; indeed, it seemed idle to expect him while this hurly-burly continued. He might not have caught his connexion in Paris, in which case he would not be here till to-morrow; or, if he had arrived, he would probably be unable to get a taxi at all in such a deluge, but be sheltering at the station, while this incessant stabbing of the lightning went on. In any case he

could not have got down to King's; if he had, he
would have been here.

By midnight the violence of the storm was abat-
ing; long pauses came between those flickers of
white-hot light, the thunder comfortably boomed
instead of cracking, and the loud drumming of the
rain subsided into a steady hiss. It had become an
ordinary storm again, the exhilaration and excitement of it had passed, and David left his post of
observation. He was beginning to give up all hope
of Frank's arrival to-night, and that was a horribly
depressing conclusion. All day, and all through
this wonderful storm, the thought that he would be
here this evening gave spice to whatever happened.
. . . There was the supper on the table, on which
by this time they ought to have been feasting, but
he had not the slightest inclination to sup alone.
Of course he might get somebody to share it with
him—Tommers, he knew, had come in, and, being
now out of training, would be pretty sure to be
hungry. But it would be a sad end for the cold
asparagus and the salmon and the chicken and the
strawberry mess, to be devoured by him and Tommers. It would taste rotten; there would be no
reason for it. It might just as well stop there, and
the more perishable portions be cleared away in the
morning. And he had chosen it with such greedy
care. . . .

David yawned and stretched himself. He would
give Frank half an hour yet, and at the end of that
time would either go to bed, or summon some
esurient neighbour, who should not, however, have
any champagne. So, feeling disappointed and

dispirited, he lay down on his sofa with his back to the
light, and a book to help him through the next half-
hour. The book, which he had taken at random
from the table, did all and more than he expected
of it, for in three minutes it had slipped from his
hand, and he, weary with excitement past and disap-
pointment present, for he no longer believed that
Frank would come to-night, was sinking through
the twilight of dozing into sleep. His last thought
was that he was quite wide awake.

Half an hour later he became conscious that there
was a bare foot straight in front of him, and drowsily
wondered whose it was or what it was doing there.
It was a large foot, and was quite inexplicable. Then
he emerged from sleep just sufficiently to conclude
that it was his own, and that he was lying on his
sofa in his sitting-room ; memory awoke, and he
was conscious that he had been waiting for Frank.
Some small noise, he thought, had roused him,
perhaps the slipping of his book from his hand, for
certainly the book was no longer there. So Frank
had not come, and he would go to bed without
getting Tommers to share the consecrated banquet.

Then there dawned on him the sensation that he
was not alone, and he lifted his heavy eyelids to see
who had stolen in while he slept. Someone was
standing by the door.

David sprang off the sofa.

" Hullo ! " he said.

" Hullo ! " said Frank.

David stood on tiptoe, with arms outstretched,
and eyes from which all the heaviness of sleep had
vanished.

" Oh, Frank ! " he said. " You old ass to steal
in like that ! I wasn't asleep, was I ? I was j-just
waiting for you. Supper ! I ordered supper. Let's
have supper ; I'm frightfully hungry."

" Ripping ! So am I . . . David ! "

" Yes ? "

" Nothing—only David," he said.

" Same here. I say, it is you, isn't it ? "

" No, it's Crowfoot."

" So it is. Sit down. I say, what an age you've
been away ! And how awfully late you are now
you've come back ! What happened ? "

" There's been a bit of a thunderstorm. I suppose you slept through it. Not a taxi to be had at
the station."

" How did you get down ? It's still pouring,
isn't it ? "

" I walked. What was the use of waiting there ?
I hadn't come back to Cambridge to see the
station."

David looked his face over.

" Black with Athenian sun ! " he said. " Salmon ? Oh, and asparagus. And luggage ? "

" Yes. Salmon and asparagus. But no luggage.
I'll get it in the morning if you'll lend me
pyjamas."

" Take them," said David. " Take anything you
like. How's Athens ? "

" All right : and Cambridge ? "

" Oh, doing nicely now," said David. " Fizz ? "

" Just about. In a tumbler."

" I've masses to tell you," said David.

" Drive ahead. So have I."

David poured out two tumblers of champagne.

"I haven't got anything to tell you," he said, "except that you have come back."

"I can't think of anything else," said Frank.

FRANK had settled to take as the subject for his Fellowship dissertation the Cult of Asclepius, and David found it far more interesting than his own work. . . . David had, as usual, brought his books to Frank's room on this August morning in the Long, and Frank had translated to him an extremely funny scene from a play by Aristophanes, in which the blind god Plutus went to be healed of his blindness in the sanctuary of the god at Athens. There were very vulgar proceedings on the part of Plutus's slave; and when the lights were put out, snakes came out of the sanctuary and licked Plutus's eyes and restored his sight.

"And now get on with your own work," said Frank, "and let me get on with mine."

"But mine's so dull," said David. "It's about Grimm's law, and yours is a sort of Grimm's fairy-tale. Why can't I do yours and you mine?"

Frank was engaged in tracing a plan of the precinct where these exciting things happened.

"Because you're not clever enough," he said. "Don't jog the table, David."

David thought this over.

"If you tell me I'm not to, I shall have to," he said.

"Very well, do jog the table. I tell you to jog the table. What a foul temper you're in!"

"I know I am," said David. "Do shut up and let me work. According to Grimm's law, you'll be pleased to hear, any consonant in one language can become any other consonant in any other, and the vowels don't count. Thus *aqua* in Latin is derived from the same root as water in English, or that of any other word you please. I call it childish."

David immersed himself in these futilities for about ten minutes, then rose to the surface and sighed heavily.

"I want a wife," he said, "and a pill."

"Well, take a wife and a pill," said Frank. "Take whatever you like, only pass the ink over here."

David pushed the ink-bottle along the cloth, and went back to his theme.

"You are like Crowfoot," he said. "Sufficient ink can make you perfectly happy. But if one's tummy's wrong one not only wants a pill, but thinks that nobody loves one. That's why I want a wife. If your tummy's right, you don't care whether anybody loves you or not. If you're quite well, that is to say, you don't really care about anything else, but if you're chippy you don't care about anything at all. It's all gastric juices. Good stuff for a materialistic essay."

Frank finished, drawing a long line to indicate a step.

"Why are you chippy?" he asked.

"Because I drank too much last night, if you want to know," said David.

"Rot," said Frank.

David began to laugh.

"But I did," he said. "And that's why I didn't come in to see you. I did it on purpose. My new missionary stunt."

He got up and, standing in front of the looking-glass over the fireplace, put out his tongue.

"Colour of mortar," he said. "Would rouge do any good?"

"Go on," said Frank.

"Well, you mustn't let him know I told you," said David, "but it was all along of Bags. Absolutely dead private, but I want your opinion."

"That means you want me to agree with you," said Frank.

"Yes, about that. Well, Bags has begun getting frightfully thirsty in the evening. He drinks a whisky and soda with one hand, and while he's drinking it, he pours out another with the other, so as to be ready. And as soon as that's ready, he drinks that, and so on, *da capo*, as they say in my sonatas. I've told him of it before, and said he was a guzzling swine, but he didn't pay the slightest attention. So last night I said that I should take drink for drink with him. It was his whisky too, and Lord, it did sink in the bottle. I don't believe he means to drink exactly; he doesn't crave, but he's just got into the habit of swallowing when he's thinking of what card to play next or what to talk about. He doesn't drink when he's alone: he told me that. It's just a sociable habit. And he must

have got an awfully strong head. We went on
drinking away, and he only became slightly mournful. But it was different with me. I hate whisky
to begin with—it's muck. I got extremely cheerful
first of all, and then I couldn't remember what I
was going to say, and then I was sick in Bags's slop-
pail. He hated that, and I'm sure I don't wonder."

" David, you ass," said Frank.

" I'm not so sure. May be true generally, but not
in this instance. He came round this morning to
see how I was, and seemed rather sorry. I told him
I should be quite well enough to have another jolly
good booze with him to-night. I say, how long does
it take to get delirium tremens ? And what happens
then ? Snakes, isn't it, like Asclepius ? "

" Bags is a rotten ass," said Frank. " Does he go
messing about with girls still ? "

" No, I don't think he does," said David. " Pretty
sure he doesn't in fact."

" And do you propose to get boozed every evening
in order to be an object-lesson to Bags ? " asked
Frank.

David cocked his head.

" Every evening ? " he asked. " No, I don't ; if
by every evening you mean lots of evenings. Bags
is an awful good chap, you know, though you may
not think it. And he hated seeing how chippy I
looked this morning in addition to my being sick in
his slop-pail. Anybody would hate that. But I
shall certainly go round and have a drink with him
to-night. Hang it all, one's got to do something,
you know, and it didn't make a particle of difference
my telling him that he was a boozy swine. He

thinks a lot of me really—that's swank—only he didn't happen to care this time."

" This time ? " asked Frank.

" Yes, this time. On this occasion," said David with so much indifference in his voice that anybody could see there had been another time. However, as he so guilelessly intended it to appear that there had never been such a thing as another time, Frank asked no further question. Besides, David, after a final look at his tongue, hurried to his seat and immersed himself in his books.

The two were up for a month of the Long Vacation term, that pleasant, leisurely time which relieves the excessive length of the Long Vacation. There were no lectures to attend or compositions to show up ; not more than half the College (reckoned either in terms of dons or undergraduates) was in residence ; you did exactly as much work as you felt inclined, dressed in flannels when you got up in the morning, and slacked about in a desultory manner. Frank was busy enough over the arrangement and composition of his Asclepius work, and David, debarred from the perusal and practice of English literature by his agreement with his father, had been paying a most respectable deference to the dead tongues. He had accepted the reason of his industry as an act of faith and of work ; he had imbibed the dead languages like a medicine which was to prove a tonic to his mind, which at present felt much the same as before. But he had written a short " Hymn to Dead Languages " which went to a tune which he could play quite fast, and began :

> David, dost thou feel them,
> How they work within ?

For the rest, the hot weather had made Crowfoot's brain to seethe with unimaginable ingenuities, and presently A. G. would be back from Zermatt, where he had been spending the day in climbing inconspicuous summits and the evening in close communion with exalted personages. At the end of August David and Frank were going down to Cornwall, which they hoped to reach on bicycles, and spend the remainder of September there, with the Dean's house as a base, and anything within reach as an objective. Just now there was nothing very exciting on hand in the way of games, since, as for tennis, who could be strenuous in a closed stuffy court, with the thermometer in the eighties, and as for cricket, King's could scarcely get a team together. A hustling captain might have done something, but the whole point of the Long was that you didn't hustle.

They worked on till one o'clock, and David ventured on a cigarette. He lit it, and instantly threw it into the fireplace.

" Garbage," he said. " I wonder, is it worth while being sick in the evening in order not to be able to smoke in the morning ? Did you ever get drunk, Frank ? "

" Yes, of course. But by accident."

He shut his books. He had not done much Asclepius in this last hour, for his mind had been occupied with David's ridiculous experiment. It was just like him : " just a rag " he would have called it, but quite serious in purpose, and somehow belonging, for all its foolishness, to the wise private David. . . . That did not prevent Frank from strongly disapproving of it. Probably David would go his own

222 David of King's

way, and though you might disapprove, you couldn't help either applauding or being amused. He was so gay when he was thoroughly in earnest.

"But that ass Bags gets drunk on purpose," Frank said. "You've told him that he's a swine."

"Rather; he doesn't care an atom," said David. "But he doesn't do it on purpose; you're wrong there. If he did, he'd drink when he was alone. He told me he didn't."

"That doesn't prove it."

David softly frowned over this.

"Well, you've got to believe what people tell you sometimes," he said. "Otherwise you don't get on. I believe what Bags says. There's the whisky, and there's somebody to talk to, and they go very well together. But if he doesn't take care——"

He rapped on the table.

"I've got it," he said. "The Spartan gents had slaves called Helots, and they used to make them drunk in order to show their sons how putrid drunken men were. That's what comes of studying Greek history. I was a Helot last night, and I daresay I shall be one to-night. But Bags will see pretty soon what an ass I look. He's just rotting, that's all."

"Well, let him rot," said Frank. "He's got a perfect right to go to the devil if he likes."

"Oh, I doubt that," said David. "Old Bags, you know. We used to keep stag-beetles together at my private school. Besides, it's such a bore for his friends."

"Well, it's a bore for me if you have to go and booze with Bags every night. And it's a bore for you, if it comes to that."

" Must do something," said David. " Any decent
chap would. And I can't think of anything else.
I'm just a Helot."

" Tell him you won't have anything to do with him
if he goes on boozing," said Frank.

" Oh, would that be any good ? Don't think so.
Because I *should* go on being friends with him anyhow.
Besides, it's rather playing the heavy father. I
don't believe in heavy fathers. Helots have a better
chance. Besides, he won't like me Helotting all over
the shop. Let me alone, Frank."

" But it's such mad stuff."

" Yes, it does seem rather mad," said David.
" But there's method, you know. . . . Anyhow it's
better than being pi."

David strolled into Bags's rooms that night, where
he found Tommers, as if nothing whatever had
happened the evening before. Bags did not seem
particularly pleased to see him, but that made no
difference to the missionary.

" Hurrah, I've found somebody at last," he said.
" Oh, and I've just heard from A. G. He's found a
Highness at Zermatt, a human one, I mean, and not
a mountain. And he's not coming back till next
week."

" Don't see the connexion," said Tommers with
irony.

" Of course you don't. There is none. Just
isolated facts. I say, wouldn't it be awfully jolly to
be a Highness and give so much pleasure ? Are there
such things as Lownesses ? Tommers, I believe you're
a Lowness."

" Why ? " said Tommers, after trying to think
himself.

" Because you're filling up all the sofa. Lord !
what a fat thing ! Shift a bit. Donnez-moi un peu de
sofère. Je veux coucher avec vous. . . Oh no,
that's something else, isn't it ? Je veux coucher sur
une pièce de votre sofère. . . . What awful piffle !
Can't anybody else talk ? "

" How much chance at present," said Tommers.

" Well, then, let's play something. Let's play cut-
throat. Bags, may we play cut-throat ? "

Bags was vexed. He had asked Tommers in to
play piquet. You always had another game of
piquet when you had finished one, and filled up your
glass. His vexation took the form of extreme politeness.

" By all means," he said. " That would be
delightful."

He put out the table and packs of cards, and
David instantly began to build card-houses.

" Bungalows of one story have become the rage,"
he said. " They're the most satisfactory to live in,
because they don't fall down so often. Crowfoot
asked me this evening why we didn't all live in
bungalows."

" He didn't," said Tommers.

" Very well, he didn't. Towers, though architectur-
ally more interesting, have an evanescent quality.
They are here one minute and gone the next. Blast !
The persevering architect, however—— Sorry. I
didn't know you were ready."

They played for a little while rather too politely for
real enjoyment, and with no other refreshment than

that afforded by cards and cigars. Bags, with the
events of last night still rather vivid, was intending
for the present to produce no whisky at all, but
probably David would go and see Frank before long,
and then he and Tommers would play piquet with the
usual accompaniment. He didn't want to make
David drink, but he was rather wanting to do so
himself, and he half wished David would go. He
had wholly wished that David hadn't come, but now
that he was here, his inimitable futility and charm
were beginning to assert themselves, and Bags was
already thinking less of the decanter and more of
him. David had grasped his psychological state
with regard to drink with great accuracy : he drank
not in order to make him enjoy himself, but because
he was enjoying himself. It was sociable and pleasant
—you enjoyed yourself more.

Then a forfeit of four hundred points to each side
on Tommers's part helped things to thaw, and the
discomfited Tommers sought consolation.

" In the highest circles," he said, " a tray of siphons
and whisky often makes its appearance about half
past ten or so with or without a plate of biscuits.
In the slang of the day, it is called a night-cap. Never
mind the biscuits."

So the hospitable duty was clearly forced on the
Honourable Crabtree. Tommers took rather a large
night-cap, called in the slang of the day a toothful.

" Whisky, David ? " asked Bags.

" No, thanks," said David. He looked sideways as
he sorted his cards to see what Bags would do. . . .
Tommers, of course, knew nothing of previous events
and present contingencies.

Bags clearly hesitated a moment, stopper in hand.
Then he poured a decent allowance into his glass.

" I think I'll change my mind," said David.

" Little or lots ? " asked Bags.

" Oh, just moderate," he said.   " Same as yours.
My deal, wasn't it ?   Three no trumps.   Not one nor
two, but three."

" Hog," said Tommers.   " Pass."

Bags took a large mouthful of his mixture.   David
permitted himself one disgusted glance at him, and did
the same.   Then he became his silly self again.   He
gathered up the trick he had just won.

" I shall now play an ace," he said.   " That's
the best thing to do, because otherwise it might be
trumped.   Oh, I forgot, there are no trumps."

He covered up the ace with his hand.

" Did anyone see that ace ? " he said.   " Was it
exposed ? "

" No, take it back," said Tommers.

David looked at him with a penetrating glance.

" Now, I wonder why you said that," he remarked.
" Oh, I see !   I'll play it.   Come on, Tommers :
out with the king, I'm sure you've got it single.
Oh, devilish cunning is Mr. Blaize, and a silly ass is
Tommers.   If you had only said you had seen the ace,
I should have argued, and maintained it wasn't
quitted, and not played it.   As it is——   Thank you.
Sorry you have been troubled, as the telephone
young lady says.   Been on the conquest among the
telephone young ladies, Crabtree ?   They wear green
helmets, like divers in deep waters, and they are older
than the rocks they sit among——"

" Crabtree's become a—a womanthrope," said

Tommers. "No—a misowench. There's not been a
fresh photo of ankles on his chimney-piece for
months."

"Youth is the seed-time of life," said David in a
hooting voice, conjectured to be meant for the
Provost's, "and so I counsel you all to sow your wild
oats in the days of your youth with no grudging hand.
And now with one voice, or rather I should say with a
great many voices, let us sing, 'We plough the fields
and scatter the oat's seed on the land.'"

Bags, out of mere inattention, had drunk the rest of
the whisky and would normally have got up to
replenish his glass, had he not seen David instantly
finish his, in order to keep level. He resented this.
What earthly business had David to interfere in his
drinks? But again, what earthly business had he
to interfere in David's? There was Tommers helping
himself to more, and that settled it. Bags would
look after his own thirst; if David didn't want any
more he wouldn't have any, and if he did, he would.
That concerned nobody but him.

Bags got up at the end of the deal, and poured an
extremely small dose into his glass.

"Jolly good whisky," said David. "Give me a
drop more, Bags."

"I thought you hated it," said Tommers. "New
stunt for you, isn't it?"

"Yes—acquired taste," said David. "Can't think
why I didn't take to it before. Wasted life. Whose
shout?"

Bags's second glass stood untasted before him;
so, too, did David's. It really was exasperating
to be controlled like this. . . . And yet Bags couldn't

call it control; he was perfectly at liberty to drink
this glass and as many more as he pleased. But it
would spoil his pleasure to see David with a wry
but cheerful face doing exactly the same.

"Awfully jolly evenings at Zermatt," said David.
"Dear old Prince Boris Bumniowsky and I are the
greatest chums, and he told me stories about his
cousin the late Czar. Then every morning we used
to climb the Matterhorn together and glissade down
on our ice-axes, and—and play the piano or dominoes,
and yodel."

David was an inimitable imitator: he really not
only sounded but somehow looked like A. G. when
he mimicked him. He was killingly funny over it,
much funnier than he had been last night when he
kept forgetting what he meant to say and was afterwards sick. . . . In consequence Bags only took a
sip of his second glass of whisky, and as David did
not see him, he took a longer one. But then even
as David was making up and recounting perfectly
unrepeatable adventures of A. G. in A. G.'s voice,
he saw that Bags's glass was half-empty, and his
own still full, and so he brought his own down to
the level of the other. He was not being a bit
heavy about it, but just drank, as part of that ridiculous plan he had started, and went on to say
what had happened in that lonely Alpine chalet on
the glacier among the gentians.

It struck twelve; this was being a good evening
for David, because he had hardly had to drink at
all, and bad for Bags because Tommers got up and
said he was off to bed.

"Twelve!" said David. "I shall go too. I say,

I am rich. Three and sixpence. Somebody will want to marry me for my money."

" Don't go yet, Tommers," said Bags rather exclusively. " Have another drink."

Tommers hesitated. Bags finished his second glass, and David with a slight sigh did the same.

" Well, it must only be a thimbleful," said Tommers. " That's the smallest sort of night-cap. The toothful, which is the size of the hole in a man's tooth, is larger than a thimble."

David, already at the door, strolled back.

" There was a man once who never ate cherry-tart, to which he was passionately devoted, because the stones stuck in his teeth," he said. " I've forgotten his name."

" Blaize !" said Tommers. " Thanks, Bags. Woa ! That's nearly a toothful."

David, with an engaging smile, watched Bags playing about with the decanter-stopper.

" Another drink, David ? " he said.

" I think I won't, thanks," he said. " But to-morrow night let's meet in my rooms. I'll get a fourth for bridge, and I'm not sure I won't give you dinner first."

" Well, make up your mind whether you will or not," said Tommers, and drank his toothful.

This offer was in the nature of a bribe. Bags seemed to understand that, and put the stopper back, thereby accepting it.

" I will," said David. " The dinner will be cheap, but a hungry man would be glad of it. That sort of dinner. And I'll win it all back at bridge afterwards. Come on, Tomlin."

" Well, I've been waiting for you all this time,"
said Tommers.

David pinioned him from behind, and pushed him
out of the door.

" I'll give you to the bottom of the stairs, and race
you to your room," he said.

Tommers began majestically to go downstairs.

" Right," he said. " But give me time to get
down."

Bags had joined him at the door.

" I wish you'd mind your own business, David,"
he said.

" I know ; but I never could," said David. " And
I've had a jolly evening. Much better than last
night, because I've not been sick. Oh, thanks for
not having another drink just now. I thought you
were going to. Eight o'clock to-morrow, then——"

" Ready," shouted Tommers from below.

" Off ! " yelled David, and dashed down stairs
with the clatter of a cavalry squadron.

Bags sauntered back into his room, rather regret-
ting that he hadn't had many more drinks, just in
order to inconvenience David as a penalty for his
interference. Yet by his horrid cunning he wasn't
directly interfering with Bags at all. He had every
right to drink as much as Bags did ; he was only
interfering with his own tastes in drinking what he
called " that muck." He hadn't preached, he
hadn't been in any way different from what he
ordinarily was, and if he chose (for whatever reasons
of his own) to drink precisely as much as Bags, it
was up to him to do so. Bags thought of finishing

the decanter all by himself more for the pleasure of
telling David so next day, and thus scoring off him,
but he didn't in the least want it. The only point
of such a proceeding would be to thwart David,
and it wasn't worth it. Of course when David had
told him that he drank too much, the only proper
proceeding was to take no notice, and, if anything,
to drink more, but this new plan of David's was
really a topper. . . . Again, another night, he might
roundly tell David that he was going to play piquet,
or had got a four for bridge, and that he wasn't
wanted ; but the objection to that was that he
would much sooner spend the evening with David
than with anybody else. He saw comparatively
little of him now that Frank was up, and in whatever blasted missionary spirit David offered his
company, he would much sooner have it than not.
And if David was there, he really couldn't go on
filling up and filling up, if David did the same. . . . .
Bags frowned at his own slowness of wit in not
being able to think of any suitable reprisal, and
went to bed reflecting that David seemed to be
cutting him off from all the pleasures of life, and
yet he himself found a good deal of amusement
without them.

"Blast his eyes," thought Bags. . . . As he
turned over to go to sleep, he found himself grinning
at the recollection of the firm fortitude of David's
face as he drank, and invented unspeakable adventures for A. G.

David, meantime, had been beaten on the post
by Tommers, and fell exhausted into his arm-chair.

" I got off badly," he said. " I should win if
we did it again."

" Come on," said Tommers.

" No, not to-night. It's late. It's always later
than I expect. How I wish the time wouldn't go
so quick ! The whole caboodle goes too quick, you
know. Here am I at the end of my second year,
and you and Bags at the end of your third."

Tommers yawned.

" All quite true," he said. " But if you're going
to gas, I want to go to bed."

David had recovered his wind, and sat up.

" Oh, no, don't," he said. " I hate going to bed.
Dull. Are you coming up for another year ? "

" No such luck, I'm going into the family business.
Tea. There's a plantation somewhere in India,
chock full of cobras."

" You might send me a pound or two from time
to time," said David. " Not tea, of course—cobras.
What rot it all is ! "

" Oh, going out into the world," said Tommers,
correctly guessing. " Yes. Nobody is anybody
in the world, unless he's clever or rich or
commits a murder, and then he's not anybody for
long. We all fade away. It's only when you're at
school or up here that you're anybody special.
There's Bags : everybody knows who Bags is, and
laughs. But when his governor dies he won't be
anybody in the House of Lords."

" Rotten world," said David.

" Well, I didn't make it. Bags is stopping up
here another year, isn't he ? I say, he didn't get
squiffy to-night."

" Bags squiffy ? " asked David, as if such an idea had never occurred to him.

" Yes. He usually does," said Tommers. " Drinks whisky till he's rather melancholy, and then has some more."

David got up.

" I never saw Bags squiffy in my life," he said. " And I should think I ought to know."

" I daresay you ought, but apparently you don't. Rather a pity when a fellow begins doing that."

" Oh, don't talk such piffle," said David. " After all, you had three drinks to-night, and Bags had only two. Supposing I went about saying you drank ? I wish you wouldn't say such things, Tommers. Somebody might believe them."

" Well, I bet you Bags gets squiffy to-morrow night when we dine with you, if you give him a fair chance."

" Done ! " said David. " Half a crown ? "

" Two."

" Very well, two. But if you're so certain you ought to give me odds."

" All right, Shylock. Three to two," said Tommers. " But you've got to be awfully hospitable. Drinks flowing."

" Rather. But don't go about hinting that Bags drinks. Why, I've known him since he was a kid."

" Well, he's beginning to play the goat," said Tommers.

David threw a cushion at him, ran upstairs, and banged his door.

" Time I intervened," he said to himself.

David kicked off his shoes, slipped out of shirt and trousers, and was ready to hop into bed almost as soon as he arrived by his bedside. But the idea of lying still, waiting for sleep to come, seemed a hopeless business, for he did not want to lie still, and he could not imagine going to sleep. Some ferment was seething in his mind, which seemed to pour restless vigour through his body, and he strolled backwards and forwards from bedroom to sitting-room, cursing the fact that it was night, and there was nothing to do. He must occupy himself some-how, for to lie in bed, all charged with potential activity, meant that he would be unable not to think and to want. Usually, by the time that the pur-suits and the diversions of the day were over, it was easy enough to lie stretched and tranquil till sleep descended on him, but to-night he was still bubbling with energy. Something had to be done: to play his piano would be almost too unpopular, to try to master the rest of Grimm's ridiculous law would be futile, and he wanted something more physically energetic than such sedentary occupations. It was a mistake to have raced Tommers down here; he should have gone to Frank's room, who was always ready to sit up till any hour, playing piquet or talking.

David had a bright idea. There was a silly game, which could be played alone, of making the circuit of your room by climbing over the furniture along the walls without setting foot on the ground. It was a strenuous affair, taxing muscle and ingenuity alike, and he thought it would just suit his needs. He had played it in Frank's room, but never in his own, and a cursory glance round the walls made it appear feasible though difficult.

He started by stepping on to a chair, and from that climbing on to the piano which stood beside it. The piano rocked slightly under him, because one castor was off, but he made the traverse with success and let himself carefully down on to the chair on the farther side. Then came the door in the angle of two walls, and beyond that the sofa. It was a long stride from the chair, where he now stood, on to the sofa, and he could not jump it, because the chair would certainly tip up and land him on the floor, but after several extensions of his leg, he got one foot on the sofa while the other remained on the chair. There for a moment he stuck, like the Colossus of Rhodes, but by clawing on to the arm of the sofa, he managed to draw his second leg after him. The sofa, of course, was easy walking, and from the farther arm of it he got on to his book-case, and there he remained, like a pelican in the wilderness, contemplating the extremely *mauvais pas* on to the window-seat. Already the game was becoming terribly important. " If I jump," thought David, " and land on the window-seat, I shall probably crash through the window, and then I shall never get round any room any more."

He whistled " Keep thou my feet I do not ask to see . . ." and the melody stimulated his brain. He shifted his position, and kneeling down on the edge of the book-case, put out a long leg backwards, feeling for the edge of the window-seat with his toes. He got one toe there, and then couldn't shift his weight so as to disengage the knee on which he knelt. His

hot hands with which he was clinging to the side
of the book-case began to slip.

" Death ! " said David, in a loud sincere voice.

He clutched wildly at the lexicon that lay on the
top of the book-case, over which just now he had
climbed, and steadied himself. But his toe came off
the window-seat, and with his back to it he had to
fish for it again. It came into contact with the
electric switch, and put the light out.

" Well, it's easier climbing in the dark," thought
the optimistic David, " because you don't see the
perils and the grim precipices around you."

Then quite suddenly he fell heavily to the ground
and bruised his knee and barked his shin. He
turned on the light, bound his leg up with a wet
handkerchief, and limped angrily to bed.

" Don't believe it's possible," he said. " Rotten
game. Golly, how my knee hurts ! I shall never
go to sleep."

In about three minutes he did so.

David was rather lame next day, but the dinner was
a great success. There was bridge afterwards,
followed by the University Indoor Athletic Sports.
Nobody else could get on to the window-seat
from the book-case, and Tommers couldn't even
get on to the piano.

That was satisfactory, and so were the three half-
crowns.

Third Year

BAGS'S birthday feast for David had become as firm an annual institution as Christmas Day, and this year it was celebrated with peculiar magnificence, for David came of age. Since he had no estates of any sort to step into, nor any tenants to present him with the very smallest piece of plate, it was clearly the part of a friend to console him for this lamentable absence of revenues by all possible sumptuousness. A. G., as usual, proposed his health, and returned thanks on his behalf; as usual, he forgot that he was speaking not out of his own mouth but David's and indulged in exotic theories and past purple memories of his own of a highly incredible nature. Crowfoot had been asked this year, and laughed in an unkind and metallic manner when A. G. made David say that he forgave the German Emperor. Frank, who was going to spend another winter in Athens for the completion of his Fellowship dissertation, had put off his departure for three days in order to be present, and a new circle of Bags's friends came. These were rather grave people, who spoke in a measured, grammatical manner, for Bags had completely deserted horsy circles, and was taking great pains with his oratory, since, preceding his ascent into the Hereditary Chamber, he was (it was hoped) to represent a constituency in the other house. His friends just now, therefore, were very serious bloods, leading lights at the Union and other debating

237

societies, who always said " and so forth," instead of
" and that sort of thing."   But they became more
accessible as the evening went on, and the porter
found a bowler hat on Henry VI's statue in the centre
of the fountain next morning.   Also a loud splash,
possibly connected with this, had been heard by the
studious and the wakeful about 2 a.m.

Bags had lately stood for the Presidency of the
Union, and had suffered so colossal a defeat that for a
while it was wiser not to mention any high numerals
at all in casual conversation. . . .   After this
greater Waterloo, Bags had shaken off the dust of
that democratic assembly, and chiefly exercised his
debating powers in the Sanhedrin, a small, very
select, and very serious body of orators, consisting
of a dozen members from Third Trinity and King's.
For a year past Bags had never missed a meeting of
the Sanhedrin, nor failed to speak at it, and at the
beginning of this term he had been elected President,
the duties of which office he discharged with impartial and laborious suavity.   Shortly after there was
to be an election of three new members to fill the
vacancies of those who had gone down, and Bags had
been persuading David to let himself be proposed as a
candidate.   Bags himself spoke rather well; he spoke
at any rate with fluency and grammar, never
forgetting his main topics, and David's entire in-
ability to string together half a dozen consecutive
sentences on any formal occasion seemed to be a
strong reason for his joining the Sanhedrin.

Bags was quite impressive on the subject.

" It's part of an intellectual training for everyone
to be able to speak," he said, " and you really ought

to learn. It's not only necessary for people whose whole career will depend on their speaking——"

" Honourable Crabtree, M.P.," said David.

Bags was a shade pompous occasionally, and he went on as if this interruption had not occurred.

"—but for everybody. It is as ludicrous for a man to call himself educated if he can't speak, as it would be if he couldn't read. Indeed I am inclined to think——"

" But I never did call myself educated," said David. " Never."

Bags pointed a forensic forefinger.

" I am inclined to think that the man who can't express his ideas in decent if not flowing language has even less claim to be considered educated than one who with an open book in front of him is unable to read it."

" If you don't stop making speeches," said David loudly, " in indecently flowing language, I've got an open book here, and I shall throw it at you. The man who is always talking as if he was making a speech is worse than uneducated : he's a bore."

Bags lowered his forefinger.

" Well, I want to put you up for the Sanhedrin," he said. " It's awfully good training. You've got to arrange your thoughts clearly and express them decently, or no one listens to you. It isn't enough just to blurt out anything that comes into your head as they do at the Union."

David's chair creaked slightly, but it wouldn't do to laugh. It was a very short time ago that Bags had said that the only real training was the rough-and-tumble of the Union. But that was before he had failed to become the President of it, and had succeeded in becoming the President of the Sanhedrin. Naturally that made a lot of difference.

" And you don't know," continued Bags, " what a sense of mastery it gives you—no, not mastery exactly—what——"

" 'How ripping it feels,' is what you mean," said David.

" Well, that may pass—how ripping it feels to know that you are speaking to a dozen fellows, all critical and eager to pick holes in your arguments, whom you are forcing by mere logic and lucid exposition and so forth to agree with you. Your job is to make them think with your mind, and see from your point of view. By degrees you learn to get confidence, and know that you'll hold them. And it gives you quickness in repartee, and in finding the telling phrase. I don't mean of course that you're slow. . . . But it would do you no end of good."

" But what's the good of putting me up ? " said David. " Of course they'll blackball me, if they've any sense. All those who were at my birthday dinner know I can't speak at all, and even if they didn't they'd soon find out. Of course they'll pill me."

Bags became a shade sublime.

" As for that, the President's candidate starts with a good bit in his favour," he said. " And you only want practice. You've got quite a decent voice——"

" Valuable member of Crowfoot's glee-club," said David. " Well, I don't mind : you can put me up if you like. If I'm pilled, it's your fault."

" Not much chance of that," said Bags loftily.

But the incredible occurred, and in spite of his

august proposer, the President had to announce to
David that the election had taken place and
that out of the four candidates proposed, he was
the only one who had not been elected. The matter
had been talked out before the ballot was held, and
several out of the nine members of whom the Sanhedrin
at the moment consisted expressed the hope that the
President would withdraw his candidate's name on
the ground that the Sanhedrin was a debating society
and David could no more speak than he could fly.
They all knew David, and wished it to be understood
that there was nothing personal intended, for there
wasn't a nicer fellow in the world. But where was
the use of a dumb member ?

" But he'll soon learn to speak," said Bags.

The leader of the opposition submitted that the
sooner he learned to speak the better. He could
come up for election then. Wouldn't the President
withdraw his candidate, for no one wanted to blackball him ?

The President wouldn't, and the ballot took place.
It showed three votes for David, and six against him,
and Bags threatened to resign, but was quite easily
persuaded to refrain from so extreme a step. The
other elections were then proceeded with, and out of
this exiguous egg of a situation there hatched the
Great Rag, compared to which all previous rags had
been " but a flea-bite in the ocean." (This fine and
expressive simile came out in a thoughtful article on
the Great Rag in the *Cambridge Review*).

The first fecund factor in the Great Rag was the
illimitable fury, chagrin, and humiliation of Bags
when the Presidential candidate was blackballed.

He had told David so plainly that his election was a certainty owing to the office and prestige of his proposer, and now he had to tell him that the only certainty left was that he had been rejected. David observed that Bags had made a big fool of himself, and a smaller fool of him, but otherwise showed no spirit. He was really rather relieved than not.

" But I'll make them sorry," said Bags. " You'll be a member of the Sanhedrin before the term's over. Blasted cheek ! I'll teach them."

" How ? " asked David.

" I don't know yet. But there's some way. You'll help, won't you, if you're needed ? "

" As long as I don't have to speak," said David. " Go away and teach them. I want to work."

The second factor was that the month was November, that there wasn't much going on, and a quantity of energetic young gentlemen pined for excitement. Bags's fury therefore fell on fruitful ground.

The third factor was that the members of the Sanhedrin were sharply divided on the question of David's rejection. Their debates lately had been very dull and academic, and this question interested them much more than German reparations and Colonial policy. . . . And so it all began.

The leader of the opposition to David's membership was a cheerful creature called Malcolm, a personal friend of David's and a Trinity undergraduate. He had been disappointed in not having been elected President instead of Bags, was delighted to have scored off the President, and rightly supposed that David didn't mind. As Secretary he strolled round next morning to inform the three newly-elected members, Hales, Morrison, and Steel, of the honour that the Sanhedrin had conferred on them. He took with him formal notices of their election. He visited Hales and Morrison first, and communicated the gratifying intelligence. Both of them in casual conversation informed him that they were going to lunch in King's with Bags, who had come round in person to deliver the invitation. Slightly perturbed and suspicious (though, after all, why shouldn't the President ask the new members to lunch ?), he trotted round to King's, to which college Steel belonged, and found Bags in his rooms. The earnest conversation that seemed to be going on ceased abruptly, as he entered.

Malcolm announced his gratifying intelligence, and Steel said, " Thanks awfully." Then, as nobody seemed to have anything else to say, and as David's rooms were quite close, Malcolm thought he would look in and explain how far from personal had been his motive in this disturbing matter.

David was quite charming about it, but seemed amused. Before Malcolm left, there came shouts of " Blaizes, are you in ? " from the court outside, and David yelled that he was. Rapid steps came up the stairs, and Bags and Steel came bounding into the room. Amid faint grins and much politeness, Malcolm then took his departure. The faint grins seemed to be succeeded by loud laughter as he walked thoughtfully downstairs.

Something was certainly a-foot—anyone could see that—but it was impossible to conjecture what it was. The impression was confirmed, though no light was shed on the nature of it, by a note from Bags which reached Malcolm late in the day, saying that by virtue of his Presidential office (see Rule 6), he summoned an extraordinary general meeting of the Sanhedrin to take place in his rooms at 8.30 p.m. the next evening, when he would have the honour of laying a motion before them, the importance of which seemed to him to warrant this urgency. Would the Secretary therefore kindly give notice of this meeting to those members of the Sanhedrin who had not yet been informed of it ? The new members, Hales, Morrison, and Steel, had already been communicated with.

The cautious Secretary first turned up the book of the rules of the Society. He found that though the President was right with regard to his power of summoning an emergency meeting, the President was powerfully wrong if he thought he could bring forward and take a vote on any motion without giving notice of it. He therefore wrote the required notices with much cheerfulness, for whatever motion Bags intended to put forward, it could not possibly be voted on at that meeting. There could be no possible doubt that the object of Bags's motion, whatever it might be, was to get David into the Sanhedrin, and it was pleasant to find that the President didn't know the rules.

As he didn't know the rules either, Malcolm sat down and studied them for ten minutes. This perusal made him acquainted with the fact that if the President summoned an emergency meeting, any member might at that meeting give notice of any other motion. And then (oh, delightful discovery !) he found that, by Rule 22, no gentleman who had been proposed as a member and been black-balled was eligible for election within a year. There-upon he danced round the room, and hurriedly went to inform some of those who, beside himself, had blackballed David that there was something going forward. Bags and those whom he had clearly suborned (the new members) probably knew what Bags's motion was.

Evans, who had been a strong anti-Davidite, was charmed with the idea of there being something stirring in view.

" It'll wake up the Sanhedrin a bit," he said, " whatever it is. Who wants to go on debating about Greece and Reparations ? "

" Looks rather like a rag," said Malcolm. " Of course Bags wants to extend the membership or something, and then propose David again. He can't do that without increasing the membership, as we're limited to twelve. If he has tampered with the three new Johnnies, you see, he thinks he can out-vote us. So he can. We were six against David, and he was three for him. Three more makes six, and as President he has the casting-vote. We'll let him do all that, and then when he proposes David, we'll gently point out that a blackballed candidate isn't eligible for election again for a year. Sucks for Bags ! "

It certainly did seem sucks for Bags and they gloated over it. With this unshakable knowledge of rules behind them, there really seemed very little to fear from any manœuvres of the enemy.

" But it's best to be cautious," said Evans. " It's

clear that Bags can carry, not at this meeting but at a subsequent one, an extension of the membership, and we ought to have a candidate."

Malcolm jumped up.

" I've got it," he said. " Look here ! Bags will propose an extension of membership and at the next meeting he'll carry it. But then we've got the right to bring forward another motion, and I'll propose that Carslake be elected. Captain of the Cambridge Boat Club, you know. Rather a smart candidate. Then Bags will propose David."

He paused a moment deep in thought, and then shouted with exultation.

" It's all right," he said. " Listen ! Bags will propose an extension of one to the membership, and he'll carry it. Then he'll propose David and get him elected. Then I shall propose Carslake, and Bags will say there isn't a vacancy. But I shall say that my motion must be voted on, and since there isn't a vacancy, I bet Bags will vote for him sarcastic-like, and probably the others as well. Then, oh then, and not till then, will I point out that David isn't eligible for election, and that therefore there is a vacancy. And Carslake, whom they've just elected, will be a member."

" Golly ! It's great ! " said Evans. " Let's go through it all again to see there's no hitch, and then I'll run round and tell Carslake."

The meeting next night duly assembled in Bags's rooms. The preliminaries were very polite and calm, and Bags brought forward the expected motion that one more member should be elected. Malcolm thereupon turned gently over the leaves of the book of rules, and rattled his pencil-case between his teeth.

" Rather a hitch, I'm afraid, Mr. President," he said regretfully. " Rule 9 states that if the President summons an emergency meeting, he can only give notice of his motion, which must be voted on at a subsequent meeting."

Bags's party exchanged little smiles. Someone had discovered this after Bags's notice for the emergency meeting was sent out, and the point was quite provided for.

Bags assumed his most suave air.

" Perhaps you would kindly allow me the ear of the house for a moment, Mr. Secretary," he said. " My motion, which I had not quite finished, is that the membership of the Society be increased by one, and that Mr. David Blaize of King's be elected. As for your point about the inadmissibility of voting on my motion at this meeting, I summon another meeting in precisely two minutes from now, in the same place. The meeting is adjourned."

" Oh, excuse me, it isn't anything of the sort," said Malcolm. " With all respect, of course, and so forth. But before you're in such a hurry to put the adjournment, I wish to take advantage of Rule 8, which, in case you haven't read it, provides that at an emergency meeting, any member may put forward, for subsequent voting, any other motion. I put forward the motion, seconded by Mr. Evans, that Mr. Leonard Carslake be elected a member of the Sanhedrin. I needn't talk much about him ; he's Captain of the University Boat Club, and so forth, and it is generally agreed that, unlike other gentlemen who have been proposed for the Society, he has a very copious flow of language and a striking power of expressing himself with great lucidity. Anyone who has ever been on the tow-path knows that."

" I suppose that Mr. Carslake has expressed his willingness to stand for election," said Bags.

" Rather. Unlike—— Well, never mind that. But he was most keen on it. You can bet your boots on that ! "

This colloquialism was a happy inspiration. Bags was standing in front of the fire and his feet were shod in gay morocco slippers. Malcolm looked pointedly at them as he spoke, and the Sanhedrin gently rippled.

Bags sat down in his chair and put his feet under the table.

" I think I am right in saying that the President's motion needs no seconder," he said.

" Quite," said Malcolm.

" So if that's all, the meeting is adjourned," said Bags, " though not *sine die* at all. Now we'll have another meeting. Minutes, please, Mr. Secretary."

"Well, give me a moment : I must write them before I read them," said Mr. Secretary.

Malcolm hurriedly scribbled the minutes of the last meeting, including his own remarks about the President's boots. He read them out, and Bags, with a broad grin, ascertained the pleasure of the meeting that he should sign them.

" The first business before this second emergency meeting," he said, " is my own motion that the membership of this Society be increased by one, and that Mr. David Blaize of King's be elected to fill it. I don't think he needs any panegyric of mine——"

" 'Paregoric,' did you say ? " asked Malcolm, who was busily scribbling.

The Sanhedrin applauded. This was all much better than talking about Colonial policy.

" ' Panegyric ' was the word I used," said Bags. " The subject of my motion does not, I was saying, need any pare—panegyric from me. The ballot-box, Mr. Secretary."

It was deferentially pointed out that the President's motion was really two motions. David could not be elected unless the first motion regarding the increase in the number of members was carried. The entire Sanhedrin voted for it. Then the vote was taken with regard to David's election, and the ballot-box was found to contain six black balls, and six votes in his favour. The President gave his casting vote for Mr. Blaize of King's.

" Mr. David Blaize is therefore elected a member of the Sanhedrin," he said. " The meeting is——"

Malcolm did not wink at anybody.

" With lots more respect, Mr. President," he said, " the meeting is not adjourned. My motion as well as yours is before the house. Proposed by the Hon. Secretary and seconded by Mr. Evans, that Mr. Leonard Carslake of Trinity be elected a member of the Sanhedrin."

" But there's no vacancy," said Bags. " He can't be elected. The meeting——"

" No, it isn't," said Malcolm. " My motion is before the house, and it must be voted on."

Bags became immensely suave again, and very judicial.

" Strictly speaking, Mr. Secretary," he said, " I'm
not sure that your motion is in order.   It implies, if
I may so word it, an inherent impossibility.   There
is no vacancy in our numbers, you see.   Your motion
is *ipso facto* nugatory.   On the other hand, your
motion was duly proposed and seconded, and so I
shall be delighted to waive my objection.   I need
hardly say what an ornament we should all feel
Mr. Carslake would be to our Society, if it was only
in our power to elect him.   Let us by all means
vote on your motion.   I see so many consenting
faces round me in favour of Mr. Carslake that I think
we need hardly use the ballot-box.   If those who are
in favour would hold up their hands——   Yes :
unanimous.   Let us by all means, without the
tedious process of the ballot-box and so forth, elect
Mr. Carslake.   The only hitch is that there is no
vacancy.   Perhaps you would kindly inform Mr.
Carslake of his unanimous election, and the sad
fact that he is not a member of the Sanhedrin.   The
meeting——"

The Secretary interrupted.

" Rule 22," he said, " on the last page.   I will
read it.   ' No gentleman who has been blackballed
for membership shall be eligible to come up again for
election within the period of one year (twelve calen-
dar months) from the date of his previous candidature.' "

He paused a moment.

" With all respect, Mr. President," he said, " I
draw your attention to the fact that the election of
Mr. David Blaize of King's is therefore invalid.
There is then a vacancy in our numbers, to which

Mr. Carslake of Trinity has been unanimously elected. Rather neat."

The smile was struck from the President's face, and the suavity from his manner.

" I'll have a squint at that rule," he said, holding out his hand.

" Oh, why squint ? " said the Secretary.

The President squinted and said " Blast," then immediately recalled this unparliamentary expression.

" The meeting is adjourned," he said. " And will everybody who voted for David just now stop behind a minute ? I hope you'll all take drinks first, or anything you want ; and then will the others clear out, as the meeting is adjourned ? Excuse me a second."

Bags bustled into his bedroom, and shut the door. Malcolm had a brilliant, beautiful brain-wave.

" I bet you David's in there," he said. " Bags meant to produce him all smiles and triumph. There's another door out on to the landing. Go and hold it, Evans. Quick. Grasp the handle tight, so that it can't be turned. Lord ! The rag's beginning ! "

Evans slid from the room, and almost immediately afterwards Bags returned, again closing the door into his bedroom. He looked slightly agitated.

" May I just wash my hands in your bedroom ? " asked Malcolm politely. " I've got some ink on them from those minutes you made me write so quickly."

Bags had no hesitation. He had told David to get away out of the other door, and come back for

conference after the enemy had gone. . . . David
had called him an ass with uncommon fervour. . . .
But he would have got away by this time; he only
had to step out.

" Rather," said Bags. " You'll find everything."

Malcolm walked through, leaving the door open.
There was David madly struggling with the handle
of the other door.

" Hullo, David," he said cheerfully. " Come in;
the meeting's adjourned. Been sitting here all this
time ? There's been a bit of a hitch in your election again. Bad luck. Won't that other door
open ? "

David abandoned the hopeless attempt on the
handle and walked into the room where the Sanhedrin
were still assembled. He was extremely cross, and
the red light of battle was in his eye.

The others finished their drinks and said polite
" good nights." There was a sound of merry laughter
on the stairs.

" L—look here," said David. " You've all made a
fool of me. What's happened ? "

Bags explained the direful situation.

" I'm awfully sorry, David," he wound up.

" I hope you are," said David. " You're an old
ass, as I told you in there. Fancy a President not
knowing the rules of his beastly society."

He looked round on the other dejected faces, and
his eye began to twinkle.

" I say, we're measly conspirators," he said. " It's
all our faults really. But I suffer most. Something
must be done; we can't sit down under this. There
was I in your fuggy bedroom, Bags, waiting to be

brought in like a blushing bride. O Lord, how funny, though ! I was sweating away to get out of the other door, and somebody must have been holding the handle. Jolly smart to think of that ! Now let's have a look at that beastly book of rules. No one seems to know anything about them, except Malcolm. Chuck it over here."

He studied them with growing gloom.

" Seems to me we're done," he said. " The Malcolmites are seven now with Carslake. I vote we put Bags in the fountain. Hi ! wait a minute."

David gave a loud cackle.

" I say, something might be done with this," he said. " I can't say what, but something. Listen ! Rule 17. ' No member who has not paid his sub-scription shall be entitled to vote at any meeting.' Well, Carslake can't have paid his subscription yet. Therefore *he* can't vote. That's something. Thin end of some kind of wedge, perhaps. Lord, I'm going to take a hand, as you're all such poops."

" Oh, David, how sharp you are," said Bags sycophantically. " I say, you chaps, Hales, Morrison, and Steel, do you mind paying your subscriptions at once ? Otherwise you won't have any vote. Only ten bob. Kemp's Treasurer—isn't that luck ? "

" Haven't got a bob," said Morrison.

" Oh, well, I'll pay for you. There you are, Kemp. Send receipts to-morrow. Now let's think. What can we do with that ripping notion of David's ? We shall be a majority at the next meeting. We might abolish the rule about a blackballed candidate not being eligible for another year."

" On which Carslake will pay his subscription and you'll be no forrader," said David.

" But the motion will be carried before Carslake pays," said Bags.

" No earthly use, fiddling about like that," said David. " Something more drastic; less red-tape; bolder lines."

Bags had found some more copies of the rules, and hey all sat round the table, feverishly studying. There was a rag somewhere in the air, if it could only be localized. And then Bags—it was only fair after his blunders and messings—made the Great Discovery.

" Rule 5," he shrieked. " There's more than meets the eye. ' The President shall be elected by the votes of the members. In case of even voting, the ex-President, if not standing for re-election, shall have the casting-vote.' "

" Well, what's there to be excited about ? " said David.

" Don't you see ? It only says that the President shall be elected by the vote of the members. It doesn't say that he need previously have been a member of the Sanhedrin at all. I'll resign, so as to get the casting vote, and propose David. Not aʃ just a member any longer, thanks awfully, but President."

At first sight the discovery looked as simple as it was certainly stupendous. At the next meeting (emergency) Bags would tender his resignation and propose David as President. Another emergency meeting would then instantly follow, and on the voting taking place, the Malcolmites would be faced with the

staggering information that Carslake had not yet paid
his subscription and was therefore ineligible to vote.
The ex-President's casting vote would be exercised,
and David elected.

"But it's too simple, it's too priceless, it's too
holy," said David. "Such things don't happen.
There's sure to be a snag somewhere. Let's all mug
up these rules for ten minutes."

Long before ten minutes were up the snag was
discovered. For (Rule 19) "a due and reasonable
time shall elapse between the nomination and election
of a new President, for the nomination of any other
candidates whom——"

That was enough.

"And you bet they'll do that," said David.

All thought of the interests and well-being, indeed
even of the existence of that small and select debating
society called the Sanhedrin was now rapidly vanishing.
A great and glorious Rag (though no one yet guessed
the magnificence of it) was swiftly flowering and the
Sanhedrin was no more than the soil out of which it
sprang. . . . Any old soil would do. At the next
emergency meeting Bags's resignation of the President-
ship was announced amid loud applause, and David's
candidature for the vacant post put forward. It
occurred to nobody (all would have scorned the action)
to find any pettifogging objection to it ; Rule 19,
which allowed time for the nomination of another
candidate, was all that heart could desire. The very
next day the Malcolmites nominated their opposition
candidate, carefully selected for purpose of scorn and
derision. His name was Sawle, and nobody had ever
heard of him. But fierce light now beat upon him

and he was discovered to be a medical student in an obscure college who collected butterflies, and who pined (no longer in vain) for notoriety. He was in his third year, wore spectacles, and was an atheist and a teetotaller. Anybody, such was the purport of their derision, was a good enough candidate to run against Blaize of King's. Another reason, no doubt, for his selection was his patronymic, for David (as he was more generally known) and Sawle were a first-rate pair of names for electioneering purposes.

The membership of the Sanhedrin was at once indefinitely extended by the consent of all parties, and the ballot abolished, for members were the first essential in a rag. The University eleven were elected *en bloc*, in David's interests, the Malcolmites retorted by electing the Rugby team, and Carslake let it be understood that any rowing man would be welcomed as a member of the Sanhedrin. Then things expanded a bit : the whole of King's joined, and the greater part of Trinity. No date was yet fixed for the election ; that could not be done till the rag had developed its full horse-power.

The subscription was reduced from ten shillings to half a crown and money poured in, for this was a very cheap price for so much pleasure, and accounts were opened at Barclay's Bank and the London & County. All this money, of course, was to be devoted to electioneering purposes, and the agents got busy. An army of small boys was provided with pieces of chalk, and engaged to write up " Vote for Blaize " on every paving-stone and every wall in Cambridge. Another army was therefore conscripted, and provided with more chalk and wet rags, with the latter of

which they expunged the word "Blaize," and with the
former of which they substituted the word " Sawle."
Then posters (a more permanent decoration, because
they could be affixed to places out of reach of the
chalk-and-rag brigade) made their appearance in
startling colours and Cambridge was asked—

" What about Sawle ?
Oh, go to Blazes."

" Sawle and the Salvation of your Souls " was the
counter-cry next day ; and presently Cambridge was
invited to cleanse itself as by fire and vote for
Blazes.

Then the cartoonists got busy, and a remarkable
picture appeared with the legend—

" Sawle has slain his thousands, and David his ten
thousands."

On one half of it was depicted a diminutive Sawle,
catching and trampling on enormous butterflies, on
the other David smoking Perpetua, and rows of
undergraduates in caps and gowns falling dead as they
came within that poisonous reek. Then there was
David sitting at his piano, playing " Once in royal
David's city," and Sawle consulting the witch of
Endor on his chances of success.

Then, on the appearance of a slightly offensive
cartoon, concerning Sawle's private life, and the
natural rejoinder about Bathsheba, it was mutually
agreed that cartoonists should confine themselves to
the glory of their own candidate, and not pour ribald
obloquy on the opposition. No funds could possibly
run to the production of all the awful things you

could invent about your opponent, and it showed a livelier imagination to praise your own candidate (especially if he was Sawle). A poster therefore (nearly complete) of David as the original D(r)avidian Swine was scrapped, and so was one of him and Bags looking through a magnifying-glass at Sawle, and saying, " Which way up is it ? "

Thus a rumour spread like wildfire about Cambridge, that there was a plot on foot to kidnap Sawle and immure him in King's, which of course was David's stronghold. Sawle was therefore provided with a stalwart bodyguard chiefly consisting of Rugby blues. David scorned to have one, until one day, on his way to a lecture, he met Sawle and his bodyguard in the Senate House passage, and being thoroughly frightened, distanced them easily in his mad flight back to King's, but was late for his lecture in consequence. He therefore lodged a complaint with his committee about personal inconvenience, and by mutual consent of the two parties it was declared in a joint proclamation which peppered Cambridge next day that the persons of the rival candidates were sacrosanct. You might not even say rude things to them as you passed, but must try to behave like a gentleman, however difficult and novel this task was. The penalty for transgressing this statute was to be paraded through the streets with a placard on the back " I am unclean " and to be cast into the fountain at King's for purification.

At this point the University authorities thought it wise to give a word of warning, and intimated that in case of any serious disturbance, such as fireworks, fights, or bonfires, those concerned would be

immediately sent down. This caused an interlude
in the serious business of the election, and the two
committees jointly consulted as to what was the proper
course. They settled that a rocket should be discharged on the front lawn at King's as a test-case,
and when the Dean desired to see the perpetrator of
the outrage, the whole college, except David, attended
en bloc, and said they had all done it. It was impossible to send the whole College down with the
exception of David, who was the cause of the whole
rag, and the Dean (not very cleverly) sent for him,
and told him that if any fireworks, fights, or bonfires
occurred, he would be sent down. David, previously
advised, pointed out that the age of perfectly
innocent scapegoats was over. He had had nothing
whatever to do with that rocket, and he had no
intention of sending up others, fighting, or lighting
bonfires. . . . The authorities, therefore, took further
counsel together, and came to the conclusion that as
there was a good deal of steam-pressure about, it
would be wise not to sit on safety-valves. " Let the
laddies have their lark," said Mr. Mackintosh on this
occasion. " They won't do any harm if we don't
seek to interfe—er with them."

David hitherto had refused to address his sup-
porters (though his ingenuity in electioneering devices
was admirable), whereas Sawle was never silent.
Sawle's speeches, from the Davidian standpoint, did
no harm, because nobody could hear what he said ;
still, Sawle was always making public appearances,
and David's silence, in Bags's opinion, was a pity.
He therefore induced David to appear one evening
at the window of his committee-rooms three stories

up, in King's Parade, and make gestures and
mouthings, while Steel, who had the loudest voice
ever known, would be concealed behind the curtain
close to him, and bawl out a tremendous fighting
speech which Bags had composed.   The Sawlites,
therefore, knowing that David was to speak from his
committee-room, arranged a simultaneous meeting on
the pavement directly opposite, at which Sawle should
speak for as long as, if not longer than David did.
But Steel's voice, even from the third floor, entirely
drowned the other speaker (who was always inaudible),
and all went well till it was clearly observed that
though David paused to drink a glass of water, his
voice boomed resonantly on. . . .   Loud hoots and
shouts of " David the dumb," and roars of laughter
. . . . It was impossible to proceed, and David
gave a sort of Apostolic Benediction with two fingers
raised, and the police cleared the obstructed roadway.

Next Sunday the preacher of the University
sermon was gratified (though not surprised) to
observe the impression caused by his eloquent
peroration. When in an echoing ecclesiastical voice
he thundered forth the words " Torn as we are, in
these unhappy controversial days, by discordant
interests, by loud-mouthed competitors, by warring
factions, we are often fain to murmur the words of
David, the sweet psalmist, and say, ' Oh, for the wings
of a dove, that I might fly away . . . ' " a palpable
stir went through his congregation, and you couldn't
possibly have heard a pin drop. There were found
some so infidel as to doubt whether the preacher

actually meant to allude to the only subject which was
of any interest (the rest of his sermon was not), but
it was made very clear how dangerous the growing
excitement was considered by truly reflective minds,
in an article which appeared next week in the
Cambridge Review entitled " Collective Emotion."
It contained the simile already quoted about the
flea-bite in the ocean, and began almost playfully
(for the *Cambridge Review*) recalling to its readers'
minds how, if anyone begins coughing in church the
infection spreads, until the whole congregation is
a-whoop. But it got very serious later on, and
talked of " the desecration of academic tranquillity
and studious shades by the introduction of rival-
ries, which, if innocent at first, are prone to flower
into the blossom of unbridled passion." The
" sweet psalmist " always denied having written
this remarkable piece, so it may still be hoped
that it was a genuine expression of the editor's
mind.

For three full weeks (and a lot can be got into a
week) the excitement waxed, and as the day of the
election approached there was scarcely to be seen
in all Cambridge a single undergraduate who did not
wear the colours of one of the candidates. Bags
went so far as to purchase a large flannel ulster in
orange and blue stripes, and wore it continuously
till it was torn off his back on a dark night, as he
returned from a dinner at the Athenæum rooms, by
several masked villains with purple and green rosettes.
The infection even spread to the sprightlier dons,
and on the day before the poll, A. G., who thought
that no pie was a true pie unless his finger was in

it, made a speech entirely about himself, in the
market-place, in support of David.

But he had better not have done that, for the rag
was an undergraduate rag, and his speech was marred
by a small but sturdy group of rowing-men who
chanted " Ha ! ha ! awfully jolly ! " in monotonous
but loud voices at frequent intervals. . . . This
meeting was attended also by a correspondent of a
leading London paper (so wide was the interest in
the election), who was instantly taken in hand by
Steel and Bags (an intelligent glance only having
passed between them) and given a mine of amazing
information. They took him to such a position
that he could get an excellent snapshot of Mr.
Gepp, whom they told him was David Blaize, addressing a mixed meeting, and the captain of the
University eleven who was standing by was kind
enough to remain quite still while a photograph of
Sawle was taken. They explained that though
A. G. looked rather old for an undergraduate, that
was due to the fatigue of the election ; his hair had
come off after an attack of typhoid. . . . They then
went for a little walk with him and pointed out the
University Church as being worth photographing as
King's College Chapel ; also the Senate House, which
was the official residence of the Vice-Chancellor.
Bags then gave him a nice lunch in his rooms in
Corpus Christi College, and was photographed, with
a bat in his hand, as the captain of the University
cricket eleven. He then so firmly introduced David,
who happened to come in, as " Mr. Nathaniel Crowfoot, one of our younger dons," that David caught
on at once, and gave him some interesting views

about compulsory Greek. Crammed with these and similar treasures of information, the unfortunate man got an early train back to town, in order to develop his photographs and write up his article for the next morning, which duly appeared and was much appreciated at Cambridge.

Then came the day of the poll. The Sawlites, confident that their man would be returned, had carried into Trinity, in small separate quantities, materials for a bonfire, while the Davidians had laid in a stock of fireworks. An amicable arrangement was come to that, whoever was successful, the bonfire should be lighted in Trinity quadrangle, and the fireworks displayed in the meadow beyond the river at King's in order not to dock the occasion of its magnificence, and the result of the poll, now that the rag was over, was awaited with a calmness almost amounting to apathy by both sides.

David was elected by a majority of seventy-three. He resigned, of course, next day, as also did the new members of the Sanhedrin, who numbered in all fourteen hundred and thirty. And the Sanhedrin, much refreshed and restored to its original numbers, resumed the deadly tenor of its debates.

DAVID had been observing the bargain he made with his father with conscientious perseverance. To devote himself to the study of Latin and Greek seemed a very singular way of fitting himself to write English (which was the avowed object of the bargain) and a directer method would have appeared far more sensible. But he had promised to take this course of treatment, and when the Great Rag was over he resumed very studious ways. Naturally, while it was in progress, everything else went to the wall, and his father, in remote Cornwall, was thrilled with it. David received a very earnest letter from him one morning when it was at its height, sending three stamped envelopes directed to himself, and an exhortation which showed a gratifying interest and a justifiable impatience. "You have not written to me for a week," scribbled the Dean, "and it is extremely remiss of you. I enclose three directed envelopes to save you trouble, and I require of you that you should write four sides at least to me every other day, beginning on receipt of them. My dear, it is the best rag I ever heard of ; it quite absorbs me. So do be punctual and regular and detailed in your letters. Form habits of punctuality now, and you will keep them all your life. . . . P.S. I hope you are working very hard."

David grinned as he read ; he could imagine his father grinning as he wrote.

So, for the remainder of that term and throughout

the next, David was so industrious that, had he not
been extremely well, you might have thought he
was ill. He made a beautiful time-table for his day
in different-coloured inks in the manner of Crowfoot,
and used all the inks for a rainbow-border. He
enjoined on himself three hours' work in the morning,
two hours' after tea, and one, with a large query
after it in green ink, after dinner. Soon afterwards
he added another query in red ink, for he had always
been sceptical about that hour after dinner, and
since experience brought no confirmation to his
wavering faith, he presently erased it altogether in
purple ink.

But it was all very dry work : his tutor, a tall,
dreary clergyman with an orange moustache, called
Giles, was a dusty, dull instructor, great on dates, and
there was no inspiration, such as Frank might have
supplied, if he had not been out at Athens, to
moisten it. David had got firmly into his head that
Latin and Greek were lessons, things to be learned,
and medicines for the mind to be taken, and consequently supines in the one and optatives in the
other were not so much modes of definite expressions as catches and traps. He had contracted a
baleful and painstaking and praiseworthy habit of
looking up every word that he came across in his
reading, which he did not understand, and underlining it, capturing it and putting a pin through
it, like Sawle with his butterflies, and his cabinet,
so to speak, got steadily fuller of these butchered
specimens. He had other collections of phrases and
strange classical constructions, and reproduced them
with his admirably retentive memory in his verse

and proses for Crowfoot and his tutor, until these
weary compositions were so full of recondite tags
that he began to be looked upon as a promising
scholar.

"But it is all Rot," said David to Bags one morning, when he had been told by his tutor that his
Iambics were a meritorious copy. "They're trying
to make me write Baboo Greek, and I'm getting on
splendidly. But it isn't real Greek any more than
the Memoir of Onoocool Chunder Mookerjee is real
English."

"What's that ?" asked Bags.

David looked at the clock: there was time for a
ten-minute interlude without trespassing on what
he profanely called the "three hours' service."

"Funniest book ever seen," said David. "I
found it on a bookstall for threepence. Here it is.
Listen to the beginning of it: 'Let me hold my
Penna after a few months to write the memoirs of
the individual above-named; but *quid agis* ? if
anyone put me such a query I will be utterly thrown
into a great jeopardy and hurley-burley and say—a
fool of myself. . . . I will tell how a single private
individual, unaided by any, by dint of nude energy
and perseverance erected a vantage-ground above
the common level of his countrymen, nay stood with
the rare, having few on the same level with him, and
sat arrayed in majestic glory.' "

David turned over a few pages.

"And here's a picture," he said, "all made of
beautiful tags. 'He was neither a Brobdignagian
nor a Lilliputian but a man of mediocre size, fair
complexion, well-shaped nose, hazel eyes, and ears

well-proportioned to his face which was of a little
round cut with rubiform lips.'"

David turned over more pages and shouted with
laughter.

"'When he was young he was filamentous,'" he
read, "'but later on he grew as plump as a partridge.'
. . . Oh, and when he died. Listen! 'His wife
and children had not the mournful consolation to
hear his last words, he remained *sotto voce* for a few
hours and then went to God about 6 p.m. . . . The
house became a perfect Babel and a pretty kettle,
of fish.' . . . Perfect English, terse and picturesque,
and you could find an authority for every word and
phrase in it. But English! That's just about as
much English as my laudable Jambags are Greek.
What was that other story about an Indian clerk
who wanted a day's leave from his office work?
The boss asked him why, and he said, 'The hand
that rocked the cradle has kicked the bucket.' But
the English for that is 'My Mother's dead.' And
I've got to devote my time to writing Greek that
corresponds to Baboo English. I know it does; I
feel it in my bones. And they tell me I'm making
great progress. Lor'!"

Bags, as usual, had been commanded to bring his
work into David's room that morning, so that the
sight of his industry might help David not to play
the piano or divert himself in flowery unclassical
pursuits. But he always welcomed any opportunity for conversation, as it enabled him to make
speeches. He had been given a constituency to
contest at the next election, and just now he dragged
every topic to an imaginary hustings.

" I'm not quite sure that I'm with you there," he said in his best oratorical manner. " It is, as regards the spoken word, at any rate, a great score to be able to state simple things elaborately. For that reason I uphold the periphrasis, ' The hand that rocked the cradle,' and so forth. It makes the hand seem of greater significance."

" ' My mother's dead ' seems to me a sufficiently significant statement, if you want to go to her funeral," said David.

" The other is the more impressive," said Bags. " The audience, if you state a bald, stark fact, receives a shock. If you elegantly and yet colloquially spread that fact out, if I may use the expression, you make the audience use their wits to find out what you mean. They do ; and that puts them in a good temper. The law of England consists entirely of phrases and periphrases and obsolete nomenclature. To accomplish a legal transaction you are bound to employ a language known only to lawyers. In fact the law of England was founded and is maintained solely to support otherwise indigent barristers."

" I don't see what that's got to do with my having to translate Shakespeare into Baboo Greek," said David.

" It has everything to do with it," said Bags. " You have to provide for the employment of otherwise indigent dons. Baboo Greek is a language only thoroughly known by them, and education is not a boon for the educated but a profession for the educator."

" That's from your last speech to the Sanhedrin," said David suspiciously.

" It's nothing of the kind. It's from the speech I'm going to make this evening."

" The principle's the same," said David.

" The principle apparently being a deplorable inaccuracy with regard to the past and the future," retorted Bags.

David tumbled a book or two down from the shelf.

" And in a year or two you'll be one of our legislators ! " he said. " Fancy being governed by you, Bags. Funny, that."

" And in a year or two you'll be writing books and forming literary taste. Excruciatingly amusing ! "

" And probably you won't get into Parliament," continued David, " and nobody will publish anything I write. So we shall be just about where we are now."

It occurred to Bags to say that there was a House of Lords as well as a House of Commons but it was wiser not to say that kind of thing to David. His respect for hereditary legislators was tempered with ribaldry, and his ribaldry was not tempered with respect. So Bags changed the subject.

" I saw Crowfoot just now," he said.

" Well, I've often done that," said David, who was feeling grumpy.

" He said something pleasant about you."

" Get on, then," said David greedily.

" Oh, nothing much. Only about your Baboo Latin prose. Said you had the makings of a scholar. But I daresay he doesn't know."

" Pooh ! " said David. " That's only because I cram it with phrases out of Cicero's letters."

" So that's that," said Bags.

David opened his Euripides.

" Euripides ! " he said. " There's a dreary dramatist for you. He writes the most measly sequels to good stories. It was exciting, you know, for Clytemnestra to kill Agamemnon on his return from Troy—Æschylus wrote that ; but Euripides goes on with it, instead of leaving it there. He goes on with the home life of Electra, after her mother has killed her father—an awful poor time she has. Then her brother Orestes comes back home. Everybody knows it's Orestes, and the one person who doesn't recognise him is his own dear sister, who has always been devoted to him. They have an enormous talk, and still she hasn't the faintest idea who he is—she's clearly deficient. Then what do you think makes it dawn on her ? She sees that his foot is like hers, and so guesses that this stranger is her long-lost brother ! Why, the strawberry mark on the arm is nothing to it."

" Seems a bit forced," conceded Bags.

David turned up a word in his dictionary.

" And I can't even attend to the play," he said, " for all the time I have to be looking out words, and seeing how they always use the optative with ϵi. I found one of the blighters, Sophocles, I think, using the subjunctive with ϵi the other day, so I made a note of that, and dragged it into my Jambags the next week. Giles knew exactly where I'd got it from, and he beamed over his spectacles at me, and said, ' Very nice ! ' It's degrading."

" You used to be rather keen about something in
Sophocles once," said Bags.

" Never," said David.

" But you did. I remember your coming into our
study one evening at school, and saying Sophocles
was a ripper. I'm sure of it, because I thought it
frightfully affected of you. Frank had been translating some chorus to you, and you said it beat Swinburne hollow."

David was beginning to have some faint remem-
brance of this.

" Yes, because he didn't bother me about
construction and particles," he said. " He just
rolled it off in topping English, and there was the end
of it."

" I expect the Greek words are just as pretty, if
you knew Greek," said Bags. " Why don't you go
on that tack ? Just read it as if it was meant to be
read."

" That's not a frightfully bad idea," said David.
" It was a chorus out of Œdipus Coloneus, I believe.
Funny that you should have remembered that
evening."

He left his high chair at the table with its dictionary and grammars and notebook, lit a pipe, picked
up a Sophocles, and spread himself on the sofa.
Then came the turning over of pages, heavily
annotated, as he found the famous chorus, and then
silence.

Ten minutes afterwards he spoke.

" I say, Bags, just take the Lexicon and look up—
no, it doesn't matter. . . ."

David's word-loving mind began to swim and

soak itself in the sparkling river of jewelled speech. . . . Ever since he had begun to work hard at his classics, in fulfilment of the paternal bargain, he had applied himself to strict academic rules, dissecting the dead, according to the prescribed plan, much in the same way as a medical student dissects, whose object is not to attain a high appreciation of human beauty, but to see how the wheels go round. David had altogether banished from his silly head the notion that the language he was trying to learn was merely the instrument of human speech in the mouth of the most beauty-loving people in the world, and not invented by them to tax the ingenuity and vex the souls of generations yet unborn. For nearly a year now he had ploughed through this arid academic wilderness, and here suddenly, at the suggestion of Bags, was an oasis. . . . Just as Frank's translation of this same chorus had been to him a revelation of the beauty which it contained, when translated, so now he found that with his expanded knowledge of Greek he could appreciate it directly, as it stood. There were words he didn't know, but whatever they meant they sounded jolly as he muttered them to himself.

It had literally never occurred to him to read Greek *in* Greek before. With the idea that Greek was "lessons," a subject for an examination, he had made English of it as he went along (for that was what you had to do in the Tripos), looking out a word here, underlining a crabbed phrase there, taking no end of trouble, in fact, to squeeze all life out of it. But now he began to perceive that these lines had beauty and significance without being translated at all. Sophocles had not written them as a cipher, which only meant something when it was rendered into an intelligible tongue. In fact it was the other way about: it was they which gave significance to the translation. You were not obliged to put English into Greek before it meant anything; why then subject Greek to a similar process before you gave it the credit of signifying anything on its own account?

It must be understood that only the most exiguous glimmer of such notions dawned on David's darkness that morning in answer to Bags's wayward suggestion, but the glimmer once kindled was likely to be fed by very inflammable stuff, namely, his own passion for the beauty of words, for the joy of painting with them, of making them the prepared palette by means of which thought became pictorially visible and glowed with its own appropriate colours. . . . . Heaven forbid, too, the idea that David put it to himself like that, though that was the process, unstated and unformulated by him, of what was beginning to happen. Vivid and impressionable all through, the last thing that occurred to him was to analyse his impressions; instead, he used them. His skylarking temperament went winging along unconscious of his discoveries, and, not less, of its growing maturity. He was far too hungry for impressions and digested them too healthily to know that he was digesting anything at all. He ate and drank and rose up to play.

One o'clock struck with astonishing unexpectedness, and reminded him of two things, the first and most important being that he should have attended a lecture precisely one hour ago.

" But I forgot," he said, " and so there's nothing more to say about that. Dreary it would have been."

He chucked his Sophocles on to the table.

" Hurrah ! the silly morning's over," he said, " and in consequence the melody of ' The Merry Peasant returning from his Work,' as composed by Mr. Schumann and performed (I might say created) by the celebrated pianist Mr. Davowski Blaizowski, shall be indicated on the instrument. What instrument, do you ask ? ' I won't deceive you,' said Mrs. Crupp, ' It's the piano. . . .' Unlike most pianists, Blaizowski gives his best recitals with the music in front of him, and his liquid eyes fixed upon it. Blast ! The text of the Merry Peasant has dropped into the instrument. How on earth can I get it out ? What would Crowfoot do ? He would saw a hole in the front of the piano, insert his hand and take the Merry Peasant out. Or, better still, he would fish for the Merry Peasant with a piece of string and a bent pin. The ordinary person, of course, would, by undoing two simple hooks, move the front of the piano, extricate the M.P.—that's what you'll become—and then put the front of the piano back again."

David adopted this mean and commonplace device.

" I went to brekker the other day with Crowfoot," he said, " and as he was pouring the rich boiling water from his urn into the teapot, the teapot lid fell back into place, and a circular cascade of boiling water played prettily over the table. Now, that might happen to anybody and to any teapot, and the

grovelling, uninventive mind would just turn off the
tap of the urn, and then lift up the teapot lid again.
But do you suppose Crowfoot did anything so efficient
and commonplace ? Not a bit of it, my little M.P.
Guess."

" Can't," said Bags.

" Well, he performed prodigies of valour, in
snatching at the teapot lid through the boiling cascade,
in order to open it again, and scalded his fingers. So
he gave that up, and had another splendid idea, all
in a flash. He pulled the teapot away, and put
the slop-basin under the tap instead. He laughed
with pleasure at his own ingenuity, and as he blew on
his fingers he said, ' Rather dodgy, that ! ' And
then at his leisure he turned the tap of the urn off,
and all was well."

" Why didn't you do that for him at once ? " asked
Bags.

" Because I couldn't," said David. " I *had* to see
how many ingenious things he would do first. And
naturally I couldn't ask him afterwards why he
hadn't done it, for that would have spoiled all his
pleasure in his dodginess. I'm going to play draughts
with him after Hall to-night. At least it's a new
variety of draughts which he's invented, called
' Chess-draughts.' . . . Sounds like cough-mixture.
. . . He told me I should understand it as soon as I
started. And much more exciting, he says."

" Lunch," said Bags, as David began to worry out
the Merry Peasant.

" Right-oh. Just two seconds. The Merry
Peasant gets home in no time."

David had a tennis-court at two, and vastly

enjoyed himself for an hour and a half. When he
came out, the abbreviated December day was drawing
to its close, and the sun like a ruddy disk just
clear of the western horizon. He walked along the
Backs where the last dead leaves had fallen from the
elms and lay in deep yellow drifts below the trees ;
it was pleasant to plough his way through them
because of the hissing noise he made as his feet kicked
them up, and because they smelt of tea. Above, the
bare branches glowed in the illumination of the
sinking sun, and a middle-aged moon, not red at all
(as surely she ought to have been if she was getting
her light from that red disk in the west), made a
strange mystification of cross-lights, for she shed
a pale whitish phosphorescence into the heart of the
shadows cast by the sun. Over the river, as he crossed
the bridge into Trinity on his way to the Pitt Club,
there was spread a web of mist in which the moon had
it all her own pale way, but above in the clear darken-
ing blue of the sky were rosy clouds where the sun
still reigned. . . . What millions of things there were
to notice !

David leaned for a little on the damp parapet of the
bridge contrasting one light with another. These
high fleecy clouds were rosy as the fingers of dawn. . .
There was a word in Homer which showed that the
same simile had occurred to that venerable
author (" or group of authors," said David to himself,
remembering a lecture on the Iliad). Homer used
a pretty word about it too : " rosy-fingered " did
not present any obvious superiority. It was just as
good in the Greek, if you said " ῥοδοδάκτυλος " and
didn't bother to translate it at all.

" Jolly nice word," said David to himself. " Why not write some more Homer ? "

Tea at the Pitt, which was David's immediate objective when he had done with the sun and moon, was always agreeable. The new Homer might describe the " butter-fingered muffins " and the " belly-burning tea." And when Blaizides, so he Homerically reflected, had taken his fill of butter-fingered muffins and belly-burning tea he would lay hands on unharvested sheets of paper, and write several letters and stuff them into the brazen-lipped post-box in the lordly club without putting any spittle-moistened stamps upon their envelopes, for the lordly club always defrayed the postal-charges of its members when they wrote their letters there. If you were a life-member you could have your letters stamped for you till the day of your death, so that if you lived long enough, and were extremely diligent, it was clear that your correspondence would account for your original subscription many times over.

In fact you might make it a habit to write so many letters every day that the Committee would offer you a small annuity to stop. You could easily write— it was all becoming rather Crowfootian—a sovereign's worth of letters a day, if you devoted your whole time to it, and it would be well worth the Committee's while, at that rate, to offer you £100 a year to cease from these epistolary activities. . . . David had once tested the scope of the Pitt's postal-system, by addressing a letter to himself at King's College, Cambridge, via Brindisi, Port Said, Bombay, Yokohama,

San Francisco, and Liverpool, and found it waiting for him on his breakfast table next morning, having been left by hand. Certainly that method of delivery had been quicker than if it had gone round the world, and he could not lodge a formal complaint.

Anyhow, there was a letter to be written to-day to Frank at the British School in Athens ; that would be rather expensive for the Pitt Club, and they couldn't get out of it this time by delivering it by hand at King's. So after a hilarious tea with a friend or two, David retired to a sequestered corner in the smoking-room, and biting the end of a quill pen began to consider what he should say to Frank. Immediately the oddity of considering what he should say to Frank struck him. It was easy enough to fill four pages, or eight for that matter, with general Cambridge gas. Usually, in fact, the difficulty was to stop, for there was always such a plethora of subjects, but to-day the difficulty was to begin. For some time, vaguely and subconsciously, but to-day quite consciously and deliberately, he wanted to tell Frank . . .

David lit a cigarette, and tried to determine exactly what it was that he wanted to tell him. He found it difficult to arrive at this, for his powers of self-analysis were delightfully elementary, and the written word demanded definiteness. But he knew that within the last year his attitude towards Frank had suffered considerable modification, and he was equally well aware that Frank's attitude towards him had not altered. For, up till now, ever since the beginning of their devoted friendship,

Frank's mind had completely dominated his own, so that whatever in tastes and conduct Frank had commended had been to him, *ex officio*, admirable; whatever Frank thought lightly of had been contemptible. But now with his growing maturity David was beginning to see that he could no longer take reach-me-down judgments, however nicely cut, and stuff himself into them. He wanted more room here and perhaps less latitude there: they had to fit him; it was no longer he who must fit himself to them. It was not that Frank was didactic or tutorial, it was rather that he himself had been rapturously surrendered and receptive. He had been eager to don the habiliments that Frank cut out, flinging himself into them with the certainty that they must and should fit him. It was not, again, that there had been open disputes or differences between them; it was mainly that David now recognized that a mental and moral independence of his own had grown up in him. For long, no doubt, it had been making root and fibre below the soil, and now, rather disconcertingly, it had put up above the ground that green strong sprouting horn that demanded light and freedom to expand in any way that its own instinct and vitality prompted. His mind was not any longer the mind of one who walked with his hand in another's, and swallowed with open mouth whatever was given him.

David laid down his quill, and took another cigarette. It was all very puzzling, and he wanted to give himself an instance of what he was driving at. His own whisky-experiment with Bags occurred to him; Frank had told him that Bags was an ass, and advised him to let Bags go his own way, and not to be so silly. . . . But David, taking his own line, had been silly; he had also been swiftly and supremely successful.

Then there was another train of thought that stood in the way of beginning this difficult letter, and how on earth was he to convey the gist of that? . . . When first this friendship began, he was a small hero-worshipping boy of fourteen, Frank the captain of the school eleven, with three years and all his athletic prowess dividing them. That element of hero-worship had undoubtedly been an ingredient, and a strong one, in their relationship, and the amazing fact that the hero really cared for this little worshipping scug had strongly coloured it. There was, necessarily, not a particle of that left now. That particular physical attraction had gradually and inevitably vanished.

"I shall never begin this blasted letter," thought David. . . . He broke away from details, and tried to sum it all up. He was not in the least less devoted to Frank than he had always been—that was sure enough and surely would always persist through any change of relationship. That male manly love might manifest itself in many mediums, but it was not changed because the mediums vanished. Above all, now, at the ages of twenty-one and twenty-four the three years that separated them were immeasurably shorter than the three years which had stood between them at the ages of fourteen and seventeen. Naturally such intervals dwindled in significance: you couldn't expect that a

man of seventy-one (as David would be in a short
fifty years) would revere the opinion of his friend
because he was seventy-four.

David finished his cigarette, and picked up his pen
again. He knew that nothing said with love behind
it ought to hurt anybody, but somehow he was
afraid of Frank being hurt. Frank was hard in
many ways, he had strong, scornful judgments when
he disapproved, and for that very reason he was
over-soft in other places. He rather laid about him
sometimes, with his nose in the air, dealing out hard
slaps. " You don't improve people," thought David,
" by slapping them. You've got to get in their
place, and imagine what it would be like to be
slapped." And Frank with all his brilliant hardness
had such a tender skin, a skin often unimaginably
tender to David's robustness. " All the more
reason," he thought, " for being careful. Let's
begin gently."

" Oh, Frank," he wrote, " I feel frightfully old.
You won't recognize me when you come back, because I've taken to spectacles, and have got a long
grey beard and gout. I work five hours a day, and
thought it was going to be six, but I was wrong.
Being twenty-one has made me feel older than the
rocks I sit among, and my eyelids are a little weary.
Did you once find that you got to a stage when you
had to make up your mind for yourself, and didn't
care a blow what anybody else said ?

" I rather wish I was older or younger. If I was
older, I should have taken a line of some kind ; while,
when I was younger, I never thought about taking a
line at all. I hate transition."

Really, English composition was extraordinarily difficult. He knew what he meant to convey quite exactly, but when it came to putting it into words, it was like trying to anchor yourself to the tail of an eel.

" I suppose the very fact of growing older," he wrote, " is the same as the fact that one changes. You can't stay still and let the years slide by ; they pick you up and carry you along, and you don't know you're being carried till they plant you down in some different place. Yet think of the dear old things here, Crowfoot and A. G., and so on. Someone in a book I read the other day says that you're born of a certain essential age, gradually live into it, and remain there. Thus if your essential age is forty, you're a man of forty when you're twenty, and remain a man of forty if you live to be eighty. It sounds awful rot, but then you do get people like Crowfoot and A. G. who remain about twenty. But then why should I feel older, as I certainly do ? "

David suddenly observed that it was six o'clock, and according to his rainbow time-table he ought to have been at work again. He thought he would take this difficult composition back to King's and finish it there, but then he would have to stamp it at his own expense, which was so bad for the Pitt Club. That would never do ; one of the first objects of existence was to make the Pitt Club stamp your letters for you, and so he made a *cache* of it on the top of a bookcase, for completion to-morrow.

The new variation on the antique game of draughts

that night exceeded David's highest anticipations.
It was refreshing after an attack of old age and
responsibility to find that when you arrived at Mr.
Crowfoot's time of life (forty or fifty or sixty, or
whatever it might be) there was a chance of still
retaining such a store of hectic excitability. . . .
David went up to his rooms as soon as Hall was
over, to wait for him there till he came out of the
Dons' Combination-room, and observed that he was to
be the only guest for this adventure, for there
was a table drawn up close to the fire, with the
draught-board ready on it and two glasses with
a flagon of Tintara wine. There were also two
boxes of draughtsmen, into which he looked, and
found that one contained the ordinary black and
white pieces, while the other was full of blue
and green pieces, which were slightly sticky, as if
they had been lately painted and had not yet
dried completely. There was also a metronome,
set ready at hand for some purpose of which he
could not form the slightest conception, and a small
dish in the fender with a tin cover to it, which
contained pieces of anchovy toast. This looked as
if the hunger of exhaustion must be provided for.
A second large table in the middle of the room,
where stood the row of polychromate inks, had two
piles of glee-books lying open on it; there were
indications that one set of these had had chunks
of the other put into it, and that the other had had
chunks of the one inserted; a gum-bottle evidently
lately used bore out this conjecture. A sheaf of
Latin proses, among which he saw one of his own,
was on the music-rest of the piano, and on the top

of it some damp lawn-tennis balls evidently put there to dry after being washed, and a pair of walking-shoes.

He had barely time to skim off the cream of these impressions when he heard the hurry of footsteps on the stairs outside, followed by the noise of a heavy stumble, and an explosive spilling of objects of some sort. Then there came a shrill, lamentable exclamation with loud clearings of the throat, and David, broadly on the grin, opened the door to see if he could be of any use.

" Oh, there you are, Blaize; capital," said Crow-foot, who was picking up a quantity of books of Common Prayer which bestrewed the stairs. " So tiresome: I thought I knew the number of steps on my staircase, but I must have counted wrong. Of course I couldn't see them over the top of the books. Yes, will you help me to pick them up? They're the prayer-books of the choir in chapel, in which the text says that they are still to pray for King William and Queen Adelaide, forsooth. After great difficulty—really some people are so antiquated and obstinate—I got the Fellows' meeting to permit me to put a slip into each of them with the names of King George and Queen Mary and Queen Alexandra. I've had them typewritten, and in case you hadn't come up yet, I was meaning to spend a minute or two in putting them in. . . . Thank you; yes, I think that's all. Let's see; you've got one, two, three, four, or rather, two, four, six, eight, for that's the easiest way to count, and I've got ten, twelve, fourteen. What can have happened to the other one? Oh no, I've got two, four—or rather ten, twelve, fourteen, fifteen. That makes it all right."

They carried in their piles of prayer-books, and perched them on the top of the piano, where Crowfoot counted them again.

" We won't trouble about the slips now," he said, " or perhaps it would be wiser to finish with them, now we're at it and there's a gum-bottle handy. And I think the lawn-tennis balls are dry, so we can get rid of them."

" You haven't been playing lawn-tennis, have you ? " asked David.

" Not since last summer, but now in four or five months' we shall be playing again—it'll be May, you know—and there's nothing so annoying if you want some Tuesday, for instance, to go and play lawn-tennis to find that you've only got dirty balls. So I always wash them towards Christmas, and there you are, in May, ready to take your racquet and begin. My shoes, too, what are they doing on the top of the piano ? Stay ; I have it : I knew that if I put them there they would catch my eye, which they wouldn't if they were in the shoe-cupboard, and I should remember to have them sent to the boot-maker's."

He peered at the proses on the music-rest, and cleared his throat.

" That's a good dodge," he said. " In case I should forget about the proses I have to correct, and sit down to my piano, there they would be in front of me, and I should get to work on them, and do my music afterwards. Now we're all ship-shape, I think. Let's get to our chess-draughts."

" Aren't we going to do the slips for the prayer-books ? " asked David.

" I think we might leave them, after all. They'll want spreading out, and there's hardly room on my table with the glee-books still gummy. . . . Shoes and proses and prayer-books : that's easy to remember. Now let's make ourselves comfortable. Tintara and small cigars and the anchovies in the fender, and the two boxes of draughtsmen all ready. We begin with the black and white ones in the ordinary way, at least very nearly ordinary. The only difference at present is that every piece counts as a crown to begin with, and can move either backwards or forwards. Shall we start with a trial game ? It gets a little more complicated further on when the chess-moves come in."

Crowfoot was completely in his element during the trial game as he explained the pleasant intricacies of his invention, and thought of a quantity of fresh ones, for future incorporation, as he went along. Every piece, as he had mentioned, counted as a crown already, while if it got safely across the board, it was then endowed with the movement of a bishop at chess, and could devastate the diagonals, capturing any piece to which the road was open. In order to show that it had become a bishop, it did not have an ordinary piece of its own put on the top of it, because that might make you think you were playing ordinary draughts, but was crowned, if a white piece, with a green piece, and if originally a black piece with a blue piece.

" Black and blue," he said—" that's easy to remember if you think of a bruise, and that leaves

green and white. Or shall we begin with green and
white pieces, and then the white become black?
Black and white, you know, like whisky. Which do
you think would be the easiest?"

David's brain was just holding on, as by claws and
teeth, to the exposition, and with a mouth full of
anchovy toast he waved the new proposal aside.

"I'm sure the first plan's the best," he said. "We
start with black and white, and they get blue and green
crowns."

"Respectively," said Crowfoot. "Very well. Or
wait a minute—no, that wouldn't do. Where had we
got to? Yes—a piece of mine—or say, yours—gets
across and becomes like a bishop. But if it ever gets
back again to its base-line, then it becomes like a Queen
in chess, and can move like a castle as well as a
bishop."

"I see," said David. "And what colour does it
become when it's a queen?"

Crowfoot laughed with pleasure.

"That's a great dodge," he said. "Now, when it's a
bishop, if you remember, it consists of a blue piece over
a black piece or a green piece over a white piece. But
when it's a queen, you reverse the pieces, and it looks
like an ordinary piece. So your adversary has to be
very careful to look whether it's green or blue below,
or else he'll walk into the jaws of a queen. Dear me,
the green and the blue pieces are very like each other
by this light. Would it be better to write a G. on
the blue, I mean the green, and a B on the blue, in
order to distinguish them? No, I don't think it
matters; it will only make us more careful. Now
let's toss for beginning. Which hand will you have?"

Crowfoot had put a green piece into his left hand and a blue into his right. David chose the left hand.

"Green," said Crowfoot. "You're green. Now let's think: green was white before it became green. Therefore you're white. Therefore you begin. Now we've started. Won't you have a glass of Tintara before you move?"

David thought it best to keep his head as clear as possible, and a scene of unparalleled confusion instantly began. Crowfoot made a breach in the centre of the board, and got three bishops. He crowned one of them with a green piece by mistake, and, thinking it was David's, laid a terrible trap for it, and captured it at the expense of two of his own men. David meantime had got a bishop of his own, and leaping down the whole length of a diagonal turned it into a queen, capturing both Crowfoot's remaining bishops in consecutive moves.

"Very powerful move," said Crowfoot, nursing his chin and adjusting the extra lenses of his spectacles. "Now I shall have to put on my thinking cap. Stay! I've got your queen on the hip. You might have taken that piece of mine, so I huff you, and down it comes and becomes a bishop. No, that would never do. Dear me, I had three bishops just now, you only took two. What can have happened to the third? However, I move that. Now what do you do?"

"I take it," said David.

"Dear me! How could I have come to make such a slip? Oh, the metronome. I've not set it going. That's a dodge to make us move briskly. You set it at Andante, and have five beats for a common piece to move in, ten for a bishop, and fifteen for a queen. If you don't move by then you lose your turn."

The weight slid down the pendulum and ticked out fifteen distracting beats, Prestissimo, before the most nimble hand could have moved anything. Crowfoot tried wedging it up with pieces of match and nibs, and weighting the top of the pendulum with the cork out of the Tintara bottle, but no remedy was efficacious for more than a turn or two, and then it was ticking away again at top speed. So after abstruse calculations Crowfoot worked out that the equivalent number of beats at this higher rate would be thirty for an ordinary piece, sixty for a bishop, and ninety for a queen. He counted these aloud as fast as he could, but no agility of lip-movement could possibly pronounce the words as fast as the metronome ticked them. It was therefore shut down and put on the piano with his walking shoes to be mended to-morrow.

Meantime the pieces flew about, changing colour like chameleons as they crossed the board and came back again, till there were three queens left on each side which sprang from end to end of the lines evading capture.

There sat Crowfoot on the edge of his chair, clearing his throat and adjusting his spectacles, with a Borneo cigar in one hand, the ash of which he flicked by mistake into his Tintara, his eyes gleaming with excitement, and his fingers not quite letting go of the piece he proposed to move while he ejaculated " Stay ! That would never do. There ! How do you get out of that ? " and making up fresh rules to fit the difficulties in which he found himself. Finally, the game had to be given up as a draw, and David, completely exhausted, lay back in his chair.

" Really it makes a first-rate game already," said Crowfoot, " and with a little more contriving it will be even more exciting. Very little apparatus, you see, just two sets of draughtsmen, one of which you enamel, and a metronome. Must you be going? Eleven o'clock, is it, already? I had no idea. We must certainly have some more games. Another glass of wine, won't you? I must draw up a list of rules, and I shouldn't in the least wonder if there was a rage in chess-draughts, just as there was in halma. Good night, Blaize. I shall just gum the prayer-books before I go to bed."

David took his letter out of the cache next day. He decided to send it, but added several pages about chess-draughts. They rather discounted the extreme seriousness of the first part, but it was only fair to give both sides.

" So it's all over except the hissing," thought David to himself, as he came out of the last paper of his Tripos. " But it's ten days before anyone can begin to hiss. . . . Wish I didn't care so frightfully."

He knew he had worked well for this last year, not

industriously and steadily only, but with all the
intelligence he possessed, " and very little of that,"
he added to himself, but whether he had done well or
not he had not the smallest idea. It was no use
thinking about it anyhow, and so instantly his
mind went back to the history paper which had
been the last of the inquisitions. On arriving
at his rooms, he consulted two compendious histories
of Greece and Rome, as to certain crucial dates,
with the gloomiest results. He gave a hollow
groan, tied the miserable little manuals together,
weighted them with the castor of the sofa that was
always coming off, and dropped them from the
middle of the bridge into the river to drown like
parricides.

" I'll larn 'em to contradict me," he observed.

A few bubbles came up on the surface from the mud
into which they had sunk.

" So *this* labourer's task is o'er," said David, "and
he's jolly well going to amuse himself till the judgment
day."

So he got up late and played his piano, and
developed a new service at tennis, and bowled rather
nicely for the University, and read a quantity of
entertaining English literature, some books in order
to see how it ought to be done and others to see how it
ought not to be done, and wrote a Shakesperean
sonnet to Bags in memory of the Whisky-crisis
beginning :

> " Shall I compare thee to a summer day ?
> Then art more thirsty and less temperate.
> Not port nor beer nor whisky nor Tokay
> But is the wanton of thy hot palate,"

and parodied Keats' " Ode to Autumn " with an
" Ode to Christmas " beginning :

> " Season of bills and yellow biliousness,
> Close bosom-friend of the hot buttered bun. . . ."

Neither of these futile compositions was ever
finished, because a touring theatrical company
came to Cambridge and played *The Second Mrs.
Tanqueray,* and so he had to set to work on a play
instead.   Then that had to be made silly too, before
he had begun to think of a plot, and it became *The
First Mrs. Crabtree* (and hot stuff she was), which
brought Bags in again, and he broke that off too with a
letter to the *Cambridge Review,* saying that its
columns often contained the news of the marriage and
death of famous Cambridge men, but never their
birth.   It was signed " M.A.Cantab," and got printed
by mistake. . . .   David sent a copy of that issue to
his father, and would have sent another to Frank, but
he had left Athens and was now on his way home.

He had never looked forward to any arrival of Frank
on the scene with such misgiving.   Frank had clearly
received that letter written from the Pitt, because,
subsequently, he had alluded to chess-draughts, but
the first half of it had remained unmistakably un-
answered.   That wasn't accidental ; it wasn't either
that Frank thought it mere piffle, for if that had been
his opinion, he would certainly have stated it with
his utmost lucidity.   But he had simply ignored it.
" So he doesn't think it's piffle," thought David,
" and what the deuce *does* he think it ? "   It was all
very harassing, but he never wished he hadn't

written it. If Frank had misunderstood him, the misunderstanding could be cleared up. If he had not misunderstood him, well, then he understood, which was precisely what David meant him to do. But, one way and another, this waiting for Frank's arrival was as bad as waiting for the lists of the Tripos.

The days dropped off, like over-ripe plums which no one cared to pluck, with misgivings and fitful occupations buzzing about them like wasps, and settling on them and nibbling them, and with the beginning of May-week Bags became the biggest wasp of all and took up a deal of time. . . . For Bags, to put it succinctly, had burst. He had for a year and a half bottled, corked up, and wired down his amorous gases, and had almost forgotten what it felt like to sit on a tobacconist's counter and try not to look foolish if a friend came in and found him gazing into a flapper's eyes. Then the pressure had proved irresistible, and with the incursion of marriageable maidens for the May-week festivities Bags had exploded with a bang. In other words, he had fallen in love, and appeared to think that nobody had ever done so before. He selected David as his confidant, owing to David's undoubted though indirect responsibility for his present disintegration, and was quite interminable. At times David almost wished he had let Bags go to the devil his own way ; at times, though Bags had clearly taken leave of his senses, David, for some obscure reason, rather envied him. It was surely enviable to be so completely absorbed in anything.

Bags did all the conventional things. He sighed and he strutted and he shaved twice a day and thought himself the most miserable outcast on the face of the earth and the lord of creation. He tried to read poetry, but dismally failed ; he wore his best riding-breeches when he made up his mind to propose and could not bring himself to the point ; and at all hours of the day he ran round to unbosom himself to David, whenever he could not be with Her. She, it may be stated, was a very pretty, sensible, and suitable girl, one of two sisters of Malcolm of the Sanhedrin, who was up here for the May-week with her Mamma. She liked Bags immensely, and was perfectly prepared to accept him when he asked her to do so.

" She dances too divinely," he said to David about half-past eleven one morning.

David yawned. The conference had been a long one, and they were really arriving at nothing.

" So you told me," he said. " ' Sylph ' was the expression. And her name's Ida. Quite a good name. ' Oh, mother Ida, hear me ere I die.' "

" She's going to be at the King's ball to-night," said Bags, " so you'll see her."

David had already said that he was not going, but Bags no longer had the faintest idea what anybody but She said.

" She says she's looking forward to it," continued Bags.

This was too much.

" If you mean that she's looking forward to my seeing her," said David in a loud, clear voice, as if he was speaking to a foreigner whose knowledge of English was imperfect, " she'll be disappointed, for I'm not going. I've told you that nine times.

Better break it to her, Bags. You mustn't en-
courage false hopes in her."

" What's that ? " asked Bags. " Oh, yes, I believe you told me you weren't going. I suppose
you're going to sit and jaw with Frank. He's coming
up this afternoon, isn't he ? What I meant was
that she's looking forward to the King's ball. Nothing about you. I wonder if she meant anything
special by that."

" Can't say," said David. " But she'd know."

Bags got up.

" Well, anyhow, you'll see her to-morrow," he
said. " She's coming to lunch with me ; they all
are. Don't forget you're coming."

" Rather not," said David.

He had thought that Bags's getting up meant
that he was going away, but it appeared to be only
a preliminary for his sitting down again. No doubt
he wanted to stretch his legs after being so long in
one position.

" She's never heard a nightingale sing," said
Bags.

" Lamentable," said David. " Take her to Crowfoot's glees. I'll be there."

Bags gave a bleat of mirthless laughter, and became
quite grave again instantly.

" So to-night after the first dance," he said, " we're
going down over the King's bridge to the gate. We
shall hear them there, shan't we ? Don't they
always sing in the Backs ? "

The ghost of a smile quivered on David's mouth.
This was food for thought. . . .

" Yes, I often hear them hollering away," he said.

" Pretty noise. I expect she'll like it awfully. It might buck you up, too."

" Buck me up ? "

" Yes ; put sóme courage into you. Poor old Bags ! Lord ! it's rather a change from the bold bad days of the cocoons."

" You've got rather coarse lately," said Bags.

" I always was," said David. " But can't you really find one drop of the old brand ? Just ask her to be yours : she can't ask you. Say you're willing. Barkis is willing, Bags is frightfully willing. It has been done, you know. I expect your father asked your mother to marry him. Telegraph to him and find out. . . . Look here, do you mind if I read ? You can go on talking just the same, and when you've got anything new to say, shout ' Hi ' and I'll listen."

Bags sighed.

" I must be going," he said. " Is your clock right ? "

" No, it's slow," said David—" ever so much slow."

Bags walked swiftly but delicately away. His shoes were lovely to look upon, but then people only judged by the outward show.

David's ghost of a smile materialized into a broad grin, and he strolled out into the town and visited various shops. It would be a great sell for Bags and Her if there didn't happen to be a nightingale singing in the Backs at the end of the first dance. Nightingales couldn't be expected to know for certain when the first dance came to an end, or how important it was that they should be punctual, and he was eager to help. He explained what he wanted at a bird-fancier's, an ironmonger's, and a music-shop, and eventually visited a toy-shop, and unweariedly explained all over again.

"It does exist," he said, "and it's a little tube, and you blow down it into a cup of water. A sort of whistle in fact, and it makes a noise like a nightingale."

"Oh, the Philomela," said a superior young lady. "Two and sixpence, or in aluminium three and sixpence."

David thought the aluminium one might be more stimulating, and the young lady agreed that it had a much superior tone.

He practised diligently that afternoon, and made the most ravishing noises. . . . Frank ought to have been here by this time, and would surely come straight to his rooms. Or perhaps he had gone to unpack first: that was possible, and David walked across to his window, meaning to deposit Philomela in the flower-box, where she was not likely to be found, and then stroll round to the rooms which he had secured for him. There under the tree in front of his window were standing Frank and Crowfoot, looking earnestly up into the thick foliage.

"Oh, he's come!" said David, and took the staircase in three leaps and ran out. That he had come was all that mattered, his misgivings and his Tripos and Bags and Philomela all went into the limbo of forgotten things.

"Frank, you old brute!" he cried. "Ripping!"

"Hullo, David!" he said. "Just arrived. I was coming round to see if you were in."

" Ah, Blaize," said Crowfoot. " Most interesting.
Maddox and I were looking to see if we could catch
sight of it. All these years I've never known a
nightingale this side of the river. Though why
nightingales I don't know: they sing equally by
day."

He adjusted his lenses as a bird flapped out of the
tree.

" There it is ! " he cried. " Oh no, that's a wood-
pigeon. It seems to have stopped singing now.
What a pity ! Why not put some groundsel or
chopped egg below the tree ? It would soon get
to understand that there was good food here, and
more nightingales would come. Then by degrees
we might lure them up into the court, and so into
the town, like the seagulls in London. It would be
very pretty to have nightingales singing in the High
Street. Have you ever heard them in these trees
before ? "

" Never," said David. " Are you sure it was a
nightingale ? "

" Perfectly certain. There's no other bird-note
the least like its ' jug-jug.' "

David's eyes cautiously caught Frank's, and seemed
to brim with some unspoken communication.

" ' Jug-jug,' " repeated Crowfoot. " They say
that if you warble ' jug-jug ' to a nightingale, you
can make it sing back. ' Jug-jug ' ! There ! No, I
think that was only a motor-horn somewhere. If
you'd go round that side of the tree, Maddox, and I
remained this side——"

David found this quite irresistible. Much as he
would have liked to stop here and listen to Crowfoot

disclose other ingenious schemes, he wanted most of all to make the nightingale answer to his juggings.

" Awfully interesting," he said. " Come up presently, Frank; I'll get tea ready."

David flew upstairs again, drew Philomela from the window-box, and concealing himself behind his curtains, poured forth a melodious answer to Crowfoot's calls. Then he stopped and listened.

" There ! " cried Crowfoot triumphantly. " I knew I should get it to answer. Listen again ! Jug-jug-jug-jug-jug."

He put his hand to his ear ; David after a short pause fluted an answer, and they had quite a beautiful duet.

" One can always do that with birds and a little patience," said Crowfoot. " I shall at once get some groundsel. A pennyworth of groundsel from the greengrocer's would go a long way. We shall have them all over the place soon."

He hurried off, and Frank skipped up to David's rooms. David's eloquent eye coupled with the fact that the nightingale ceased when he came out of his room, and instantly began again when he got back, made it pretty certain that he knew a smattering about nightingales. . . . As usual they plunged straight into this subject of current interest without wasting breath in saying how pleased they were to see each other.

" David, you little devil, was it you ? " he asked.

" Yes, of course," said David. " I say, you do look brown ! Oh my, how funny he was ! "

" But did you plan it all ? Did you get the night-

ingale and then sit at the window waiting for Crowfoot to come ? "

" No. All a fluke—a blessed, beautiful fluke,"
said David. " I got the nightingale because of
Bags——"

" Get on—when's your Tripos result out ? "

" To-morrow. Don't interrupt. You see, Bags
is taking his girl—Bags is madly in love, by the way
—to the gate into the Backs to-night to listen to
the nightingale, because she's never heard one. So
just in case there weren't any I thought that sooner
than disappoint them, I'd produce one. I shall sit
in a tree and sing and watch them spooning. Do
you think he's really gone to get some groundsel ?
—Crowfoot."

" Yes, and a hard-boiled egg. Is there something
in the air of King's that makes everyone slightly
cracked ? Go on."

" Bags !—about Bags ! " said David. " He's sick
with love, but can't bring himself up to the scratch.
So I thought I'd kill two birds with one nightingale.
She'll hear the nightingale, and the moon and nightingales do ginger a fellow up, don't they ? Just a
little pipe, you see—aluminium gives the best tone
—and some water and me to blow. The young lady
at the shop said it was a Philomela."

" And you're making it a—a galeotto," said
Frank.

" Am I ? What does it mean ? "

" It means a pimp," said Frank.

" Oh, I see. Just to put it before them as an
idea. Quite. You never saw a man in such a
state as Bags. Dotty. Let's come down to the

gate and find a thick suitable bush for the gale—galeotto. No, I think we'll wait a bit first and jaw, and see if Crowfoot brings the groundsel. Going to the dance to-night ? "

" Lord, no ; I hate dancing. We'll dine to-gether."

" Rather. I say, those Tripos lists to-morrow. Do you remember two years ago when you were in for your archæological stunt ? We picnicked the day before at Byron's pool, and ants crawled over me. Two blooming years ago ! I should rather like to say ' Encore ' and have it all over again."

Frank came across to the window-seat.

" I wonder if you would say ' Encore ' if you knew you'd have it all over again," he said. " I rather doubt it. I think you want to get on, and grow up and spread your wings."

He paused a moment, and laid his hand on David's arm, which lay conveniently along the window-sill. David saw at once that they were already on the subject on which he had written to him one day at the Pitt. Frank's reticence had filled him with vague misgivings, but that gesture showed him that he need not have any about the discussion of it.

" David, I got that letter of yours," he said.

" And you—you didn't mind ? I was afraid you did, as you didn't answer it. And I expect I put it badly."

" No, it was pretty clear. But I knew I could answer it better in talk. First thing is, that I knew already what you said. You've grown up more in this last year than in all the years we've known each other. But it was much better that you should find

it out for yourself. Also much better that, when
you'd found it out, you should have told me. I
should have hated it if, when you'd found it out,
you had let me guess it."

" I nearly did," said David. " But then I had to
let you know. Beastly hard to explain, though."

" Well, I knew it before. You always were an ass.
You thought that I should always want you to take
my word for everything, and not to think and choose
for yourself, didn't you ? "

" About that," said David. " Sorry."

Frank's eyes began to twinkle.

" Granted, I'm sure," he said. " And then you
used to make an A1 copper-bottomed hero of me,
you know, and I loved that. Who wouldn't when
he was so fond of anybody as I was of you ? That
was games chiefly, and jolly good things they are.
. . . Oh, I forgot to ask. How's your tennis ? "

" Not so very bad," said David.

Frank shifted his position a little, and extended
his hand round the back of David's neck.

" David, old chap," he said quite gravely, " we've
had such a dam' good time—you know it as well
as I do—that all these years I've never wanted it to
be anything different to what it was. But it belonged to boyhood, and now it has changed ; it
couldn't possibly help that. But as for my disliking
it, how could any decent fellow dislike his friends
growing up ? We've loved each other, thank God ;
I've been first in your life, and you in mine. Soon
now, I shouldn't wonder, you'll meet a girl, and fall
madly in love with her and be frightfully happy, and
you must think me a pretty good stinkpot if you

imagined I should mind that. Very likely I shall do exactly the same. . . . Besides, our friendship is built into us. It's all there. . . ."

" That's all right, then," said David quietly.

" I should just about think it was. I say, it was a pretty good thing we met—eight years ago, isn't it ?—when you came down to Marchester to try for a scholarship."

David leant his head back against Frank's hand.

" I was a little scug," he said warmly.

" Yes, but not hopeless."

" Should have been if you hadn't whacked me into shape more or less. Lord, I was keen on you. Thought there'd never been anyone like you——"

David turned his head a little. " Nor there ever was," he said.

A merry chirping sound of " jug-jug " came from outside, and simultaneously they reversed themselves and peered through the flowers in the window box.

" Too good to be true," whispered David, " Gosh, where's my Philomela ? "

The incredible Crowfoot was flitting about with a small bunch of groundsel in one hand, and a saucer with hard-boiled egg chopped up fine in the other. The saucer he tried to balance on the railings and it upset. He picked up the larger pieces and restored them to the saucer, which he put on the ground ; the groundsel he strewed about the grass. From time to time he looked brightly up into the tree and said " jug-jug-jug " an incredible number of times. David replied with a few polite and melodious phrases, but then so exploded with silent laughter that he blew all the water out of Philomela's little cup. Crowfoot, after trying in vain to entice more melody out of the nightingale, looked at his watch, and went away in a great hurry, clearing his throat.

David, when he had passed out of hearing, laughed till he ached, and then became quite serious again.

" That's a long jaw for us, Frank," he said.

" I know. Rather a record. We never did jaw much to each other, except about books and games and piffle."

" No. Case of understanding each other," said David. " Besides, when one means anything tremendously, one doesn't jaw. One has a cigarette, and says ' Blast.' Much the best plan. But only friends can do it."

" I had to explain this time," said Frank. " You didn't seem to have the faintest notion——"

" I know ; but you've called me an ass for that. I say, come out, and let's find a tree for my galeotto-stunt."

They found an admirable tree, a thick-foliaged yew obviously designed for galeottos, with a convenient bolt-hole at the back, so that if the enamoured couple showed any signs of wanting to hear the nightingale at close quarters, that accomplished bird could slip away unseen. They hatched a simple but effective signalling-system : David, on the bridge, was to have Philomela ready at halfpast ten, and Frank would be stationed at the entrance of the marquee where dancing was in progress. When the objects of all these arrangements emerged at the end of the first dance, Frank would with a wave of his handkerchief (like Isolde) signal that they had started towards the bridge on their romantic expedition. David would then have time to ensconce himself in the galeotto-bush, without having to wait indefinitely, perched spikily in a rather precarious fork of the yew-tree. Frank would follow down in the wake of the lovers, give one loud whistle to indicate that they had passed the bridge, and that the music might begin. He would then go quietly back to David's room to await the arrival of the nightingale, after it had done its best to aid and abet.

Isolde waved his large handkerchief and David from his observation-post on the bridge hurried down to the amorous rendezvous. A small cup, Philomela, and a liniment-bottle washed out and filled with water jingled in his pocket, and he shinned up into his tree and gingerly seated himself in seclusion. Presently a whistle sounded, and footsteps came along the path. In the deep dusk of his densely screened perch he could not be certain if they were the right ones, for Bags and She, having crossed the bridge, might be lingering, and the footsteps be those of others. But immediately he heard Bags's loud, silly laugh, highly charged with nervous excitement. That would not do at all; Bags mustn't laugh on the threshold of such a beautiful adventure, and Bags mustn't be nervous. So to pull him together, Philomela sang two or three short and stimulating phrases, ravishing fragments, like a pianist running his hands over the piano before he really began. . . . Apparently that had an excellent effect, for the laughter ceased, and the footsteps, though still approaching, were tiptoed for fear of frightening the bird. Very soon they were opposite the tree, and

20

yet the embowered songster could catch no glimpse
of them. "Therefore," thought David, "they can't
see the embowered songster. Now we'll give them
what for."

He burst into full-throated melody of the most
superior aluminium tone; he bubbled and jugged
and whistled in a transport of judicious blowing.
Three lungfuls of song he gave them, and then,
for fear they should think that this was too
much of an "immortal bird," he stopped. A girl's
voice in an enraptured whisper answered him.

"Oh, but how perfectly lovely, Mr. Crabtree!"
she said. "How darling of it! I believe it's
in that yew-tree."

"Did you say 'yew-tree' or 'you and me'?"
asked Bags. . . . Such flippancy! Bags must be
serious and brave, thought Philomela.

"Oh, how silly you are!" said the girl.
"Almost as silly as the things you told me about
your friend David. Do be quiet. I'm sure it's in
that tree. Delicious bird!"

"I'll pay you out for that," thought David. "And
what the deuce does she mean by calling me by my
Christian name? If I said 'Yes, Ida——' But
let's get on."

David made it quite clear that the delicious bird
was where she thought it. He poured forth a fresh
torrent of melody.

"Oh, I could listen for ever," said Ida.

"So could I," said Bags, "if you were here."

The nightingale applauded this statement. That
was what it was here for.

"But I would sooner hear you talk than listen

to a nightingale," said Bags when the song ceased again.

David gave them another stave. He had expected that his galeotto-stunt would be the most killing joke, but now he found that he didn't feel the least amused. There was something serious and beautiful going on, and he had imagined it would be merely funny. And then immediately he heard Bags's voice again. It must be Bags's voice because there was no one else there, but it wobbled and croaked in a manner that made it quite unrecognisable.

" Ida," he said, " Miss Malcolm—no, Ida, I wonder if you could possibly think of—well, think of me at all. You're absolutely the most ador-able——"

David hastily put down Philomela's cup between his legs, and stopped his ears, just as he did when he was singing glees. Whatever Bags was saying, whatever Ida might answer, wasn't for him at all. It wasn't fun to hear them " spooning," as he had anticipated ; it was too dreadful that he should be eavesdropping. He had only meant to be an encouraging bird, but he felt he would become an awful cad, if he listened. All the same, the nightin-gale seemed to have been pretty useful. . . .

When he unstopped his ears, they had moved a dozen yards away up the path. He pressed the branches of the yew apart, in order to see when the coast was clear for the descent of the nightingale, and saw them moving slowly and very close together towards the bridge. Once they stopped and turned, as if listening for more music, but it really looked as if they had had sufficient. When they walked on again, it was quite clear that Bags's arm was round her waist, and David dropped down from his perch, and proceeded cautiously till they crossed the bridge and turned off where the path ran alongside the river. So he went back to his room and found Frank.

" Gosh ! There never was such a galeotto," he said. " Powerfullest galeotto ever recorded. I hadn't sung more than three minutes when Bags got bang in the middle of the track. Took a header ! Splash ! "

" What did she say ? " asked Frank.

" Don't know. I had to stop my ears."

" What for ? "

" You'd have understood if you'd been there. It suddenly became frightfully private. Bags's voice croaked like a frog, and had an awful wobble in it, sort of bleat, like that stop on the organ—' Vox humana,' isn't it ?—that sounds like nothing human at all. Well, Bags was just like Vox humana amorosa. It sounded too killing, but I didn't want to laugh a bit. I just stopped my ears in order to hear nothing more of it. I want a drink. It's thirsty work being a nightingale. But I believe I've done Bags a good turn. Lord, how they admired my voice ! I felt like a prima donna singing ' Home, sweet home.' They ought to have handed me up large wreaths and bouquets, and I'd have smiled and kissed my hand, and sung some more——"

" David, you're a pimp," said Frank.

" Devilish good profession for once. But fancy needing to be bucked up by an aluminium pimp in a

yew-tree, when you'd got your girl all to yourself
in the dark. . . ."

David and Frank sat up till some timeless hour, for
it was really very little use going to bed while the
band at the dance blared on; but probably they
would not have parted any sooner if there had
been no dance in King's at all. There was a lot to say,
and food for silence in between, and what not. In
consequence David slept late next morning and
had a violent dream about an earthquake,
which resolved itself into the banging of his outer
door. Bags burst in.

" I'm engaged," he said, and broke into that loud,
silly laugh which had annoyed the nightingale last
night.

" Oh, I say, how ripping ! " said David, sitting up.
" Congratters. You won't be such a bore now. How
did it happen ? "

Bags sat down on his bed and embraced David's
knees.

" I don't know *how* it happened," he said. " It
just happened. We just strolled down across the
bridge, and just then——"

" If you say ' just ' any more, I shall scream,"
said David.

" Don't be so beastly. And just—no, and before
we got to the back gate one began. Nightingale,
I mean. Ida had never heard a nightingale before.
Oh, my God, you never heard anything so beautiful. It was in a big yew-tree, and we never saw it
at all. She was frightfully taken with it. It was
absolutely divine, and we're going to listen again

to-night. David, do attend; don't bury your face like that."

" I am attending," said David. He pulled himself together and raised his head.

" Well, you were quite right. It did buck me up like anything. It sounded as if it was singing at me to go ahead. Have you ever heard a nightingale ? Really listened, I mean ? I felt as if it was put there to shout at me ' Get on : it'll be all right ! ' "

" Just what I always told you," said David.

" Well, you did happen to be right. But if you'd jawed for ever, you wouldn't have bucked me up like that blessed bird."

David couldn't stand such injustice.

" I bet you I helped to buck you up," he said. " You're an ungrateful swine, Bags."

" No, I'm not. You only yawned and laughed at me. I always felt worse than ever after I'd been talking to you."

" So did I," said David. " If it had gone on much longer, I should have hated you. Well ? "

Bags's rather goat-like face assumed an expression of radiant imbecility.

" Nightingales are always supposed to say ' Jug-jug,' " he said. " What they really say is ' Love-love.' "

" Oh, I shall be sick," said David.

" But they do," said Bags. " You don't know. How can you know ? "

(" Aluminium, three and six ; superior tone," thought David.)

Bags gave a sort of bleat.

" Well, I listened," he said. " And then all of a

sudden I knew. And I asked her, and she said
' Yes,' and I'm cracked with happiness."

" Good old Bags," said David, " I'm awfully
glad."

" Thanks, and I had to come and tell you. It was
partly your doing, too, another way round. If it
hadn't been for you I should have gone on mucking
about and messing round——"

" No, you wouldn't. You'd soon have seen what a
rotten game it was. I say, I must get up."

" Right. I just had to come round and tell you.
You are a brick, David. Lunch at half past one,
and you'll see her."

The news had been so thrilling that not till David
was in his bath did he remember that at ten o'clock
precisely, in an hour from now, the Tripos lists would
be read out. At that thought, though the cigarette
between bath and breakfast was the most fragrant
of the day, it suddenly tasted like " odour of poisonous
brass and metal sick," and he threw it, scarcely
begun, into his basin, where it spread itself among
soapsuds like strands of brown seaweed.

And then all the malicious deities of inanimate
nature awoke. He dropped his tooth-brush into the
water where the soaked cigarette lay, and the bristles
got threaded with limp strings of tobacco and pieces
of soaked paper. His collar-stud, after splitting his
thumb-nail, came in half, and when he thought he
had successfully screwed the two mean pieces of bone
together, and buttoned his collar and tied his tie,
it came in half again, and he had to take off his tie
and unbutton his collar. Then the lower disk of it
slipped down inside his shirt, and he had to execute

a sad dance till it rolled out of his trouser-leg. He
could not find another stud, so he tried to put the two
pieces together again with sealing-wax, and dropped
a flaming blob of it on the back of his hand. This,
as is well known, is far more painful than anything
that ever happened to early Christian martyrs, but
it is not mitigated by the ardent faith which rendered their sufferings so much more tolerable. However, the stud, when cool, seemed to hold, but the
split edge of his nail caught in the fabric of his tie
and set all his teeth on edge. Since the injury was
on his right hand, he could not trim it with his left,
for the scissors, instead of cutting, shut down sideways. Then his shoe-lace broke, and after bending
down to tie the sundered ends together, he found
that he must have cut himself shaving under his
chin, for the edge of his collar was stained with
blood.

David decided that the best thing to do was to
have breakfast and finish dressing afterwards, for
whatever torturing misfortunes fate holds, they are
less shattering after food, and especially after hot,
sweet, strong tea. But, thinking of the Tripos, he
forgot to put any tea-leaves in the pot, and poured a
stream of crystal-clear water on to the four lumps of
sugar he had put in his cup. And his egg leaked at
the bottom, and all the good strengthening food
inside it ran out into the egg-cup. Between whiles
he licked the raw place on the back of his hand where
the molten wax had burned him.

It will hardly be credited that another disaster,
as appalling as any, awaited him, but so it was. A
drop of marmalade fell from the loaded toast

he was carrying to his mouth, between his wrist and his shirt-cuff. He tried to wipe it off, but it was no use ; if he turned his hand an inch, he felt the cloying stickiness. This broke him up altogether, and he gave one despairing cry and rose from the table. He had had to change his bloody collar already, and now he must change his shirt as well, and he had had no true breakfast, and his thumb-nail was like a hook of which the barb was embedded in his flesh, and the Tripos list was to be read out at ten. It seemed as if all the powers of darkness were sent to chasten and subdue him into a state of mind sufficiently humiliated to receive the final blow at ten o'clock. Of all the mornings he had ever known, this was the beastliest, and if at that moment a tooth had begun to ache, he would not, as Lord Tennyson observed, "have found it to be strange."

It was better to sit quiet for a minute or two, so that the malignant powers might think he was quite flattened out, and so pass on to other victims ; clearly to do anything at all during this assault was to court disaster. So he sat down softly on the window-seat, wondering why people in distress were always supposed to " fling themselves " on to chairs and sofas and floors, and said " Hell " under his breath at short intervals. . . . Presently there was the sound of the window below his being thrown open, and David remembered that Tommers had come up last night for the King's ball, and was lodged in his old room immediately below. Tommers confirmed his presence by shouting out " Blazes . . . David . . . Son of Jesse," in the usual manner.

David felt too depressed to give any cheerful response, but he peered cautiously out through the window-box, and saw the back of Tommers's black head immediately below.   For one moment he thought of getting him to come up and cut his thumb-nail for him, but before he answered, his eyes happened to fall on the egg-cup which contained the whole beautiful contents (minus one spoonful) of a soft-boiled egg.

" God hates me this morning for some unknown reason," he thought, " but at any rate I can pass some of it on."

One step took him to his table, and another back to the window again, and carefully aligning Tommers's head he emptied the egg-cup on to it.   Tommers was already beginning to grow a little bald in the manner of a tonsure, and the contents of the egg-cup fell on that very spot.   " It droppeth like the gentle dew from heaven," thought David, as he saw Tommers's hand clapped to the place, and withdrawn covered with cold yolk of egg and little bits of shell, and heard one magnificent outburst of Elizabethan vexation. . . . So he crossed the room and softly sported his outer door, so that in case Tommers came up-stairs (which seemed highly likely) it would look as if David had gone out or wasn't up yet and could not possibly be responsible for this extraordinary occurrence.

David's spirits rose, and he proceeded to change his bloody collar and his sticky shirt with a reviving cheerfulness.   Soon there came the thump of angry footsteps on the stairs, and Tommers battered at his closed door and said rude loud things.   Not a sound came from within, and David, remembering that he was to lunch with fascinating females, put on his smart new Zingari tie and a shirt with a gay stripe in it. The contrast, of course, of his own case with Tommers's bucked him up, for of all the beastly things that had happened to him that morning there was none that could really compare with having a cold soft egg plump itself down in the middle of your baldness. Not all the malignancy of Providence had invented for him such a nasty fate as he had invented for Tommers.

Life, thought David (beginning to construct an elegant English sentence), was full of deceptions and tangled webs, and its crazy confusion made it very difficult to remember all the things you had to forget. For instance, he had to remember to forget that he had been a nightingale when he was talking not to Bags only, but also to Crowfoot, who might be expected round again this morning with some more hard-boiled egg. And, thinking of eggs, he must remember never to have heard of such a thing as a soft-boiled one when talking to Tommers. . . . Then with a sinking of the heart he saw that in ten minutes' he must start for the Senate-house, and after that he would probably have to forget that he had taken a miserably bad degree, and try to be cheerful at lunch. Bags would certainly give them champagne at lunch, by way of being festive and engaged, and champagne at lunch, though quite irresistible, always produced in David a feverish torpor and a dry mouth (he had got that already with thinking of the lists), and he would be expected to be bright, and to stagger round the sights of Cambridge, with Mrs. Malcolm and the

other Miss Malcolm, while Bags and His Own walked
behind and got separated from them and were found
kissing each other in a side-chapel. . . . Well, Bags
was happy, anyhow.

And now it was time to go to the Senate-house,
and to do that it was necessary to pass Tommers's
room without attracting his notice, or so fast that
he couldn't be stopped. David chose the first line
of tactics, and so, when he was dressed, he let himself
out very quietly and tip-toed downstairs with his
shoes in his hand. He saw, while still a few steps
above Tommers's landing, that his door was ajar,
which looked rather ominous, but he had only just
begun to guess how ominous it was, when it flew
wide open, and a soaking bath-sponge hit him in the
face, and a piece of Windsor-soap rapped him smartly
on the nose, and tennis-balls and oranges and things
darkened the air. He gave one loud scream, and
hurling his two shoes one after the other through the
open door, to drive the enemy off, leaped in after
them.

Tommers, like a sound strategist, had ambushed
himself behind the door, as the two shoes flew by,
and sprang on David from behind, grasping him
firmly round the arms. If he had only tripped him
up at once, all would have been well, but that
moment's dilatoriness enabled David, though pinioned,
to pick up a siphon and discharge its exhilarating
contents over his shoulder into Tommers's face.
Some, of course, went down his own neck, and Tommers, letting go of him with one hand, thrust a
spoonful of brown sugar down after it. David picked
up a sofa cushion and held it tight round Tommers's

face, with the intention of smothering him, and
Tommers got hold of his nice Zingari tie, and pulled
the slip-knot tight. For fear of strangulation David
had to let go of the cushion and get his neck free,
and then they fell on each other, and wrestled, and
things were spilt and a chair broke, and they rolled
about on the floor till exhaustion set in.

" And all because of what ? " panted David, as
he lay on the hearthrug beside the inert Tommers.

" Egg," said Tommers feebly.

David could just manage to laugh between his
sobbing breaths.

" Perfect shot, wasn't it ? " he said. " Lucky,
but perfect."

" But why did you do it ? " asked Tommers.

" Because I was suffering. Bootlaces, collar-studs
sealing-wax, tea, thumb-nail—every blooming thing
had conspired against me."

" But what had I done ? " asked Tommers.
" Why bring me in ? "

" I had to. Couldn't bear it alone," said David.
" Why am I so sticky down the back."

" Syphon and sugar, I shouldn't wonder," said
Tommers. " It gets gluey."

David jumped up.

" Oh, you shouldn't have done it," he said.
" That'll be my third shirt to-day. And I've got to
go to the Senate-house to hear Tripos lists at ten."

" Ten ? " said Tommers. " It's ten ten now."

From outside came Frank's voice.

" David ! Hi ! David ! " he shouted.

David ran to the window ; perhaps Frank had
been there.

" I say, did you go to the Senate-house ? " he cried. " What's happened ? "

" Yes, I looked in. They were reading out some old Tripos. Dull work."

" Oh, get on," said David.

" Why such a hurry ? King's did pretty rottenly. Two second-class and a few thirds——"

" Oh, which is it ? " said David.

" Don't interrupt. Two seconds and some thirds and one first."

" W-w-what ? " said David, suddenly stammering. . , .